I0749208

TRILOGY

By Kathleen J. Shields

This book is a work of fiction. Places, events, and situations in this story are purely fictional. Any resemblance to actual persons, living or dead, is coincidental.

HARDBACK TRILOGY
ISBN-13: 978-1-941345-45-0 **Hardback**
ISBN-E: 978-0-463935-99-6

PAPERBACK BOOKS
ISBN-13: 978-1-941345-26-9 **The Painting 1**
ISBN-E: 978-1-310661-32-7

ISBN-13: 978-1-941345-32-0 **The Painting 2**
ISBN-E: 978-0-463161-09-8

ISBN-13: 978-1-941345-47-4 **The Painting 3**
ISBN-E: 978-0-463855-60-7

Canyon Lake, TX
www.ErinGoBraghPublishing.com

Table of Contents

PREFACE

When I started writing *The Painting* there was no plan for it, no outline. It came to me as a dream, or a sign. All I knew was I was lead to the computer, and just started typing. I honestly did not know why. As the story progressed I found huge aspects of my life were making their way into the story, who I was, at the time, was Gerald in the story. I even started wondering if I was writing this as some sort of catharsis, a way to release or work through my grief and depression. I had many unanswered questions, but I wrote nonetheless.

His name, *Gerald Oliver Delaney*, was "given" to me during this process. I didn't know why it had to be THAT name, but I knew deep down in my soul, it did. It never made any sense until the end of the story when Gerald signed his artwork with his initials. I was bawling; tears streaming down my face, as the story poured from my fingertips onto the keyboard; because I was reading it as it appeared on my computer monitor the way a reader would read it in a book. I had no idea what was happening, until the completion of the story presented itself. I consider the book my miracle.

When the idea of the trilogy was presented, I studied, I contemplated, I procrastinated, and then, I wrote it - each time, in many instances, being astonished by the testaments that worked their ways in. Each story that held similar circumstances that coincided to my own life, that it again, became a therapy of sorts.

The most notable of experiences were detailed in the *"Who am I to write this story?"* epilogue, where I ask this question and answer it with my impressions at the time. Each book I posed the same query, and each response was distinctly different; fraught full of meaning and emotion that only my current life situations could produce. I listened to God, I tested my faith, and I learned how to believe. That is what I learned in this book.

What will YOU take away from this trilogy? I can't tell you. What you get from this story will adversely affect you in connection with where you are in your life. Just like if you read this story again years from now, the details that you NEED to see will be more apparent.

They say the Bible works that way... but don't go by MY words, learn through His.

The Painting

Introduction

Our lives are like a blank canvas…

It's the paints we add to it, the colors we chose, the brush strokes we decide to take – our life's decisions - that create the painting that is our existence. For some there are dark shadows that diminish any light and blot out our promise and possibility. For others, the light is blinding, and we go in search for some darkness to dull the pain, while others still find a happy medium between the two and yet allow life's distractions to sway our final outcomes.

There are various mediums we can use on our canvas. Each type of paint or material or application offers its own unique outcome with an undefined result. Choosing your medium is choosing your path in life.

Do we opt for an oil based paint, a heavy slow drying pigment where it will take time and heat to cure, where the only way to limit the wait is to use the colors sparingly and miss out on the bold textures of the scene? Do we choose pastel sticks or chalk, soft, powdery rods that can be blended together with the tips of our fingers? Softly smoothed, and yet the excess dust is simply blown away with a gust of wind. A substance that would need a fixative sprayed on it to make it permanent and then our canvas could never change. Do we prefer watercolor, something that can be washed out, faded and muted? When applied to an absorbent canvas, the edges fan out and are undefined. Or when applied to a smooth plastic paper, the paint can be washed away with a moist cloth as if it never existed in the first place? Do we pick crayon, simple, child-like and innocent? Do we decide on marker, permanent and doesn't allow for errors? Or do we select pencil with which we can lightly sketch and erase if we don't like where it is going?

What about the foundation of our work? Our life's "canvas" could be made of paper, cloth, wood, glass, plastic or metal. Each option provides for a unique foundation. Each decision we make will inherently alter our final design. This is why we are all so very different from one another. Our life's canvas begins its journey from the day we are born. The first few years of laying the groundwork isn't even our decision. We have to take the base we are given and do with it what we can. ***This is why emotion is so important.*** Our feelings, insecurities, and joys all add to our canvas. We paint a world within each of us that is uniquely our own.

What follows is Gerald's world – the creator and painter of a universe so complex it needed a second canvas.

Chapter 1

Loneliness is not only isolation;
it's an inability to blend into the world.
No matter how much you want to be a part of life,
loneliness is caused by the continued
disappointments in others.

- K

Gerald wasn't alone or isolated. He was surrounded by others. Children from school, teachers, his family, even townspeople, all collectively going about their busy lives, not noticing Gerald.

Of course, not being noticed was better than the alternative.

"Look guys, it's that weird kid."

Gerald knew from the gruff voice the speaker was Derek, the boy whose life's mission was making him feel bad.

"I wonder if he's going to cry today."

Gerald endured the verbal torment. That was difficult enough to walk away from, but lately, Derek and his buddies had added physical suffering as well.

Gerald listened to the boys laughing behind him. His heartbeat quickened as did his breathing. Dread filled his churning stomach as he began walking faster.

"I think the little twerp is scared," Derek added as the boys began chasing after Gerald.

The boys tackled Gerald to the ground. Face in the dirt, notebooks and pencils scattered, tears in his eyes, Gerald stayed down as the boys laughed, kicked dirt towards him and left.

When they were far enough away, Gerald slowly gathered his possessions and got back to his feet. His heart ached. His cheek hurt and his elbow was scraped.

Gerald didn't understand why they persecuted him. He couldn't comprehend what it was about picking on him that made them feel better. What he did know was it brought them joy to bring him gloom. The idea that his misery gave pleasure to others perplexed him.

Gerald saw the world differently. He loved to watch the animals carry out their daily tasks. He wished he could join the fish as they swam in the cool waters. He longed to be a bird flying freely in the sky. He thought it would be fun to be a bunny and hop away from it all.

As Gerald walked towards his house, he dusted himself off. He reorganized his papers, and wiped the tears from his eyes. Walking up the steps of his front deck, he slowed, making sure his cheeks were dry. As he stood there, he felt the sun beaming down on him. It warmed him inside and out. The brightness brought a smile to his face.

He sat down on the deck, breathed in the day, allowed the warmth to lift his spirits, and then noticed an inchworm, inching its way across his boards. He watched it slowly straddle a small crack between the panels and pull itself over.

Gerald realized this tiny crack was like a massive cavern to the inchworm. He looked at the length of his deck and realized that this was like a barren desert that would take all day if not multiple days for this little guy to navigate across. He knew he wanted to help it, but he didn't want to interfere.

If he carried the inchworm to the end of the deck, he might end up taking it too far. If he left it at the end of the deck, without the value of the journey, it might become lost and not know where to go from there.

Gerald also knew that, like the butterfly who must be left alone to strengthen its wings when it emerges from the cocoon, he needed to leave the inchworm alone as well.

However, as he watched that little worm slowly make his way across each deck board, surprise caught him when he noticed the inchworm suddenly seemed stumped. The separation between the board he was on and the one he intended to reach was huge. It was wider than the inchworm's entire body. There was no way he could make it across. Gerald realized that without help this little guy would have to turn back around. He would have to travel a day back the way he came.

He then observed the inchworm looking left and then right. It studied the situation and decided to travel down the board parallel to the cavern in hopes of finding some other way across. *He wasn't willing to give up.* This made Gerald smile. The determination this little insignificant inchworm had in getting to his ultimate destination was strong. The pride Gerald felt for it grew more in that moment.

Since Gerald was larger, able to see so much more, he glanced down at the cavern on both sides of the inchworm. He realized that no matter how long it took that little guy, he would not find a way across. Gerald instantly felt sad. He wanted so much to help, but he also didn't want that worm's determination to let him down.

Gerald stood up, reached for a nearby tree and shook a limb enough to loosen a leaf. He watched that leaf spiral through the air down towards the ground and land a foot in front of the worm.

Its landing startled the inchworm, but once he realized it was safe he continued towards the leaf. Gerald watched for quite some time as the worm investigated. It maneuvered around the green obstacle, and then inched on top of it. Gerald was amazed as he watched the worm push the leaf over the cavern to create a bridge.

As he watched the worm accomplish his task and move forward, he knew he had helped by supplying an opportunity that the worm was able to use.

It was tasks like these simple, incon-sequential, trivial things that made Gerald the happiest. He couldn't understand it when he watched children running around and accidentally stomping on a grasshopper. He was distraught when he witnessed children shove sticks in ant piles and destroy the homes they'd worked so hard to build. It broke his heart when he watched them throw rocks at bird nests.

When he said something to the children about what they were doing, the ridicule began. They couldn't understand why it was so important to him. They couldn't comprehend why he would cry for broken eggs or appreciate the value of bugs. They laughed at him.

Some of them didn't like the fact that he made them feel bad about what they did, and they took out their aggressions on him. They poked fun at him instead of the ant pile. They pushed him away and ignored him. And when they were forced to play with him, or to choose him for a team, they'd choose him last or not at all.

It made Gerald very sad.

It made him lonely.

Gerald's loneliness was like the milk in the refrigerator slowly going bad. He seemed happy left alone to enjoy nature uninterrupted, but he didn't realize what else it was doing to him. A hole was being formed within his soul; a hole that needed to be filled. A hole that could only be filled by love.

Not a girl/boy love but rather the love of friends, of a true human connection. Love that comes with sharing joys and disappointments with someone else - expressing ourselves with another, laughing... that's the kind of love he needed.

He missed companionship, yet he was completely unaware of needing anything in his life. Gerald had absolutely no idea how lonely he was, but he was about to find out.

CHAPTER 2

During recess, instead of playing with others, he went off to be by himself. He'd find the shade of a nearby tree and sit down under it. He'd stare up into the limbs and watch squirrels working away. He'd watch birds take off from the limbs, spread their wings out and soar into the beautiful blue sky.

He'd get lost in the clouds, imagining them into shapes, animals and faces. He returned to the ground to peer deep within the grass at the bugs collecting food, ants carrying twigs and then out to the birds collecting fluff.

Every once in a while, he'd look out over the field to the playground and watch the children playing; swinging, hanging off of monkey bars, running and jumping, laughing and screaming.

He watched them and felt so far away, so distant from that scene of craziness. He was never a part of it, and he never wanted to be. Since he was picked on - in gym class or recess, he stopped caring if he was chosen last or not at all.

"We don't want him on our team," they'd say, or "What good is he? He's worthless."

Instead of feeling bad, Gerald found the silver lining and learned to enjoy the solitude instead.

When he walked by, they'd trip him and then laugh at him when he fell. It made Gerald cry. When he'd walk into the cafeteria with his lunch tray looking for a place to sit, he'd watch as empty seats filled with bags, extended elbows and others to make their table appear full.

The teasing, name calling and mean acts isolated Gerald from this world and pushed him further away into his own world, a world of no humans – no one to ever hurt him again.

That afternoon, when Gerald walked into his home, he was quiet as usual.

"How was your day?" his mom asked from the kitchen.

"Fine," he replied, trying to sound upbeat.

She knew he was sad. She wished she knew what to do for him. But unfortunately, the only time she ever saw him smile was when he was alone, with his eyes closed, surrounded by the sweet sounds of nature.

That evening, Gerald's dad came home late. Carrying a huge package wrapped in brown paper, he struggled to get through the door. He also carried a large sack of supplies. After he manhandled the large, flat package into the house, he leaned it up against a nearby wall, Gerald's mother walked out of the kitchen and spoke.

"What is that?"

"I got a gift for Gerald."

"Gerald, can you come out here?" his mother called him from the other room.

Gerald slowly meandered out of his room and gazed upon the large object leaning against the wall. His eyes widened.

"It's for you," his father said.

Gerald half smiled and then cocked his head to the side, wondering silently what could possibly be wrapped inside that brown paper.

"Go on, open it," his father encouraged him.

Gerald slowly, carefully, peeled back the brown paper wrapping to expose his gift... a large, textured, white canvas that was almost twice as tall as Gerald stood. He turned and looked back at his happy parents holding each other's hands and gave a shy smile.

His father then handed Gerald the bag of supplies. Gerald looked inside and took out the objects one at a time, inspecting each item: various containers of paint with shades of every color, a pallet he could hold, mixing bowls, and multiple sized brushes; some with large heads and some with very fine tips. He laid everything out on the table and gazed upon it all, eyes wide with wonder.

Kneeling next to Gerald, his father placed his hand on his son's shoulder.

"I know this world is hard on you. I know that you feel more deeply than others - you hurt and care. I know you like to escape into your imagination and, at times, even that gets taken away from you, so I bought you this. I thought you could paint your own world - a world of your own design. A world into which you can escape, a world you can make your own. Where you can find happiness.... Would you like that?"

Gerald smiled and nodded. His mother stood there with tears in her eyes as she watched Gerald comprehend this project. He picked up a paintbrush and stared at it. Then turned to his father and hugged him.

"Thank you, Dad."

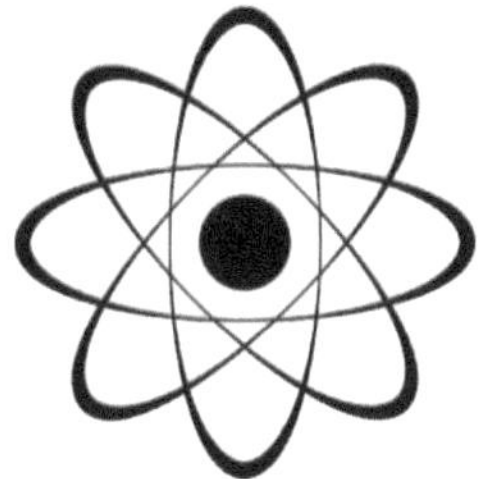

Chapter 3

Gerald peered at the large white canvas and wondered where he should start. He had never painted anything in his entire life. It was so big, it almost overwhelmed him. The canvas seemed to speak to him. It said, "Make it good." And this feeling made Gerald shiver.

He realized he needed to start at the top, so he found a step stool, dragged it to the canvas and climbed up.

So far away from the ground, face to face with this large monstrous canvas, Gerald picked up his paintbrush and pallet. He closed his eyes. He took a deep breath, slowly exhaled and made his first stroke.

One large thick black streak went completely across the canvas. Then, he painted another long streak, and another. When the top of the canvas was covered in shades of black, he dabbed his brush into the blue and began mixing it in as he proceeded down the canvas. He was laying the ground work for something, and currently, that something was very dark.

As night approached, his father called for him to get cleaned up for dinner. He climbed down from the stool, closed up his paints, washed out his brushes and looked up at what he had started.

It resembled a separation of light and dark. Darkness covered the deep and all of a sudden the canvas spoke to Gerald again. It said, "Let there be light." And Gerald knew, tomorrow, he would need to do something to brighten up his world.

The next day at school, Gerald couldn't help but think about his painting. He wanted nothing more than to run home and paint. He stared out the window of the classroom noticing at how the sky seemed to darken toward the top and lighten closer to the ground. How the clouds brightened the blue, and how the sun sparkled golden in the sky.

He knew what to do when he got home, and he couldn't wait to accomplish his task. But first, he had to endure hours of ridicule from his peers. He heard the snickering of boys behind him. He felt the eyes of the class turn and stare at him when the teacher asked him a question. He felt so small and so insignificant, and yet he wanted to become smaller and disappear entirely.

The day was long and daunting. When he finally made it home, Gerald was almost exhausted. Almost, but not too exhausted to escape into his room to work on his painting.

With paintbrush in hand, Gerald mixed the blacks and blues and whites together. He worked diligently, painting the most beautiful blue sky with fluffy white clouds. He even added a bit of panache when he dabbed his brush into the white dollop of paint and flicked it towards the top of the canvas. He flicked it again and again, sending sprays of little white flecks that filled the dark black.

Time after time he sprayed the canvas with hundreds of white dots of all different sizes. The effect was that some looked brighter and closer, while others looked less bright and farther away. When he was done, he gazed upon his creation and said, "That looks good."

Then Gerald mixed the white and blue together, to create a much brighter blue. He continued down the painting, brightening it until it seemed too bright. Gerald felt a little darkness needed to be painted back in.

For some reason, Gerald felt there needed to be equal parts dark and light. Since it was so dark at the top, it needed to be dark at the bottom, to balance it out. So he began darkening the blues until he finally made it to the bottom of the canvas.

When he stepped back to view his canvas, he realized what he had painted. Above was sky, the dark of the universe, the bright of the day. From the bright of the day to the bottom of the sea, he had painted the waters of the ocean, the ocean whose depths were just as dark and unknown as the void and cold of space.

That evening at dinner, Gerald's father asked about his progress with the painting. Gerald had only painted the base of the painting. He hadn't added any dimension, nothing truly interesting but the smile on his face beamed. "It's a work in progress," said Gerald proudly, "I think it is coming along quite well."

"Well, that's wonderful." His father smiled.

With delight, Gerald added, "I am really looking forward to getting back to work on it tomorrow!"

"Gerald, we're going over to my sister's house tomorrow." His mother watched Gerald's smile fade away. She knew he was disappointed and tried to lift his spirits. "It'll be nice to see your cousins, right?"

"Sure." Gerald spoke glumly. His cousins were not high on his favorites list, but worse than that, Gerald realized that tomorrow he wouldn't get to paint. As his happy expression drifted away, his stomach began to churn.

"May I be excused? I'm not really hungry."

"Of course." His father noticed the abrupt change in his son's demeanor.

Gerald stood and walked to his room.

He put his paints away.

He washed his brushes out.

He hung his pallet to dry.

He did all of this methodically as the disappointment worked its way through him.

CHAPTER 4

Gerald's Aunt Cath was an odd bird, at least that's how his father described her. She had a way of wrapping herself around you in the biggest most comprehensive hug ever.

"Oliver!" she exclaimed brightly, raising her arms into the air to give away one of her massively encompassing hugs.

Gerald never understood why she called him by his middle name. His middle name was his late grandfather's first name. When his grandfather passed, it seemed only fitting, to his aunt, to keep the name alive. She'd explained it once to Gerald. By using his grandfather's name, it was like her father was still there during the family reunions. And while his mother found that to be a beautiful sentiment, to Gerald it was as if he wasn't as important as the dead. Enveloped within his aunt's bear hug, he heard her speaking through his muffled ears.

"Oh how he's grown," she said, referring to Gerald but speaking to his mom. "He's almost as big as my youngest. I'll bet he can't wait to go play with his cousins." Then she called her three sons – Robert, Riley and Reed.

When she pulled Gerald out of her arms, she smiled at him, "How have you been young man?" Yet before Gerald could even contemplate answering, the three R's ran up and she told them all to go off and play.

Gerald knew if he dwelled on what his Aunt Cath had just done – attempted to show interest, only to show him she didn't really care, it would add to his growing disappointments. He decided not to dwell on it. Besides, her three sons were almost worse than the mean kids at school. As soon as they were outside of their mother's sight, he knew they'd do something.

"Do you want to play hide and go seek?" they asked.

Gerald was refreshingly stunned. He smiled and nodded his head.

"Great! You go hide, and we'll count."

Gerald turned to find possible hiding places when he heard them counting up in unison. He ran towards the woods, and when he was just outside of earshot, they began to laugh.

"How long do you think it'll take him to figure out we aren't looking for him?"

"Hopefully all afternoon." They laughed loudly, then walked the other direction.

An hour later Gerald returned to his aunt's house. His mother noticed him walk in as her sister continued to talk.

"So the lady pushed her cart as fast as she could and slammed it into the other woman's legs."

Gerald thought it was a horrible story but his aunt laughed as she told it.

He walked up to his mom who shared her glass of lemonade with him and had Gerald take a seat next to her. They both listened to his aunt finish her story. She turned from the kitchen sink to see Gerald sitting there as well.

"When did you get here?" his aunt asked.

Gerald shrugged his shoulders.

"Hmmm," she groused as a tight smile spread across her face. "Guess adult talk is over now that there are little ears in the room." She turned back to the sink.

Once again, as it often happened at school, Gerald walked into a room and the conversations suddenly stopped. At school it felt as if he weren't welcome with the other children. With his Aunt Cath, it felt like he wasn't welcomed at all. He looked over to his mom who smiled kindly at him. She saw Gerald's sadness and confusion. Standing up, she walked over to his aunt's kitchen window where four little brown pots rested on the sill.

"Do you see these tiny seedlings?" she asked. "They need to be planted. Would you like to take care of that for us?"

Gerald nodded, and his mom handed him the plants. As Gerald left the room, he heard his aunt speak up. "What a great idea, Sis. You are always so good to him."

Gerald's mom had once told him his aunt didn't mean anything bad or mean, that she just didn't have the filter in her brain other people have. To Gerald, it seemed like quite a few people in his life were missing that filter, and there was a part of him that wondered if he was the odd one out.

As he sat in the garden, Gerald placed the tools he needed around him to transplant the young plants. The practice of sowing these small sprouting seedlings into the ground energized him. He dug the hole in the cool moist dirt, and carefully brushed aside the pile of soil. With tender support, he pulled the seedlings root ball from its temporary pot and cradled it as he slipped it into the hole. Finally, like tucking a baby into bed, he covered the root structure with the dirt and packed it in. The quiet of his mind allowed the birds singing in the distance to fill his ears. He felt the warm rays of sunlight kiss his face. He closed his eyes and smelled the musk from the dirt, the pollen in the air, the grass in the distance. It was quiet moments like this that left Gerald feeling the happiest. He could never be alone when so much beauty surrounded him.

Crunch-squish.

"Ha ha!"

Gerald opened his eyes and saw his freshly planted seedling flattened under his cousin's shoe. He followed the line of the boy's leg up his torso to his face that was darkened into a silhouette by the sunshine above him.

"Oops – did I do that?" The boy feigned an apologetic comment while snickering under his breath. He looked ovcr at his brothers and laughed with them.

Gerald sat back and yanked his small shovel out from under Ryan's shoe. He watched as the boy twisted his foot, pressing the plant further into the ground.

Then almost comically, his middle cousin stepped backward onto another plant, then lifted his foot up as if he had stepped on dog poo. "Oops – did it again."

The brothers laughed louder as the instigator stomped out of Gerald's garden, kicking another seedling as he exited. "You should really watch where you plant those things."

Gerald crawled closer to the first seedling and noticed its main stem had been snapped in half. Its leaves were torn, folded and flattened into the dirt. Gerald could almost feel the young plant's pain as he lifted its lifeless sprouts off the ground and into the palm of his hand.

How could they be so mean? Don't they know that they killed this young plant? A tear slipped down Gerald's face as he carefully placed the plant back onto the dirt and then leaned further to see the second ravaged plant. It was bent, not broken. A couple of leaves had been lost but the main stem still flexed back into place. It had a chance of survival, so Gerald attempted to save it.

He cupped his hand and scooped a pile of dirt under the plant to support its stem and poured an extra bit of water over it to replenish it. Gerald closed his eyes and hoped silently that this small young plant would make it. He wanted to escape back into that pleasant, peaceful moment he had enjoyed a few minutes earlier, but it was gone. He could almost hear the plants screaming. Bird songs now seemed like cries. The wind felt cold and hard as the sun sank behind a cloud. Now, all he felt was darkness, and Gerald knew his peace was gone.

How quickly it all goes away, he thought. I wish those boys would disappear.

Chapter 5

With the mutilation his horrible cousins had inflicted on those young plants still fresh on Gerald's mind, he approached his canvas that night with a plan.

He painted land and hills and mountains, some large and close up, others further away. Then he began dotting his landscape with plants and trees. He got lost in his painting as he planted his paintbrush onto the canvas and twirled it through his fingers, spinning large branches with tons of leaves.

For hours, Gerald created the vegetation in his world. Various kinds of plants and trees, some with flowers, some bearing fruit. Seeds would sprout and blow in the wind and land in the freshly painted dirt. Then they would sprout and grow and flourish in this incredibly vivid world of Gerald's. That thought made him happy and satisfied.

As bedtime crept closer and his eyes drooped, Gerald stepped away from his painting to take in his work.

While exhausted, both emotionally and physically, he found himself smiling.

This painting project had transformed him. His world was blue and green and tan and brown. The colors were vibrant – they expressed a renewal in his spirit.

This is good, Gerald thought as he washed his brushes.

At school the next morning, his science teacher discussed life cycles of frogs. Gerald found himself enthralled in the idea of watching tiny tadpoles hatch from eggs and grow into the frogs that could leap great distances, croak loudly and live in the water or on the land.

Gerald was deep in thought about how wonderful it must be to be a tadpole, to be swimming in the cool shallow waters and to revel in the quiet. He longed to be able to breathe underwater, never needing to come out of the water or hear the children laughing.

"Mr. Delaney!" the teacher barked loudly, apparently for the third time, although Gerald only heard her once. "I'm waiting."

"Waiting for what, Ma'am?"

She shook her head with frustration, "For the answer."

"I'm sorry. I didn't hear the question," Gerald admitted shyly, knowing he was in trouble.

"Pay attention, Mr. Delaney." The teacher scowled at him.

This was a look he'd seen many times but never directed at him. She called on another student, and Gerald sank further down into his seat.

Tadpoles were still the topic of conversation; it was not like he had ventured away from that. The boys behind him snickered under their breath. Gerald wished he could take a deep breath and dive down into the depths of the waters past the tadpoles and disappear.

That afternoon, as soon as he could, Gerald went down to a nearby pond and started looking for frog eggs. He walked all around the pond searching for tall grasses, twigs or logs or rocks, anything that stuck out of the pond and provided a safe area for eggs.

Finally, near a nice shade tree, ten feet down from a nearby pathway, he spotted the foamy tangle of frog eggs. They were stuck to a plant in the shallow waters of the pond. As he leaned in, he noticed the clear round eggs, hundreds of them, and within, small black tadpoles growing and getting ready for life.

The next day Gerald checked the eggs and noticed a few tadpoles had hatched. He knew the rest would soon follow. They would eat the remaining eggshells for sustenance and nutrients and then gradually grow in this shallow water. He knew it would take time for them to grow into the frogs they were destined to become, but he looked forward to it.

He became enthusiastic about the idea of returning to the pond every afternoon after school so he could watch them. He was eager to watch them grow their little legs out and take their first steps onto land. To Gerald, it would have been like watching a child take a first step.

That afternoon, however, a group of kids came to go swimming in the pond. The first few ran and leapt into the waters with so much exuberance that they created large waves that washed many of the unhatched eggs away.

"Stop!" Gerald pleaded. "You're going to kill the tadpoles."

Some of the kids looked at him, shocked that Gerald had even spoken to them. But a couple others didn't seem to care at all. They kicked and punched the waters, splashing Gerald and creating large ripples and currents that swept away the tadpoles.

When Gerald looked back down at the now ravaged and empty bank where the tadpoles had been, he saw nothing but devastation. There were no signs of life. He searched and searched, and then, he spotted a tadpole flopping on the ground just far enough away from the water to die.

Fading away quickly, Gerald knew he had to save the little guy. He tenderly scooped the small tadpole into his palm and carefully released it back into the water. The violently rocking waters though, swayed under the force of the kids playing. It washed over the tiny tadpole, and spun him violently in the current. Gerald watched as the little guy quickly lost his fight for life and sank further and further down into the darkness of the waters.

Gerald ran home crying.

How could those children not care? Gerald wondered. How many animals had been harmed by them and their families over the years?

Chapter 6

Over and over again, Gerald witnessed the destruction of so many things he loved. Humans constantly ruined what this world had to offer without even so much as an acknowledgment of these tiny plants and animals. Yet, it wasn't limited to small things.

He watched adults tear down trees, leaving animals homeless. They'd destroy complete forests to build their buildings and then be shocked when the animals came looking for food and shelter. He watched people litter, throwing away trash that choked and strangled the animals. He read stories of people mistreating animals, tying them up, starving them, and neglecting them - just because they were bigger than other animals.

Gerald couldn't believe what he saw of this world. He couldn't believe how horrible people were. He couldn't understand why anyone would want to live in a world with all of these terrible humans. That's when Gerald realized what he wanted to do with his painting. For weeks, he worked on his painting in silence. He painted birds in the sky, hundreds of types of birds, big and small, of all sorts of colors, shapes and sizes. They soared through the clouds and landed on the tree tops. They were happy.

Then he began painting the fish in the sea, large and small, whales and dolphins, octopus and crab. Every sea living creature he could imagine he painted, and even some new ones. He filled his sea down to the depths of the dark waters where the colors of their bodies seemed to illuminate the depths in which they swam. Mixed with colorful corals and seashells, the ocean was as colorful and vibrant as the land.

Then he began painting the animals on the land, from the very small to the very tall. Big animals like elephants and rhinos to small animals like mice and rabbits. Then he painted every single animal in between. He painted white animals and black animals, brown and green and orange animals. Animals of every color of the pallet dotted each aspect of his painting. There were monkeys in the trees, badgers underground, squirrels in the sky, and absolutely everything in between.

These animals lived peacefully among each other. The tall ones helped the short ones; the strong ones helped the weak. They all worked in unison with each other. There was order and understanding within a quiet solitude. Each animal family had a love and understanding for each other. They all spoke their own similar language, and this tied them all together.

Gerald had spilled every ounce of love and caring he had into this world. He willed it to be beautiful and peaceful. He willed it to grow and flourish. His spirit instilled blissfulness throughout it. The birds sang the most amazing songs. The crickets chirped their calming tunes. Flowers bloomed and slept and bloomed again. There was color and life and delight. He was determined to make this world a sanctuary, and so it had become his paradise. It was a beautiful world Gerald had created. When he finished, the picturesque scene danced on the canvas and brought such pleasure to Gerald that he couldn't help but want to stay with it forever. It was peaceful and tranquil. There was harmony and serenity. It stilled his heart and filled his soul, and as he sat there staring at it, he found contentment.

The next thing he wanted to do when he was completely finished with it, was share it with his father. He ran out to the living room, and with the brightest, most thrill-filled face he had ever expressed, Gerald announced his news.

"Dad! I've finished my painting!"

"You have?"

"Yes! I can't wait for you to see it."

"Well, let's go." He smiled as he took his son's hand and led him into the studio. When his father walked in and saw that giant canvas with so many colors and shapes and so much detail leaning up against the wall, his mouth gaped open. He stared at it in silence for the longest time, marveling at it.

He got lost in the scene. His eyes slowly scanning the entirety of the piece, and while he saw so much, he knew he wasn't seeing it all. It was too vast.

He couldn't believe the marvelous work Gerald had done. Not a detail had been missed. Every tree, every flower, every leaf and blade of grass had been painstakingly painted. Every animal of every size and every shape and every color he could possibly think of and some he hadn't seen in years could be found hiding, playing and walking within this miraculous painting. The detail was astonishing. It was realistic yet expressionistic.

He could tell that Gerald had created the world based on what he knew but also made it his own. It was like nothing he had ever seen before and yet it seemed familiar. It was...

"Incredible," he finally breathed after many minutes of staring at the piece.

"You like it?"

He began to say, "I had no idea...," yet paused in order to hold back a tear. Gerald glanced up at his father who stared at the painting. "I had no idea."

Gerald realized his father couldn't see it the way he did. He knew his father only saw the paint, and he wanted nothing more than to share the magic with him as well. He took his father's hand into his.

"Dad, I want you to truly experience it."

Gerald's dad turned to face his son, who smiled. Gerald stared at the painting, closed his eyes and inhaled deeply. His smile broadened as a gust of wind blew the hair on his head. Startled as to the source of a wind in a room with no windows, his dad turned his gaze back to the painting. He looked upon it and watched as it came to life.

The tree branches were swaying in the wind. Birds started soaring across the sky and dolphins leapt out of the ocean waters. He could smell the salty air, the flowers in bloom. He could feel the temperature cool and then heard the repetitive caw of a peacock's cry.

His mouth opened as more individual sounds rushed to his ears. A jungle of acoustics and smells flooded his senses, and he felt the world call to him.

He released Gerald's hand and walked closer to the painting. It was a massive canvas, he knew, but once it was painted it seemed even larger than he could comprehend.

The closer he walked, the more he was immersed into the world. It sucked him in. He soon realized he was actually standing inside. He looked all around. It was as if nothing else existed outside this world.

Looking up into the branches of the trees, he saw the most colorful parrot. As soon as the parrot spied him, it spread its dazzling wings and leapt off the limb to soar high into the air.

As he watched the parrot fly off, a movement caught his peripheral vision. He returned his gaze to the tree's canopy and saw a long thin tail sweep through the leaves, rustling them as it moved.

He watched and waited patiently until a small Howler monkey peaked his head out from behind a clump of leaves. Gerald's father let loose a hearty laugh. As soon as the sound escaped his father's lips, the Howler monkey vocalized loudly in return. Instantly, a swarm of small birds flew out of the tree and toward the sky.

Amidst the echo from the Howler monkeys screech, land animals of all sorts came out of hiding. Rabbits and squirrels scrambled to alternate locations. Turtles and lizards crept into the midday sun. Raccoons and skunks meandered toward the pathway along with foxes and badgers. Ferrets, prairie dogs, chipmunks and weasels gathered around him. Wolves, goats, deer and elk gathered behind them. Lions, tigers, cheetahs and jaguars also emerged; rhinos, hippos, elephants and bears lined up behind the large cats.

Then, when his father was completely surrounded, two large giraffes leaned their heads and necks over the massive crowd and parted the pathway so he could walk the path that stretched out before him.

He moved forward through the animals to journey deeper within the painting. As he approached the ocean's shore, crabs and turtles scrambled over the soft white sand and into the lapping waters.

He watched turtles float and swim over the waves further out into the sea until his eyes caught sight of a shark's fin. Then two dolphins leapt out of the ocean and flipped in the air. As they dived back into the ocean, their spray of water was dwarfed when a large whale exhaled from his blowhole. A massive spray of water shot up into the sky and sparkled in the mid-day sun.

Swarms of fish of varying colors, sizes and shapes swam by. As one swam relatively close to the top of the water's edge, three seagulls dove down to splash the water. As the gulls took off to fly back into the brilliant blue sky, puffy white clouds caught his eyes.

His attention was then captured by a massive bald eagle swooping through the scene and back toward land where it lighted upon the side of a massive mountain.

Right above him on a cliff's edge stood a mountain elk, tall and proud. He was perched on a ledge that seemed dangerous yet was home. Even higher, sat a wolf and cub. At the crest of the snow topped mountain were polar bears and penguins. They all observed the visitor with curious expressions.

"Whoa...," his father exhaled as he took in the most vivid and lively, colorful and dazzling world he had ever seen.

CHAPTER 7

As Gerald's father took a step backwards, he found himself back in Gerald's room. He realized he had actually walked inside the painting. He had entered the world and experienced it as if it were reality. What a magical experience. He continued to stare at it and tried to wrap his head around it. He rubbed his chin.

"That is brilliant."

"Thank you."

He heard his son's voice but continued to stare at the painting. From out here, close enough to see the brush strokes and paint, he couldn't quite wrap his head around it. He had just been inside. He had smelled the sea air. He had felt the cool breeze. He had heard the sounds of a thousand different animals, and yet he stared at the canvas.

"It's magical!" he exclaimed brightly. "What an enchanting talent. You literally created a world from a blank canvas and brought it to life."

He pulled his gaze from the painting to notice Gerald looking up at him, adoringly. Those eyes, his son's eyes, reminded him of the intense love he felt for his son. The joy and pride he felt overwhelmed him, but then another emotion drifted in.

He observed his son's smile and realized how long it had been since the last time he saw it. Gerald was always so quiet and so alone. He had no one with whom to share this joy, no one else to whom he could reveal this magic. Gerald had such a dislike of his peers. His father felt a profound sadness for his son.

"I see you didn't paint any humans."

"That's right."

"May I ask, why?"

"Why would I?" Gerald countered. "Humans are mean."

Those words clawed at his father's heart. The ache nearly buckled his knees, but he persisted. "Humans can care for your animals."

"They would ignore the animals, or hurt them or kill them."

"Not all humans are mean." He kneeled down to be at eye-level to his son. "I'm not mean." Gerald didn't reply to that comment, so his father continued. "You could paint yourself inside to tend to the animals."

"I don't ever want to go inside this world. I just want to watch it, to enjoy it."

"Seriously?" his father spoke quizzically. "Why is that?"

"It brings me pleasure; the animals and colors and sounds and smells. They fill me with this sense of completion, of absolute bliss. It's a feeling I never feel out here. A feeling that so completely overwhelms me with happiness that I know, without a doubt, if I stepped into that painting, if I walked inside and experienced it as real life, if I truly felt that contentment, I would never want to come out. I would get lost within that painting, never to be seen again.

Although so much of me, almost every fiber of my very being wants more than anything to run into it and never return, I know I can't. I need to be here with you and mom. I need to learn more about this world of ours. I need to understand why it is so harsh and painful and emotional and dark. I need to understand why I was chosen to be here and experience this as well as why I would be able to paint that world – a world that is perfect."

Gerald pointed to his painting. "Why do I have this alternative, this ability to paint beauty of which that I cannot be a part? That," he pointed again, "is so different from what I experience in life. It is so much more elaborate, but it's so incredibly simple, too.

"Without humans, there is no evil. There is no one to make me feel small and insignificant. No one to disappointment me, to get my hopes up and then shatter my dreams. No one to push me around, or to kick me or destroy my work. No one to stomp on my plants, tear down my trees or litter my world. There is no one to hunt down and kill my animals. No one to start fights and wars, no one to blow up bombs and start fires.

"This world can stay perfect. Why would I want to insert the imperfect into a perfect world? That would cause chaos and destruction. Wouldn't it?"

How can I counter that question? his father pondered. How can I help Gerald understand that with the bad, there is also good? How can I explain any of this when my son has never seen even the slightest ounce of good?

Gerald's father sighed. He knew Gerald needed to understand, but he needed to learn it in his own time, and in his own way. *There is good in this world. I just have to hope Gerald will be presented with the opportunity to see it.*

"Those are excellent questions. Questions that *can* be answered, but I can't just tell you those answers, that wouldn't help you. As much as I wish for you to be able to learn the lessons of this world without getting hurt, I realize now that you must seek out your own answers."

He took his son's hand. "You do know there is good in this world, right?"

"There is?"

"Yes," he laughed, "there is a lot of good in this world."

"Where?"

"Everywhere. You just have to be able to see it. Yes, there is bad, quite a bit of bad, but you can't have good without bad, just like you can't have light without dark. One day, you are going to experience good, and you are going to understand."

"I look forward to that day."

Smiling sadly, Gerald's father viewed the painting again and then asked, "Do you believe your painting is complete?"

"I do."

"You don't think you will ever want to paint humans in it?"

Gerald thought about it carefully. While he truly believed his father was telling him the truth about good, he still didn't think he would ever want to paint humans in his world.

"No, I don't."

"Never want to watch a child climb a tree or swim in the sea?"

"I don't think so."

"Never ride a horse or pet a tiger?"

"Nope."

"Well, do you know what you must do next?"

"No." He looked into his dad's eyes with curious wonder.

"Every artist must sign his work."

"Sign it?"

"Paint your name."

"Where?"

"Where ever you would like, but most artists sign their work in the bottom right corner."

Gerald inspected his painting. He glanced down at the bottom right corner and felt a shiver go down his spine. There was so much in the picture, even right there. Seaweed and coral surrounded by colorful fish and eels. *My name? My very long name. It will destroy the work.*

"I can't do it."

"Why not?"

"My name's too long: Gerald Oliver Delaney. I could mess up the coral, dirty the waters or accidentally paint over a fish."

"Then paint it small."

"I'm not sure I can."

"Well then, what about your initials?"

Gerald considered that. "I could paint my first initial, my G, that wouldn't take up much room. But why sign my work in the first place?"

Smiling knowingly, his dad answered, "Signing your art is an important part of the creative process. The instant you apply your name to your work, you declare it officially finished and ready to be seen by the world. No matter what your signature looks like, what form it takes or where you put it, no work of art will ever be complete without one. Your signature identifies your art for all time as having been created, completed and approved by you and you alone. You are the creator for now and all time."

"Wow," Gerald whispered.

He walked up to his canvas. He picked up his tiniest paintbrush and lightly dipped it into the white paint. Kneeling in front of the bottom right corner of the canvas, he placed his brush tip above the corals and the fish in a very small section of dark blue sea. With light simple strokes, Gerald painted his initial:

CHAPTER 8

The next day at school Gerald smiled as he thought about his wonderful world. He couldn't wait for school to be over so he could return to the painting and watch over his world. His imagination could escape this reality. He could enjoy life and nature without anyone interrupting his happiness.

He walked through the hall carrying his stack of binders when Derek, the bully, reached out and knocked the books from his hands. Stray papers floated to the tile as Gerald's binders clattered to the floor. As Gerald watched his books and folders fall, his mood fell with them. He suddenly was ripped from his happy place and thrown back into harsh reality. His smile faded.

Boys pointed and erupted in a chorus of laughter as Gerald dragged his thoughts away from his peaceful world to the one in which he was picked on and ridiculed. Frowning, he bent down to pick up his math binder just as one of the kids kicked it out of his reach.

The binder slid three feet away, and Gerald watched as it slowed and stopped at a girl's feet. She stopped walking to examine the scene before her. Gerald returned his gaze back to the pile of clutter; he didn't notice her pick up the book.

The sound of mean laughter filled the girl's ears. She shook her head and glared at the boys disapprovingly. They paid no attention to her.

As the bell rang for them to go to class, the boys walked off leaving Gerald on his knees collecting his stuff. Walking over to Gerald, the girl handed him his binder and said, "Hi. I'm Tiffany."

Gerald took his binder from her hand and added it to his disheveled pile.

"And you are?" she asked after waiting for him to reply.

"Gerald," he mumbled, his eyes on his papers and not her.

Tiffany kneeled and helped him gather his papers. He glanced curiously at her a few times as she helped him collect his things.

Is she planning on taking them or throwing them further away?

He prepared for the worst. They both stood, and she handed him his things.

He took them, staring at her in wonder.

Noting the confused expression on his face, she smiled and asked, "What's wrong?"

"Why are you helping me?"

"Why wouldn't I?"

Her answer stunned Gerald. He stared at her silently, trying to decipher her true evil intent until she finally spoke again.

"I've got to get to class. I'll see you later, Gerald."

As she walked away Gerald stood there waiting for the other shoe to drop. For a frog to leap out from under his papers. For the secret ink she spilled in his binder to start oozing out. For her to turn around and shoot a spit wad at him... something! But she turned the corner and left him standing in the hallway all by himself.

Why did she help me?

"Mr. Delaney, you're late!" the teacher snapped as Gerald walked in the door. He immediately heard the boys in the back laughing at him which made him feel smaller than getting in trouble with the teacher.

As he made his way to his desk, Gerald spotted that same girl looking up at him with a shy yet pitiful smile on her face. Though she attempted to give a sympathetic look, all Gerald could think was she was somehow making fun of him.

He sat down wondering about her for the longest time until the assignment was passed out and he turned his attention to it.

At lunch, Gerald carried his tray feeling that same heavy pit in his stomach as he scanned the crowd of students for some place to sit.

If he hadn't been so hungry, he'd have skipped this part of the day and hidden in the bathroom, but even the bathroom held dangers for a small shy kid like Gerald. How he wished he could go home and escape into his world and stay there forever.

He made his way past the masses when he heard his name being called. Certain that his ears were fooling him, he kept walking, but there it was again.

"Gerald."

He glanced up from his tray and followed the sound to a hand waving in the air.

"Over here," she said, shocking Gerald as he realized it was the same girl from this morning.

Though she looked and waved in his direction, Gerald was absolutely certain she must be talking to someone, anyone other than him. He turned to see who was behind him, but there was no one.

He turned back to face her curiously. She smiled and waved again.

"Gerald, would you like to sit here?"

He was stunned. It must have shown on his face because she smiled at him and stood from the table. She took him by the hand and said, "Come, sit with me." She dragged him to her table.

No one had ever asked him to sit with them. No one had ever remembered his name. No one had ever offered to help him without wanting to do something mean. As he sat down with his plate of food, he covered it with his hands so she wouldn't spit in it or drop a bug into it.

"What are you doing?" she asked as he stared at her suspiciously.

He took a bite of his bread, without taking his eyes off her. She spoke again.

"I'm Tiffany, remember?"

"I remember."

"We met this morning."

"I know," he admitted with apprehension.

"I'm new here."

Gerald was shocked. "You are?"

"Yeah. My parents just moved to town. I'm finding it hard making friends."

"Tell me about it," Gerald grumbled.

"I miss my old school. I had so many friends there. Now I have to start over again and that is so hard. Do you have any friends?"

Gerald sadly shook his head.

"Well, you do now." Tiffany smiled.

"Why would you want to be my friend?"

"Why wouldn't I?" she countered. She looked at him waiting for his answer, but he just stared back at her.

"You do that a lot," she said as she took a bite of her chicken salad.

"Do what?" Gerald asked as he took another bite of his own lunch.

"Stare at people, well, me at least. Why are you staring at me?"

"I don't understand you."

"What do you mean? We speak the same language, right?"

"Yes, of course, we do."

"Then what don't you understand?"

"Why you are being nice to me? No one has ever been nice to me."

"No one?" Tiffany repeated in disbelief.

Gerald shook his head.

"No one has ever what, talked to you?"

Again, Gerald shook his head no.

"No one's ever been kind to you?"

He continued shaking his head.

"No one has ever invited you to sit with them?"

Gerald began to get dizzy shaking his head.

"No one has ever helped you gather your books?"

Gerald stopped shaking his head. Now Tiffany stared at him. Her brow furrowed slightly as she cocked her head to the side.

"What?" Gerald asked, feeling very awkward at that moment.

"That is so sad." Tiffany spoke, putting her utensil down. She took Gerald's hand into hers. "Gerald, that's not acceptable. You can't let people be mean to you."

"It's not like I let them do it or ask for it."

"But you don't stand up for yourself. You don't tell them not to."

"How can I do that when there's only one of me and there are so many of them?"

"Because now it's not just one of you, it's both of us. And Gerald, I'm going to show you what friendship is supposed to be like."

CHAPTER 9

Tiffany proved to be true to her word. They played together and talked during recess. At the end of school, she joined him on his walk home from school. They discussed their favorite foods, things to do, favorite animals; they told jokes and shared stories about each of themselves. Granted, Tiffany told more stories than Gerald because he couldn't think of much to say. He didn't want to depress her with stories of his dead tadpoles or the young seedlings his cousins stomped. He couldn't imagine her wanting to hear much of anything in his life.

But then, she surprised him.

"Gerald, I've been doing lots of talking. Tell me something about yourself."

"There's really not much to say," Gerald admitted. He wanted to. He'd been wracking his brain all day trying to add to her conversation, but he couldn't think of anything happy he could offer. He enjoyed listening to her stories, sharing her joys and life's excitements. He longed to feel that way, and as they walked and talked - he did.

But now Tiffany wanted to know something about him. Something joyful and happy... "I love nature."

"I do, too," she declared as she began regaling him with stories of finding a bird's nest full of eggs. She explained how she brought it to school and used the science lab heat lamp to hatch the birds. Then, all of the students took turns feeding the young birds, tending to them, raising them.

Gerald was entranced at the thought that children were so thoughtful and caring in her old town. "I'd love to meet those students, so many good people in one place. I long to go there and meet others like me."

"People like that can be found here, too, Gerald. You just have to see them."

"Oh, I've seen them all right, the people here. They are horrible and destructive. They don't care about nature or life or plants. They really don't care about me or my feelings, and I hardly believe they even care about others."

Tiffany was appalled at what Gerald had just said. She had met quite a few children that day at school and thought many of them were delightful. Why had Gerald not seen that? She thought carefully and then asked, "What are your parents like?"

Gerald smiled. His eyes even smiled as he inhaled and spoke happily. "They are wonderful. In fact, my dad...," Gerald began with excitement, but then paused. He trailed off not sure he wanted to share. His smile faded, his eyes became wide, almost as if he were afraid. Tiffany grew concerned.

"What about your dad?"

"I don't know. Never mind."

"Oh, come on," Tiffany insisted. "You sounded so excited, happier than you have all day, and then...you stopped. Please tell me what you were going to say."

Gerald thought carefully about what he was going to say. He then quietly spoke with a shyness to him. "My dad bought me a canvas to paint."

"So you are an artist?"

"No. I don't think so."

"Have you painted on it yet?"

"Yes. I painted an entire world and signed it."

"Then you are an artist. I'd love to see it." Tiffany smiled in a way that seemed to warm his heart, but that heart was still very cold and hard. It had not completely opened to the idea of trusting another human.

"Oh, I don't know if I ever want to share it with anyone," Gerald admitted shyly.

"Why not?"

"Because people are mean."

That single phrase pierced Tiffany's heart. She had never felt that way. She knew there were mean kids and bad people, but she could never group all the people of the world into that one category. Yet Gerald could.

How sad it must feel to truly believe that all people are mean, never to have experienced enough happiness to at least give pause to a thought like that. Tiffany knew she had to do something for Gerald to change his perspective on people.

"Not all people are mean."

"Really?" Gerald asked with complete bewilderment.

"Of course not!" She smiled at him. "I'm not mean."

Gerald tilted his head a bit, "Well, you've been nice to me. ...*So far.*"

Tiffany exhaled through a bewildered smile. "I don't know how, Gerald, but I'm going to prove to you that people are good."

Gerald stopped and stared at her. "You just said people are good."

"That's right."

"But I said people are mean."

"Right."

"So when I said *mean*, did you hear *bad*?"

"No. I heard you say *mean*. But you categorized ALL people as mean, which to me means bad since I categorize all people as good."

"But not ALL people are good. What about those boys at school who always pick on me?"

"They are not being nice, but that doesn't mean they are bad. There is always good in people."

"My father said that, but I guess I didn't understand. I asked him to explain but he said I needed to figure it out on my own."

"He wanted you to learn that there is good in people. Just like there is good in those boys."

"How can you say that? If there was good in them, they wouldn't pick on me."

"They are misguided, but not all bad. I am certain if you got to know them, you would find good in them."

"Why would I want to get to know them when they've always been mean to me?"

"I don't know, Gerald. Why would you discount each one of them forever for a few bad actions?"

Gerald thought about that for a few moments. Tiffany had a point. They began walking again as Gerald thought. Tiffany gave him the quiet time to think. Finally, Gerald came back with another question.

"So being mean does not indicate they are bad people?"

"Right." She smiled.

"So does that mean that being nice does not necessarily suggest that you are a good person?"

Tiffany now stopped and stared at Gerald. She was a nice person; she and he both knew this. She would never consider herself as a bad person, and she would never intentionally do anything bad.

Gerald could sense that she was suddenly feeling conflicted, so he explained.

"My dad said - there is always good and always bad and always light and always dark. He explained that you can't have one without the other. If I were to apply that to people, that would imply that everyone who is good can also be bad and everyone who is bad can also be good. Likewise, every kid who's ever been mean to me also has the capability of being nice but they choose to be mean so they are deciding to be bad."

"I guess that makes sense." Tiffany watched as Gerald walked over to a nearby tree.

"But animals and plants don't have that capability." He pointed to a couple of squirrels in the tree. They watched as one squirrel offered an extra acorn to the other. Gerald continued explaining in a whisper.

"That squirrel could have chosen not to share his food. He could have decided to run off or push the other squirrel away but he didn't."

"Maybe they're friends."

"So only if you are friends, you are nice to one another? Why can't you be nice to complete strangers?"

"But you can. That's how you make friends. You give someone a chance."

"I've met quite a few people, mostly students at school, but even cousins in my own family have been mean to me. Besides you and my parents, no one I have ever met has attempted to be my friend. Even the ones who weren't mean, who simply ignored me, I consider mean. They proved they weren't good by not giving me a chance. So as far as I am concerned, I stand by my previous phrase that all people are mean."

They both stood there thinking. Gerald was quite impressed with the philosophical conversation they had just had. He was intrigued with Tiffany. She had brought up some valid points, points that made him think, maybe even reconsider for the slightest moment.

Tiffany, while also consumed in thought, was still concerned with proving to Gerald that people are good. She felt they had come a good ways today but she hadn't successfully swayed Gerald's opinion. She believed in time she'd be able to help him understand. She then began wondering again about the painting. She was curious about what it looked like.

"So you won't show me your painting?"

"Not today."

"But someday?"

Gerald felt a goodness about her and wanted to believe. He smiled. "We'll see."

There was a small part of him that wanted to share his painting with her but he still worried. He barely knew her. He didn't know if she would or could turn mean. He didn't know how she would act or what she would say if she didn't like the painting. He didn't know if she'd be able to see it as he saw it or appreciate it.

Gerald would have to test her first. She'd have to prove herself worthy of seeing his painting. If she could see the world he knows out here and understand, if she could prove her heart was good and her intentions pure and her desire to be nice, sincere, then maybe, Gerald would share his world with her.

The next day before school began, Gerald noticed Tiffany talking with another student. Hesitantly, Gerald walked up to them. He listened to their conversation, trying to smile and listen like he was interested.

The other student didn't look at him. Tiffany hadn't acknowledged him. He was certain what he dreaded had already started, the ignoring of Gerald - a long time favorite activity of any team he had ever been chosen last for.

Feeling sheepishly embarrassed as if he were standing there unwanted, literally eavesdropping on a conversation of which he obviously was not a part, he started to back away. Tiffany though, reached for his hand. She held him there, still not looking at him but refusing to let him leave. Gerald didn't know what to think.

Finally, when the student stopped speaking, Tiffany surprised Gerald.

"That is so interesting. I'll have to fill my friend in. Gerald," she turned to him, "this is Sam, short for

Samantha. She, too, is an artist, or at least hopes to be one someday."

Gerald smiled. She held out her hand to shake his. "Nice to meet you, Gerald." Gerald shook her hand noticing there was dried paint on her fingers. In fact, as he looked at her, he noticed she had flecks of paint on her freckled face. Her hair was sloppily pulled back into a bun and a dry paintbrush was shoved through it to hold it in place.

"Tiffany told me about your painting. I'm quite impressed." She spoke to Gerald.

"You are?" Gerald asked, knowing Tiffany hadn't even seen his painting yet. "What about?"

"The fact that you've finished it."

"Sam started a piece of artwork last month but never finished it," Tiffany explained. "She just told me how she wasn't sure what it was missing, so she decided to walk away from it and try her hand at something else."

Gerald was intrigued. "Would you be interested in showing me your artwork? I could maybe...," but then he trailed off nervously.

"I would love to show it to someone! Maybe a new set of eyes will help me." Samantha gleamed. As the girls continued to talk and discuss plans for meeting after school, Gerald couldn't help but feel amazed.

He hadn't been ignored. He had been included in a conversation. He had received a compliment and respect, and he had been invited to someone's house. Gerald had never experienced anything like this.

Maybe there is some good in people?

CHAPTER 10

That afternoon, Gerald and Tiffany followed Sam back to her home. It was a quirky little place filled with color. An array of sculptures and ornaments decorated the yard. Each exterior wall of the house was hand-painted with spirals and shapes that decorated the edges of the windows and doors.

When they walked into the house, they saw beads hanging from door jams like curtains and a collage of paintings, sculptures, and hand-crafted items completely covering the walls.

Sam showed them into her studio, which was lit by a variety of lamps and lights, and they took sight of many canvases. They were much, much smaller than Gerald's massive canvas. Some were hung on the wall; some were sitting on easels. Some were lined up against one another on the floor.

"To the left is the painting I started on last night, but right here is the pastel vase I began last month."

Gerald gazed upon the canvas. It was a chalk interpretation of a vase of purple and yellow silk flowers that sat on the table about four feet away.

She had carefully sketched and blended the blues of the vase, adding the darker blue shadows around the rim and base. She had painstakingly blended the purples and yellows of the flowers in it, and it was very nice. Yet Gerald noticed that it seemed to be floating in midair. It wasn't sitting on anything. There was nothing but white canvas all around it, and while the white helped the colorful vase of flowers pop off the canvas, it definitely didn't feel right.

"You can't have light without dark," his father's words spilled out of his mouth.

"What do you mean?" Sam asked as she turned to Gerald.

"My dad tried to teach me something about opposites. You can't have good without bad, and you can't have light without dark."

He thought about his own painting. How he had started with the dark because that was how he felt. He considered himself a good person, but his emotions and mood drew him to the dark colors.

Suddenly he understood something about himself, which in turn helped him to understand something about others. It was the situations in his life that made him go dark. He closed himself off to others for fear of ridicule, and when Tiffany tried to befriend him he was standoffish.

Maybe he was at least partly responsible for his loneliness?

He thought about his painting, and how after he brought in the lighter colors, it seemed to come together. It also helped him realize that after he opened himself up to Tiffany's light, other good things seemed to come with it.

He looked back at Samantha's painting and spoke. "You have painted this beautiful vase of flowers, but they are basically floating in midair. It's not realistic. Light can't exist without dark."

Gerald pointed to a bright spot on the vase. "This light is wonderful, but you aren't showing any dark. Maybe what your painting needs is shadowing. Shadows under the vase as it sits on a table. Shadows behind the vase as it blocks the light from hitting the wall." Gerald moved so he could cast a shadow on the wall. "The darkness will help it feel more real and help the beauty of the flowers shine."

Tiffany stared at Gerald. "That was so deep," she said, truly impressed.

Sam looked back at the painting, picked up a black chalk stick and began sketching some shadows around the vase. She drew a darker line horizontally a quarter way up from the bottom of the vase, skipping over the vase to make it seem as if the vase were sitting on a table. Then, she added shadow to the wall behind it.

She sketched quickly but with determination. When she stepped away from the painting a few minutes later, the trio could see the truth. The shadows gave the painting depth and personality. It made the subject matter real.

It was a remarkable contrast.

"Gerald, thank you." Samantha spoke sincerely. "I never would have considered adding darkness into my painting. I wanted it to be bright and good and thought the only way to keep it that way would be to avoid the dark colors. Yet they complement each other. The shadows did the exact opposite of what I had thought they would."

"I guess sometimes it takes someone else's perspective to solve some of the simplest of problems." Tiffany smiled as Gerald caught her eyes.

Gerald smiled with a sigh. He was beginning to understand what his father had been talking about. If it weren't for his negative experiences in life, he wouldn't have such a strong appreciation for this friendship with Tiffany. If it weren't for Tiffany's kindness, he wouldn't have understood the meaning of friendship or felt the joy of helping someone else.

Tiffany and Gerald both watched as Sam pulled out her chalk sticks and began to work. A few moments later she turned back to them.

"Oh, you are still here!" She giggled. "The canvas is calling and I'm here to answer. You two can show yourselves out, right?"

Tiffany glanced at Gerald and shrugged her shoulders. They left Sam's studio in silence. Once outside, Gerald spoke quietly.

"That was rude."

"She's just excited about her project."

"Yes, but she just forgot about us. She basically kicked us out. I thought she was nice and she turned out to be like everyone else."

"How do you mean?"

"She needed something. I thought she wanted friendship, but she just wanted insight. As soon as she got what she wanted, she discarded us like an empty tube of paint. I've been used many times in my life. It's not fun. I get my hopes up. I feel like I have finally made a connection and then they just drop me."

Tiffany listened as they strolled through the park.

"Worse than that, I've had people lie to me after I helped them. They claimed they'd be there for me. They'd tell me if I need anything, just ask." Gerald sat down on a bench near a cluster of trees and Tiffany sat beside him.

"I'm not one to ask for help. But I would hope that if they saw that I needed it, they would offer."

Gerald turned to Tiffany, who was listening. Her smile was small, but she was still there for him. He worried he would scare her away with his negativity, so he stopped speaking.

"Gerald?"

"I'm sorry." He spoke softly, his head down and his eyes focused on his lap.

"For what?"

"I shouldn't have said those things. I don't want to bring you down."

"Gerald, we are friends. You can tell me anything."

"Can I? Can I really?"

"Of course," she said, touching his chin with her finger tips and pointing his face to hers. "I am so happy that you are finally opening up to me. That you are finally telling me something about yourself."

"But my stories are always so sad. I have bullies and isolation, disappointments and letdowns. I feel so alone. I feel like I have nothing positive to bring to a friendship. Your stories are always so bright and cheerful; they make me smile – but my stories make you sad, they make ME sad. Why would you want to do that to yourself?"

"Because I care about you."

"I don't understand why. No one else does. Everyone else just goes about their lives as if I don't exist… like Sam just did."

"You helped Sam see something she couldn't see for herself. You brought an excitement to her that she had lost. You gave her a gift, one that she won't forget."

"She forgot about us pretty quickly."

"Don't give up on her." Tiffany glanced up into the trees. Gerald followed her gaze to a couple of squirrels. They both watched as one squirrel handed another an acorn.

Gerald then noticed how the recipient then took off with the acorn leaving the other squirrel sitting there alone. His heart broke for the squirrel sitting there by itself, but Tiffany saw something different.

She watched as the recipient squirrel ran down the tree to the ground. She quietly directed Gerald's focus on that squirrel. They both watched as it buried the acorn in the ground, then ran back up the tree branch to sit with its friend.

"He came back," Gerald spoke.

"I saw your focus stay on the giver just now. I sensed your sadness for him as he was left alone, just like you had been left alone. But what you wouldn't have seen was that he gave his friend a gift; something that brought him joy.

"That squirrel took that acorn and buried it in the ground to keep it safe, to get to it later. He was so happy, that yes, he momentarily forgot his friend, but only for a moment. He did come back. That's what real friends do.

Yes, it was on his time. Yes, it very easily could have taken much longer and yes, there are situations in this world that could have kept him from coming back. His parents could have called him home, a cat could have chased him away, it could have started raining and he'd have to seek shelter, but eventually, when life allowed, he would have come back. That's what friendship is all about."

Gerald understood. He sat there in quiet solitude reflecting on this for a spell. He thought about his past, of the friends who weren't friends, and he tried to understand why they never came back.

He realized that life had gotten in the way. Sam's painting called to her, but maybe tomorrow at school, she would come back to them. He thought about the bullies who would knock his books from his hands and the one whom he'd once helped standing with them. He never really thought about it until now, but in those moments, the one that should have helped him, who never did, never acted with the others. He just stood there watching.

While, to Gerald, a true friend wouldn't have let it happen, or stick up for their friend, he realized fear could have kept him from standing up. He couldn't blame him for the bullying, but he still couldn't forgive him for his complacency either. Gerald suddenly felt better about the situation. By allowing his darker feelings to lighten the pressure on his heart, he suddenly felt something new.

Forgiveness.

All in all, it had been a wonderful day. The pleasure Gerald felt in seeing the sparkle in Sam's eyes as she expressed her thrill in solving her problem was a truly rewarding experience. He could sense her elation when the painting came together. It was a delight to see her smile. It was an experience he, too, would like to feel.

"Do you think Sam will ask us back to see her finished painting?"

Tiffany smiled at Gerald, "I bet she will, but it may not be tomorrow. You know well these things take time. But, I bet when it is time, she will."

Gerald grinned. "That would be nice."

He had something to look forward to. He had another chance at happiness, at feeling more amazing emotions. It gave him a longing, an eagerness to feel more. It gave him the desire to want to open himself up in the same way. He found that he wanted to share his own painting with Tiffany and before he could think twice about it, he spoke.

"I want to show you my painting."

Tiffany stopped. "You didn't want to show me your painting yesterday."

"But I want to show it to you today. Would you like to see it?" Gerald asked with a large smile on his face.

"Of course! I would be honored."

Tiffany witnessed a light shine from Gerald's eyes, a light she had never seen before. The smile on his face was brighter than the sun. His passion was strong and she understood the importance of this moment for him.

Tiffany followed Gerald to his home, and he announced their arrival when they walked in the door. "Mom, I'm home."

His mother stuck her head out from the kitchen and smiled, then saw Tiffany behind him. She finished drying her hands, tossed the towel to the counter and walked out. "Who is your friend?"

"This is Tiffany. She was nice to me at school."

"That is so wonderful." His mother smiled and shook Tiffany's hand. "Welcome, Tiffany."

"Thank you, Ma'am."

"Can I get you kids anything to eat or drink?"

"No thanks, Mom. I want to show Tiffany my painting."

"You do?" She asked knowing her surprise was apparent. She watched Gerald lead Tiffany into *his* studio and decided to follow. When Tiffany walked into the room and took sight of the massive canvas, she gasped loudly. Her mouth was completely open, and her eyes as wide as they could be. She stared and then stared some more. She was completely mystified.

When Gerald couldn't wait another second to know what she thought of it, he asked.

"So what do you think?"

She continued to gaze at it as if she were hypnotized. Gerald waited a few seconds, then asked again.

"Tiffany?" Her silence started to worry him. What if she didn't like it? What if she was trying to figure out how to let him down easily? What if she were actually a mean person, preparing to turn on him?

Gerald was near sick with worry when he took a step forward and turned to face her. When he gazed upon her face, he saw an expression he wasn't expecting. Her mouth was still open, her eyes were still wide, and she was crying.

Softer, he inquired carefully, "Tiffany, what's wrong?"

She blinked her eyes and then wiped them with the back of her hand. She gave Gerald with the biggest smile he had ever seen – ever!

"Gerald, that is the most astonishing painting I have ever seen. It literally takes my breath away."

Gerald smiled and looked back up at the painting. Tiffany stared at it for a few more seconds, entranced before she spoke.

"There's so much beauty. So many instances of love and caring. Not a line of detail has been overlooked. It's as if you created an entire world from scratch."

"You should witness it from within," he spoke quietly.

Tiffany turned to him with confusion on her face. He glanced over at the painting and spoke again.

"Walk closer to it."

Tiffany took a step closer, then another, then another. She was so small in comparison to it, and with each step she took she felt even smaller than before. The closer she got to the painting, the more it seemed to encompass her. The more it seemed to speak to her.

With another step, she felt a cool breeze. Then, she heard the shuffling of the leaves. She caught sight of something moving in a plant by her feet. A small green lizard scurried under the plant which scared a rabbit that hopped across the path and into a log.

She stepped backward, afraid to step on something. In doing so, she came out of the painting and turned to Gerald with the oddest expression on her face.

"That is amazing, Gerald. You HAVE created your own world!"

CHAPTER 11

She took Gerald's hand and started to pull him toward the painting. "Come on, let's go in together."

"Oh, I don't want to go into the painting."

Tiffany turned to stare at him dumbly. "Why not?"

"It's hard to explain, but I'd much rather watch over it from out here."

Tiffany tried but didn't truly understand. She released his hand and stood there next to him, gazing at the massive canvas.

A few moments later, though, Gerald realized she didn't seem as happy as she had been. "But you could go back in."

"Oh," she slowly acknowledged. "I don't want to leave you by yourself."

Gerald was puzzled by her comment. She could be in there experiencing something magical. In fact, she could be anywhere, with anyone, and yet she stayed with him. No one had ever wanted to just hang out with him.

A few minutes later, the clock struck five, and Tiffany realized she needed to go home. She explained that her mother would be expecting her for dinner. Turning back, she asked, "Can I come back tomorrow?"

He smiled. "Of course, I would love that."

The next day Tiffany didn't mention the painting to anyone. Gerald had completely expected her to tell Samantha, a fellow artist, but she didn't. It almost hurt his feelings to think that she had so quickly forgotten about his masterpiece.

At the end of the day, he was already heading home, alone, when Tiffany ran up to him.

"I can't wait to see the painting again."

"Really?" His surprise was evident.

"Of course! It took every ounce of restraint I had not to blab about it to everyone in school."

Gerald seemed perplexed.

Tiffany explained. "You said the other day that you didn't want to share it with anyone."

"I did."

"But you shared it with me."

"Yes."

"That made me feel very special."

Gerald smiled.

"But I didn't want you to feel pressured to share the painting with anyone you didn't want to share it with, so I kept it our secret."

Gerald stood a little straighter. His smile spread across his face. Tiffany had put some real thought and consideration into his feelings. Something no one had ever done before, besides his parents.

That afternoon when Gerald and Tiffany entered the house, Tiffany greeted Gerald's mom.

"Hello, Tiffany. It is so nice to see you again. Can I get you kids anything to drink?"

"Sure."

After a quick snack, Gerald and Tiffany went back into the studio to observe Gerald's painting. Tiffany immediately walked right up to it and felt herself become encapsulated inside this magnificent world. She heard the birds singing, smelled the musk of freshly fallen rain and felt the warm breeze on her skin. It was the most incredible feeling she had ever experienced.

Tiffany felt as if she could easily become a part of this world, wanting to stay forever. For a brief moment, her thoughts turned to Gerald's statement the night before about wanting to watch over it from outside. She couldn't understand why he wouldn't want to experience the thrill of his world from within, but she let that pass for the moment.

"Ooh-ooh" came the sound of a small chimpanzee climbing down the limbs of a nearby tree to take a closer look at her. She smiled at him then said, "Hello," which made him hide behind a branch.

She grinned at him and then continued walking down the trail. She watched as bunnies scurried into their holes, birds flew out from their nests and turtles pulled into their shells.

Not able to understand why the animals seemed to be afraid of her, Tiffany turned back around and came out of the painting to ask Gerald.

"Done so soon?"

"The animals seem skittish, more so than they did yesterday."

Gerald wondered but didn't have an answer. He shrugged. Tiffany didn't know what else to add to that so she changed the subject.

"Tell me why you won't go into the painting, Gerald."

"I already did. I want to watch over it from out here."

"Yes, but why?"

He shrugged his shoulders again.

Tiffany sat down next to him and studied the painting from his perspective. It was still an incredible sight. It was a beautiful painting, so much color, so vibrant and radiant, but...

"Oh, my gosh!"

"What?" Gerald turned to her concerned.

"I just saw movement." She gasped with her eyes wide open.

Gerald smiled knowingly.

"You can see everything that happens inside there from out here?"

"Yep."

"Why didn't you tell me?"

Gerald shrugged again.

"So you saw me walking down the path?"

Gerald nodded.

"You saw the animals fly away or go into their shells?"

Gerald cocked his head to the side. Tiffany looked as if she were hurt. He couldn't understand why until her next question.

"Did you make them run from me?"

"Of course not." Gerald looked troubled. "I want everyone to have the same wonderful experience but I cannot control what happens in that world just like you can't control what happens out here."

Tiffany grew confused. "But you painted the world. You made it from your own two hands and imagination. How can you not control what happens inside?"

"I wouldn't want to. It's the same reason I don't want to go into it. I want to enjoy it from afar. To let it surprise me, to fill me with unexpected pleasure. But I never intended for humans to be a part of it.

Humans are so mean and uncaring. They scare the animals and trample on the plants. I may trust you to go inside but they don't know that. They know that I don't trust people - so I guess they don't either."

Tiffany tried to understand his feeling rather than focus on her own hurt feelings. She remembered that before her, Gerald hadn't found the good in humans. That's why he painted the picture the way he did.

Tiffany wondered silently if there was something she could do to change his mind. But she knew not to pester him or force his decision. She asked about something else.

“What does it look like when I’m in there?”

“Well, it’s neat to see you explore my world, but there is so much to marvel at. I don’t watch you the entire time.”

“Oh.” Confused but not necessarily surprised, she changed the subject again. “How many people can enter your world?”

Gerald shrugged again. “I don’t really know. I guess, since it’s an entire world, with depths far beyond this garden area you can see, an infinite world of possibilities and space, well, a whole lot of people. But why do you ask?”

“I know how you feel about humans. I understand why you’ve chosen not to share your world with humans, but you shared it with me. What is it about me that other people don’t have?”

“I guess it’s that,” Gerald thought for a moment, “that you’ve shown me your heart.”

Tiffany blushed as he continued.

“You were nice to me and welcomed me as a friend. No one else has ever done that for me. You’ve proven that you are kind and good.”

“What about Sam? She was nice to you, wasn’t she?”

“Well, yes.”

“She shared her artwork with you, didn’t she?”

“Yes, she did.”

“What about sharing your artwork with her? Only her?” Tiffany asked in sincere wonder.

"Well... I guess I could, if you think it would be okay."

"I do." Tiffany smiled. "And do you know what I think?"

Gerald shook his head.

"I think she is going to love it as much as I do."

"Do you think she will tell others?"

"Oh, I don't know," Tiffany admitted. "But we could ask her not to."

"Yes. That would be good. If she doesn't tell anyone else about the painting, I'll let her see it."

"Cool."

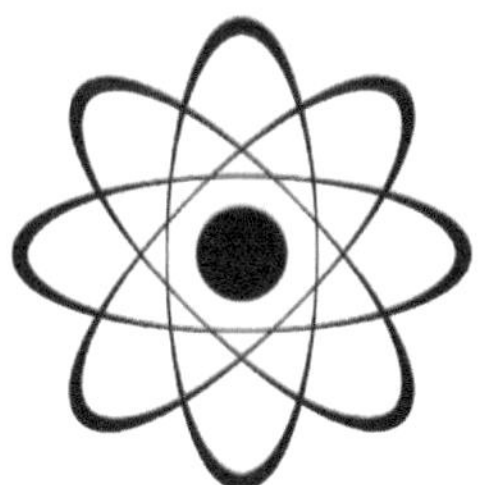

Chapter 12

So the next day at school, when Gerald saw Tiffany talking to Sam, he quietly walked up to them. Tiffany stopped talking and she and Sam both looked at Gerald expectantly.

Feeling Tiffany and Sam's eyes on him made him feel nervous. The fact that neither of them were talking, made him uneasy. "What?"

"Isn't there something you want to ask Sam?"

"*You* aren't going to do it?"

"Why would *I* do it? It's your painting to decide what to do with." She smiled again, urging him to proceed with hand motions.

He glanced up at Sam shyly and twisted his foot sideways while fiddling with his hands.

"Uh, Sam...?" he trailed off into a question without stating one.

"Yes, Gerald?"

Gerald felt so nervous. He wondered if Tiffany felt this way the first time she talked to him. "Sam I was wondering..."

"Yes?"

"If you would like to see my painting?"

"Ohh, yes! I sure would." Sam beamed brightly.

Sam's smile was so large and pleasant, Gerald forgot his stipulations. Her enthusiasm filled him, and it gave him a thrill. He actually felt a desire to share. So, as soon as school was out, they ran to Gerald's and in through the front door.

"Hi, Gerald, who's your new friend?"

"This is Sam, short for Samantha. I'm going to show her my painting."

"You are? Well, that's wonderful. Would your friends like something to drink?"

"Yes, Ma'am."

When they finally made their way into Gerald's studio, the anticipation was simply killing Gerald. He was so nervous and excited at the idea of showcasing his work to a fellow artist, he almost couldn't breathe.

He turned to Sam to take in her facial expressions as she absorbed his work for the first time. Her eyes widened, and her mouth dropped. There was no indication of how she felt about the painting. She simply stared at it.

What is she thinking? Gerald thought. Does she like it? Does she hate it? Oh gosh, what will I do if she hates it? What will I do if she says so out loud? What if she says, it's horrible. Will I cry? What will she say if I cry? Will she pick on me?

Gerald gulped. He felt so vulnerable. As the milliseconds passed, he grew angry at Tiffany for talking him into doing this. If she hadn't insisted, he wouldn't have shown Sam, and Sam wouldn't be getting ready to laugh at him. The terror and fear and pain he felt was excruciating. Why couldn't she just rip off the Band-Aid and get the ridicule over with?

He was about to turn and run out of his own room when he heard Sam sniff. He glanced over at her and saw her shake as if a chill had gone up her spine. She wiped her eyes with the back of her hand.

"Gerald, that's..."

"Amazing right?" Tiffany threw in her two cents.

Gerald waited to hear what adjective Sam planned on using, wonderful, horrible, dumb... he braced himself as she inhaled before speaking.

"Miraculous."

A flush of relief washed over him as he waited for her to say something else, but she didn't. She continued to stare at it. She was speechless.

Knowing how much the painting had to offer, Tiffany took Sam's hand and led her closer. "Wait until you see it up close."

"But it's so big. If I get closer I won't be able to see everything at once."

"You don't want to see everything at once; you want to experience it from within," she explained as she dragged Sam closer.

"I want to watch everything at once." Gerald spoke low, but Tiffany didn't hear him. She continued pulling Sam closer and closer until she too experienced the painting as it enveloped her.

At first, Sam couldn't understand why Tiffany insisted she get closer. Now, as she smelled the sweet fragrant flowers blooming and heard the water trickling down the stream and felt the warm sun beaming on her face, she couldn't help but marvel at the wonder of it.

"What in the world?"

"This is Gerald's world. He painted it. He created everything in it from the birds in the sky to the fish in the sea and everything under the sun. Isn't it wonderful? I think it's absolutely marvelous."

"Well, that's one way to describe it," Sam declared as she walked down the pathway leading to the trickling stream. As she approached, a few turtles dove into the nearby waters, and she looked up as a couple of squirrels scampered up into the trees. As an acorn dropped on her head, she realized that this was more than a painting, more than anything she could ever comprehend. All she knew was it was here, and she couldn't be happier.

The pair spent quite a bit of time inside the painting exploring. Sam was amazed at its beauty. She couldn't fathom how anyone could do something this magical with a paintbrush and paints. Gerald was a miracle worker, a magician... he was divine.

Finally, Sam turned and emerged from the painting. She had so many questions. She had a hard time wrapping her head around the magic she had just experienced.

Noticing Gerald sitting down at the back of the room, watching his world from afar, she joined him. She sat down next to him and examined the painting from his perspective.

It was just as beautiful far away as it was close up, but there was something odd. Sam was deep in thought when she saw movement from within.

"What's that?" She sat up and leaned forward.

Gerald smiled. "That was Tiffany. She just leapt from one of those big rocks and scared a jaguar higher into that nearby tree."

"You can observe the movement of the painting from out here?" Sam marveled aloud. She thought about that for a moment, now able to watch the birds flying in the blue sky and the dolphins leaping from the ocean waters. Then it occurred to her why something about the picture seemed off.

"Gerald, you made this remarkable world. You created all of this beauty. And yet, you sit outside it. You watch from afar. It's as if you are not part of that world...," and then it made sense as she finished her sentence, "and not part of this world either."

Gerald caught her eyes for a moment, and Sam could see the twinkle of a tiny tear form in the bottom of his eyes. She looked back to the painting, and he, too, looked away and wiped his eyes with his arm.

There was silence between them for the longest moment, and then Tiffany emerged from the painting.

"I could live in there!" Tiffany exclaimed as she skipped over to the two of them and plopped down. "I could set up a tent and literally move in." She spun on her behind to turn and face the painting, then scootched between Gerald and Sam leaning against the wall.

"Wouldn't it be awesome? Can you imagine it? A world with no teachers or homework? No parents telling you to clean your room? No brothers leaving their gum in your hair? It would be a sanctuary."

Gerald heard her word *sanctuary* and realized how right she was. This was his sanctuary, his refuge. He had painted this world for himself, so he could escape the realities of his own life. He had never intended to share it with others. Of course, he had never thought he would ever find others with whom he *could* share it. Now he had two.

As a whale blew water from its blowhole, a rainbow formed in the sky. All three of them oohed and ahhhed at the remarkable sight. Gerald noticed the smiles on Tiffany and Sam's faces. He saw the twinkles in their eyes. He witnessed the delight his painting gave to them and he realized even two people who seemed to be perfectly happy out here in the real world secretly needed the escape. They, too, needed the happiness.

Gerald realized instantly that he wasn't alone. He may have felt alone, downright lonely at times, even before making two new friends. But he wasn't the only one. Even those who seemed happy, even those who seemed surrounded by friends, laughing and sharing and enjoying what life had to offer, were still, at times, just as lonely as he.

Gerald began to wonder who else needed this enjoyment. Who else out here needed an escape into a magical world that could put a smile on your face and warm your heart. Who else was dying on the inside but hiding it on the outside? Who else should he invite to see his painting?

CHAPTER 13

The next day after school Tiffany ran up to Gerald. "Ready to go?"

"Go where?"

"To your place, silly. To see your painting."

Gerald smiled. "I would like that, but I have something to do."

"Oh," Tiffany pouted. Gerald saw her disappointment and smiled.

"It's a surprise. For you and everyone."

"A surprise?" Tiffany beamed brightly.

"You'll see." Gerald was so energized and eager. He'd come up with a plan the night before. He knew what he wanted to do. This afternoon he would put his plan into play. He had much to do to prepare, and this afternoon, that was exactly what he was going to do.

Toward the back of his property stood a large green house. It was tall enough to be two-stories but there was no loft or second floor. The clear glass made the house bright, even through the years' worth of dirt. It belonged to the previous landowner, whom Gerald had never met. He was gone long before Gerald was born. All Gerald knew was no one ever came out here. No one ever used the greenhouse. That was about to change.

He ran into his house, asked his mom for a whole slew of cleaning supplies and ran off. He threw everything he had collected into a wheelbarrow and pushed it out across the field.

His mother watched from the kitchen window, curious as to what he was doing but not worried. She was thankful he was happy for a change. He had something to do to keep him occupied, and he was smiling. That was good enough for her.

Sweat poured down Gerald's face as he approached the large green house with his wheelbarrow full of supplies. He set down the barrow and approached the clear glass doors. They were very dirty and needed a good washing. He could barely see through them, but as he opened the doors, he could see his plan coming together.

Without a moment's delay, he grabbed a water pail and filled it at the outdoor faucet. He then squirted some soap into the water and dipped a large sponge into the pail to wash the windows.

As the soapy waters cleaned the dirt away, the sunlight began to brighten the greenhouse. Gerald saw that the floor needed to be swept and mopped, the walls cleaned, and the dead vines and vegetation cleared. He knew it would take a great deal of work. He knew it would take many days. He also knew that everything worth doing took work and time and patience.

Over the next week, Tiffany and Sam kept asking about the painting and his surprise project. Gerald wouldn't tell them a thing but that it was almost ready. He'd smile the largest smile they'd ever seen on his face, and he'd say, "I can't wait to show you."

Tiffany kept wondering if he was working on another painting. Sam kept wondering if he was changing something on the painting. The only thing they both knew for certain was that Gerald was excited, and so, they were excited, too.

Each afternoon Gerald ran to the greenhouse to work. The first day was preparation – out with the old dead plants, in with the new fertile ones. By day two, he saw green buds sprout from the ground. The next day, the vines started growing up the walls. By the fourth day, their tendrils began uncurling, spiraling around support poles and framing the windows.

By day five, their leaves began to unfurl and beautiful green heart-shaped leaves began to pop open. By day six, beautiful purple flowers opened their petals to the soft sunlight falling through the now spotless windows. Gerald spent the rest of the afternoon collecting chairs and setting them up inside the greenhouse. As evening came, Gerald went to his dad for help.

"Dad, can you help me move my painting?"

"Move it? Where?"

"To the greenhouse at the end of our property. I cleaned it up and setup chairs so I can display it there for everyone to see. But the canvas is so big, I need help moving it."

Gerald's father could sense his son's excitement. He was proud of his son for wanting to share his work with others. He nodded his head with delight.

The sun was setting as Gerald opened the doors to the greenhouse. Gold and pink rays of sun shone through the windows, casting an entrancing glow on the vines and purple flowers, the chairs and easel. Gerald's father rested the painting on the make-shift easel Gerald had made for the massive canvas. Then he stepped back and took it all in. Again, his son had created his own beautiful world. The pride he felt, the delight in Gerald's eyes, the fulfillment this project had given his son, was overwhelming.

Feeling his emotions building, his heart bursting with enthusiasm for his son, his tears flowed freely. "Remarkable." He spoke in barely a whisper. "Simply remarkable."

The next day, Gerald found Sam and Tiffany in the hallway. "It's ready," he said excitedly.

"Your surprise? What is it?"

"I can't tell you. You have to see it. But there's a catch."

"What?" They both asked in unison.

"I need you to tell others – to invite others, but only those you trust. Only those who will appreciate it. Only the kind and loving; the ones who care for others." Gerald was so serious. "Only those who are worthy."

Tiffany and Sam glanced at each other curiously then back at Gerald.

"Have them all meet me at the greenhouse at the end of my property after school."

He described a bit more to the girls, then watched as they ran off to tell others about his big debut.

Sam told her entire art class. Tiffany told the entire drama department. The nature artists told the gardening group. The costumers told the sewing classes. The gardeners told the shop class. The sewing class told the quilters and crocheting club. The shop class shared the news with the journalism department, and the journalists sent out a massive announcement.

Gerald was waiting by the doors to the greenhouse when almost every kid from school approached.

Gerald was shocked.

He wasn't sure he was ready for this. He wasn't sure he could handle so many people at once. He didn't understand why so many showed up.

His stipulations specifically declared only the people who could care, who were kind, who could love. Only the worthy, yet almost everyone showed up!

How could they all be worthy? How could they all care, when Gerald had felt so alone and unloved for so long?

But then it occurred to him. Maybe all of these people, with friends and without, all feel they are worthy.

Maybe they all really do care. Maybe they all really do love. Maybe they all could benefit from what Gerald had to offer.

He was so nervous.

Excited with anticipation, he looked forward to everyone's response but he was also terrified. His stomach fluttered with fear. His heart beat rapidly. As the huge group of his peers gathered and stood before him, Gerald paused, unable to move.

Tiffany realized he was in shock. She knew how he felt about sharing his painting with others. She knew how shy he was. She walked up next to him and took his hand.

He turned to her. Her smile melted the ice that froze him in place, and he remembered why he was here. He remembered all of the hard work, the excitement that had been building, the eagerness he'd felt in wanting to share his painting, and that's when he found his voice.

"Thank you for coming everyone." Those who were talking, quieted. "My name is Gerald Oliver Delaney. I go to the same school as you, but many of you don't know me. We're in many of the same classes, but most of you have probably never even noticed me. You don't know of my loneliness. You don't know of my isolation." Gerald took a big breath before continuing.

"You don't know how much I hurt and feel and ache for a friend. Maybe that's because many of you are in the same boat, feeling your own isolation and fear.

I realize that now.

I'm sure you're wondering why you are here. Let me explain. A while back, in my lowest point, someone who actually cared about me did something for me. They gave me a present. It was a small gesture, but through their gift I learned something about myself. Something that I didn't know existed.

My dad gave me a blank canvas – a really huge blank canvas. It needed something. It needed paint, of course, but it also needed passion. It needed someone to help it grow, to nurture it, to give it hope and encouragement." Gerald looked out at the faces standing before him. He hoped they understood.

It needed layers of color, of depth. It needed a foundation on which the world could develop on it. A place where plants could grow. A place that could provide shelter for all of the animals. Where trees could spread their branches out and provide the security we all are striving for in life.

This canvas needed love, just like we all do. I gave it love through my paints.

When I first started, it felt as if it wasn't right, that something was missing. Sometimes, the areas of its base were so dark, it felt as if the light couldn't work on it - that the light paint would mix in with the dark and become muted, like it would also go dark.

The dark tried to consume the canvas, to blot out all of the light forever... but the light succeeded.

The light gave the darkness depth, shadowing, definition..." Gerald saw Sam nod her head with a smile; she understood so well. He continued.

"The light gave it a foundation to grow on. It brought life and hope that seemed so far away."

Gerald paused, and the silence was deafening.

"In the end, as it all came together, my passion for this project, the devotion I had in seeing it through - I triumphed over my worries. I accomplished something that no one could imagine possible, because no one had ever spent the time to even consider it was necessary.

What I'm about to share with you is very close to my heart. It is my masterpiece. I had once thought it was complete just the way it was, that I was finished with it, but I now realize it was missing something. You."

Gerald heard the crowd murmur as many discussed or agreed with his message.

"No world could ever be complete without someone to share it with. A world that isolates you is a prison. I don't want to be a prisoner any longer. I don't want to be alone. I want to feel the love that I gave to this painting by witnessing the joy it brings to you.

So, without further ado," Gerald opened the doors to the greenhouse, "please take a look at my painting and let me know what you think."

As the crowd of students began to walk in, Gerald remained outside. He had opened himself to a vulnerability that he had absolutely no way to escape.

Gerald didn't know that his parents had heard his speech, that they stood hand in hand, at the back of the crowd, overwhelmed with emotion and tears and pride for their son.

All Gerald knew was that he was standing here, surrounded by people, and feeling more alone and afraid than he had ever felt in his entire life.

CHAPTER 14

Once everyone had shuffled into the greenhouse, Gerald closed his eyes and took a deep breath. He could hear conversations and murmurings from inside, but he hadn't stepped inside himself, yet.

He exhaled slowly, opened his eyes and put on a brave face. As he stepped inside the greenhouse, he saw everyone viewing his painting. The looks on their faces varied from wide eyed wonder, to aghast amazement, to complete shock and awe.

"Look there," someone said and pointed to the sky in the painting. Others gasped as they saw movement, birds flying in the sky.

"Did those trees move?" someone asked as the students expressed admiration and wonder, bewilderment and surprise.

"It's beautiful."

"It's astonishing."

There were discussions, commentary. "It's animated yet it's not. It speaks to me."

Wild remarks and bold observations continued. "You can see the paint, the texture of the canvas, and yet the world moves as if it is alive."

"I feel so warm and comforted."

"It's as if I am alive for the first time ever."

Gerald heard no criticism.

The crowd gawked as they witnessed the miracles within. They watched as birds launched from the branches into his sky. They stared at the tree limbs that swayed under the weight of gorillas and at giraffes popping their heads out from the canopy of the forest.

Many of the students sat in the chairs that Gerald had provided. Before long every chair was occupied. Others leaned against the walls, and many kneeled down on the floor in front of the painting.

They watched it like a movie, reacting to its ever changing landscape. With the intensity and wonder of small children, they all watched the world, Gerald's world, exist.

Tiffany found Gerald at the back of the greenhouse. Just as he had watched his painting from afar, he watched the audience from afar as well.

"Don't you want to go up there and talk to anyone?"

"They can come back here and talk to me," he countered.

"But you could go up there and ask if anyone has any questions, get a conversation started."

"They heard my speech. There's nothing more I can say."

"They can ask you questions. Get a take on why you did it. You could explain the answers to their questions."

"If they have any questions, I would love it if they came back here and asked them."

"But if you go to them…"

"I've told them all they need to know," Gerald admitted. No one besides Tiffany had ever approached him for anything before, and he had no expectations that anyone would do it now.... although he hoped they would.

"Why are you so afraid, Gerald?"

"Afraid? I'm not afraid! I should be afraid though. I opened myself up to potential ridicule and hurt. But I'm not afraid. I am sharing this world for everyone's benefit.

I've let them know who I am and asked them to let me know what they think. I'm standing here alone, eagerly waiting on anyone to make me a part of their conversation; their lives. I shared my masterpiece with all of them and now it is up to them.

If they like it, if they appreciate it, if they want to thank me or ask questions or talk to me, all they need to do is come to me. I'm not hiding. I'm not hard to approach. I'm right here, waiting enthusiastically for someone, anyone, to talk to me, but I am not going to demand it, or get in their faces. I want them to WANT to come to me. I want them to WANT me in their lives, to become my friend. That's not being afraid - that's hope."

Tiffany understood. She nodded her head and leaned back against the wall with Gerald. She surveyed the painting and the crowd from back here. It was an interesting perspective. The painting seemed so much farther away. You could still see it, but it lost all of its detail.

"Gerald, what about suggesting they get closer to the painting? Go inside? Experience it from within?"

Gerald knew that question was bound to be raised. He wasn't sure he wanted to explain all of the wonders of the painting. He could tell them, but he would rather they discover it for themselves. He hoped they'd be intrigued enough to investigate this world on their own or better yet, ask him directly.

It didn't seem right to take the joy from those who were looking at it as others would block their view who wanted to venture into it. He didn't want to tell them or suggest what to do next, how to enjoy the painting - these people had free will. They could do what they wanted. If they wanted to enjoy it from afar, who was he to stop them?

Of course, Gerald began to wonder silently, did he not tell them because they would leave him?

He looked at the painting, then out to the crowd. Right now, as it stood, any one of them could turn around, notice him standing here and walk up to talk to him. They could casually say hi or mention how they liked the painting. He stood right by the door – they couldn't leave without noticing him.

But they could.

Gerald knew how hard people worked to ignore him. No matter how much he wanted them to notice him, they wouldn't. No matter how much he willed them to choose him for their team, they would refuse. They could easily walk out the door and never so much as glance up at him. Why give them even more of an opportunity to ignore him?

If they could enter the painting, they could easily be gone forever. They could leave this world and enter his. They could move in, build a life, build a home. They would cut down his trees, kill his plants and animals for food, and litter. There was no way he'd want to encourage that.

Tiffany could see the perplexity of confusion and uncertainty on his face. She realized he was conflicted on the subject so she let it drop. She turned and sat next to Gerald up against the wall and took his hand into hers.

She gazed back up at the painting and spoke quietly, as if just saying something, not necessarily to anyone specifically.

"It is truly a marvelous sight to see."

As the day came to a close and the evening light faded behind the trees, the people left. Gerald returned to his home after closing up the greenhouse to find his parents waiting for him.

"How was your day?"

Gerald told them all about it over dinner. He spoke of the greenhouse and the school of students that came out to see his painting and what he said during his speech. He thanked his dad again for believing in him. He even suggested they come out to see it tomorrow afternoon.

"We look forward to it."

The next day, Gerald went home from school and walked with his parents to the greenhouse. When they arrived, Gerald was amazed that another huge crowd of people had gathered, waiting to go in and see his painting.

There were more people than before -more students, teachers, other parents, reporters… a whole slew of people, practically the entire town. Gerald was stunned.

He walked through the crowd to the door and unlocked it. Before the doors were even open, the crowds pushed their way in to see the magical painting he had created.

Everyone gawked and stared. They pointed at the animals and discussed the scene. They talked amongst each other. They overheard complete stranger's comments and added their own two-cents to those conversations.

They sat and enjoyed Gerald's world. Reporters took pictures and video of the canvas. They reported the mysterious moving painting and interviewed the spectators, recording their thoughts and feelings.

The reports each night gathered even more exposure for Gerald's work. Each day, more and more people came to see it. From all over, people flocked to see the painting, walking past Gerald who watched it all quietly.

None of the new people had heard his original speech. None of the old ones had thought to tell others about him. Everyone was consumed with wanting to experience this miraculous piece of artwork, but none of them had thought to inquire about the creator.

Gerald had been forgotten about, again. He was adored and loved silently while being ignored and forgotten at the same time. His work was appreciated, but he wasn't. He felt a new kind of hurt inside. A prideful hurt that was too strong for mere tears to drown out.

Tiffany came by to check on him regularly. Sam did as well, albeit not as often – she was working on a new painting. Many of the regular attendees began to drop off in time. They started to go back to their lives, their projects, whatever they did to keep themselves busy and preoccupied.

Soon, Gerald didn't recognize a single face that came by to see his painting. He was almost completely ignored. The only time anyone said anything to him was when they realized they were standing in front of him and apologized and moved to the side.

There was a small part of Gerald that wanted to voice his outrage and to yell at the top of his lungs, "Hey! I'm Gerald Oliver Delaney! I'm the creator of this painting! Pay attention to me." But he didn't. He wanted so badly to be loved, but he wasn't going to try to force anyone to love him.

That evening as the last person left, Gerald and Tiffany stood from their chairs in the back of the room and stretched. Tiffany walked up closer to the painting, enjoying it from out here but wanting so much to go back inside.

"Gerald, since no one is around, can I go inside the painting?"

Gerald smiled. He nodded and watched as Tiffany walked closer and closer until she was enveloped within the leaves of the painting. He smiled as she disappeared in the underbrush but turned when he heard the door click behind him.

It was closed. No one was back there, or anywhere. He turned back around and watched his painting with satisfaction as Tiffany enjoyed it from within.

A little later, Tiffany emerged from the painting and Gerald stood. "I love it in there. I still can't understand why you don't want to go in."

Gerald shyly shrugged his shoulders and the two of them walked out. Gerald was very grateful Tiffany was his friend.

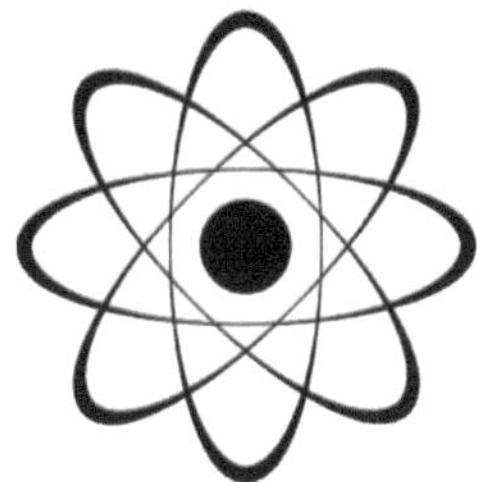

CHAPTER 15

After dinner, Gerald's father sat down to watch the news. Before the commercial break they did a quick teaser about a story coming up.

"A magical painting with a huge secret."

"Gerald, come in here!" his father called. Gerald walked into the room as his father turned up the sound. Gerald recognized the reporter who had been at the greenhouse earlier.

"The miraculous painting that has touched the lives of so many has a hidden secret that no one knows about - until now! Find out about this mysterious secret after the commercial break!"

Gerald couldn't fathom what was going on. So many people had seen the painting. People had come from all over. Reporters had stopped reporting on it weeks ago. The people had slowly stopped coming. What had this reporter discovered? Then it came to Gerald like a slap of cold water flooding his face.

Today, when Tiffany went into the painting, Gerald heard the door close. He hadn't seen anyone but it must have been that reporter. Did the reporter witness Tiffany go inside? Was he going to report on that? What would happen if everyone realized they could go into the painting? To escape reality and life and live in this beautiful garden? What would happen to Gerald's world?

Gerald was panicked. His father could tell. He took Gerald's hand and spoke. "It'll be all right."

But how can it be? wondered Gerald. His biggest secret was about to come out and this could ruin everything.

The commercial break ended. The evening news music came back on, and the reporter stepped in front of the camera.

Gerald's heart raced.

"Good evening! Today I had the honor of going down to that oh-so-popular greenhouse at the edge of town and viewing that miraculous painting for myself. It truly is unbelievable. An inexplicable example of one person's phenomenal talent. If you haven't seen it, you truly should.

That being said, there is more than meets the eye when it comes to this painting. They say beauty's in the eye of the beholder, behold this."

The camera panned over to a monitor where a shaky clip of Tiffany walking into the painting played.

"That's right folks," said the reporter as the camera shifted back to him, "that young girl walked into the painting. You may be thinking that was trick photography or a doorway leading to a jungle – it's not; it's the painting.

But it CAN be considered a doorway if you think about it. This painting that clearly a painting that moves and sways in the breeze, that has animals calling and trumpeting in the distance, that has whales and dolphins swimming in the sea – is actually the entrance to a new world. A world that the artist created. A world we all can enter. Don't believe me?"

The camera panned back to the monitor where the reporter stood in front of Gerald's painting. The video was dark, with only a little bit of sunlight illuminating the greenhouse. It was obviously taken shortly after Gerald and Tiffany had left.

Gerald watched as the reporter turned and slowly walked towards the painting. As he neared the painting, viewers saw the wind from within the painting ruffle his hair. And, as he walked inside disappearing from view behind the vegetation on the primary pathway, Gerald knew his secret was out.

The camera panned back to the reporter who continued, "I stayed in there for about ten minutes until it got too dark outside to see. I imagine one could stay inside as long as they wanted. So if you thought you had seen all you could see of that phenomenal painting, you'd be wrong!"

Gerald stood as the phone rang.

"Gerald, it's Tiffany," his mother called out from the kitchen.

Gerald walked to the phone and immediately heard Tiffany crying.

"Gerald, I am so sorry. This is all my fault. I never should have gone into the painting tonight. I should have stayed out like you wanted. It's just that I wanted to experience that perfect world..."

Gerald listened as she went on but became lost in his own thoughts. Tiffany was not at fault. All she wanted to do was experience his world completely. It WAS perfect, his world. Who was he to keep it from everyone? He had opened it up to share but had never let go of the keys. It was like freeing a horse but never letting loose of the reigns.

Maybe this was a blessing in disguise. Maybe it would rekindle people's interest in his painting – and therefore in him.

In bed that night he could hardly sleep. Instead, he wondered what tomorrow would be like.

Would it all be okay?

Or would it be a catastrophe?

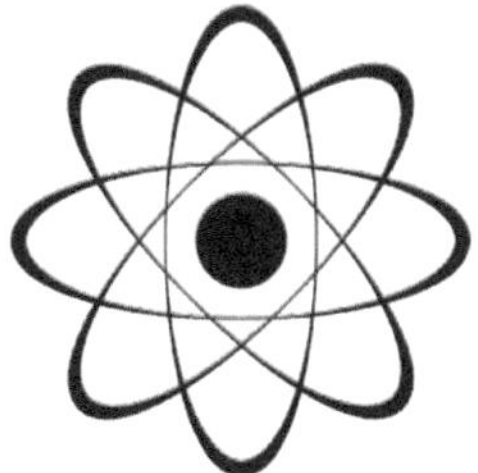

Chapter 16

As Gerald walked to school the next morning, he noticed large crowds of people walking the other way. When he entered the school, he realized it was mostly empty.

He walked back out of the school and noticed more people walking the same direction. He followed them, out of curiosity.

When they reached his field, Gerald realized what was going on. He ran to the greenhouse as fast as he could. The doors were already open. The greenhouse had been broken into. Swarms of people were barreling into it - way more than it could hold.

He pushed his way inside to witness hordes of people pressing themselves into the painting. More and more people came in, crowds of them, and they were all stepping into Gerald's world.

He watched helplessly as his world was overrun by people. They didn't ask if they could go inside. They were intruding - stomping on his grass, swimming in his sea, climbing up his trees. They were riding his elephants and posing for pictures next to his peacocks. They were picking his flowers and eating his fruit and drawing on his rocks.

Tree limbs were being broken, grass trampled down to dirt. Frogs and turtles and snakes and toads hopped, crawled and slithered to safety. He watched as people cut down trees to construct rafts so they could explore the ocean. Other people had brought baskets of food and drinks and ate picnics in his prairies but then left trash all over the ground.

Others even climbed up his mountains, knocking loose rocks that tumbled to the ground and hurt the people walking below.

So many people had entered and paused to take in the scenery; they were now being pushed down as others pressed their way in. Many were trampled.

As the people screamed, so did the monkeys. The birds all flew away. The larger animals scrambled to the far edges of the canvas.

Past the commotion of the entrance, he saw a group of children stumble upon a cave of lions. A blond headed boy picked up a small lion cub to show the others. Gerald watched in horror as the mother lion poised, crouched on a rock, ready to attack.

"Look out!" Gerald yelled.

The wind picked up.

It brushed harshly against the boy who turned into it in time to see the mother lioness. Wisely, he put the lion cub down and ran.

Gerald watched helplessly as his world was being destroyed. He pleaded for everyone to stop.

"Listen to me, please!" He ran closer. He tried to block the new people from going inside. They pushed him away.

"Please don't scare the animals!"

"Please don't cut down the trees. Please don't hurt each other."

But no one listened.

Gerald's tears began to flow as he wept for his world, his plants, his animals, and for the people within.

"Why?" he asked hoarsely.

Still, no one listened to him.

The day within the painting became shadowed with a single dark cloud. A mellow rumbling of thunder gave warning to an approaching storm, but the people did not take notice.

He watched helplessly as the carnage continued. People cried for help. They were being pushed, stepped on, brushed aside and their cries ignored.

Gerald knew he had to do something, but what? He surveyed his surroundings. Chairs had been knocked over and pushed into piles, and people tripped over them and fell onto the pile as well. Others tried climbing in through the windows, arms and legs flailing.

"Stop!" Gerald yelled at the top of his lungs. "Stop it!"

Instantly, from the painting's clear blue sky, lightning struck. It struck near the most chaotic area inside the painting. It surprised the people. A nearby patch of grass caught fire and began spreading quickly.

Gerald panicked. Something had to be done – but what? He looked around the room. He spotted his cleaning supplies in the wheelbarrow in the corner. The broom handle hung over the edge and the mop, its head in the bucket of water, leaned against the wall.

Water!

Gerald ran to the bucket, and dragged it to the painting. When he was close enough, he gripped the bucket's edges with both hands and slung the water toward the painting.

It splashed on the painting but became more than just a bucket of water as it entered. It became a torrential rainstorm. The water washed over the people and the trees and the ocean and the mountains.

It doused the fire, but the water continued to grow and spread. It flooded the pathway, turning it into a rushing river. It rained harder and faster. It washed the people inside down the pathway and right out of the painting.

Those that could - ran. Others crawled over the pile of people who had slopped out of the painting and made their way out of the greenhouse. Everyone fled the area. They dashed past the hurt. Scuttled by the scared. They rushed past Gerald.

No one looked back.

No one, except Gerald.

He inspected the remnants of his painting. His entire world had been flooded. He had successfully removed the people, but he had also lost the animals. The trees were submerged. The water's destructive force washed debris downstream and oddly, it continued to rain.

Gerald didn't know how to stop it. His world was flooding, and he had caused its demise. He watched helplessly as the saturation continued. The rain continued pouring down. Soon, he couldn't tell whether it was the flood waters rising or his own tears. The devastation was more than Gerald could handle.

He ran from the greenhouse as fast as he could. He ran to his home, flung open the door and ran to his bedroom. There, he collapsed onto his bed and sobbed uncontrollably into his pillow.

The people he didn't trust or like, who had always been mean to him and ignored him and made him feel so alone, had destroyed the only thing that had ever truly made him happy.

In their haste and persistence, their eagerness to experience the magic of his world, their impatience to wait and be calm and walk in carefully, the crowds had caused chaos.

Their disorder and selfishness destroyed the peace and tranquility of his world. The serenity of his realm had been taken from him. His heart had been shattered and his hope lost.

Gerald cried into the night. He wept for his plants and animals. He wept for the demise of his world. He had lost everything. His heart had been shattered, and he didn't know what to do to fix it.

As he tried to fall to sleep, his head hurt, his eyes hurt and his heart hurt.

The night was dark, darker than ever before. Gerald had lost all hope.

Chapter 17

The next morning, Tiffany came to Gerald's house to check on him. She blamed herself for exposing the entrance to his world and for anyone who might have been hurt.

Tiffany had heard rumors about what had happened. Some of the story themes varied drastically, but most had common similarities. She had heard a tornado touched down. There was a lightning strike. Animals attacked some hikers. There were multiple mauling's. An avalanche happened. A torrential rainstorm caused massive flooding and destruction.

But Tiffany didn't know which was true or false. That morning she went to Gerald's as soon as she could to find out the truth for herself.

"Gerald, your friend Tiffany is here," his mother called to him. He didn't answer. She looked at Tiffany's face which held so much concern. "He came running home crying last night. He wouldn't come out for dinner. He wouldn't tell us what happened. Everything we've heard was awful... Tiffany, why don't you go back there and visit him. Maybe a friendly face will help."

Tiffany walked back to Gerald's room and found him lying face down on his pillow. "Gerald?" He didn't move. "Gerald?" she called again, this time louder. When he didn't stir, she went to him and shook him. "Gerald, are you okay?"

"No, I'm not," he mumbled, keeping his face turned away from her.

"Could you tell me what happened?"

"It was horrible. A nightmare. I can't even begin to explain it."

"Did anyone... die?"

"No, I don't think so."

"How is the painting?"

"I don't know. It was still raining when I left."

"It rained inside the painting?"

Slowly, Gerald turned to Tiffany. Her sweet, caring eyes gave him the strength to discuss what happened. He told her the entire story, and when he was done, they both sat there in silence.

Finally, Tiffany broke the silence with a question. "Do you think it's still raining?"

"I don't know."

"What about the animals? Do you think they survived?"

Gerald heard Tiffany's words and began to cry again. The idea that any of his animals might have been killed devastated him. It further crushed his already broken heart. He began to wonder, worry and speculate about what might have happened to his world.

Finally, he realized his curiosity needed to be satisfied. Whether the results were good or bad, he had to find out.

"I guess I should go check."

"You probably want to go alone," Tiffany added. Truly insightful, she understood Gerald's feelings. Maybe she was afraid to see it herself, or maybe she realized it was something Gerald needed to do alone. Either way, he appreciated her not making it any harder on him than it already was.

After Tiffany left, Gerald headed to the greenhouse to check on the painting. As he approached the massive greenhouse, his stomach grew queasy. Glass windows were broken, chairs were overturned and scattered across the lawn in pieces. The doors had been left open. From afar Gerald could see the painting was still inside.

As he walked closer, he saw that it looked very different. Many of the trees were gone, struck down and pounded by waves and debris. The beautiful plants and flowers and grass had been washed away. It had stopped raining and the flood waters had subsided. But now all Gerald could see was a muddy mess.

What trees were left standing were the tallest, strongest ones, though many of their branches leaned in the direction the waters had flowed.

He searched the painting for movement. He searched the ocean, but jostling waves were the only movement. He searched the trails, but no animals crept along them. He searched the sky for birds in flight, but the only movement was that of grey clouds floating on the breeze.

Just as Gerald was about to hang his head in sadness, he saw it, the slightest stirring of some leaves in a tree far, far away.

He strained his eyes to peer at the tree, hoping to see that movement again. He waited and waited, almost ready to give up, when – there it was again.

A long grey elephant trunk peeked out over the canopy of the tree.

"Are you okay?" Gerald asked as the elephant lifted its head to see Gerald standing there. The animal trumpeted his response, a loud, honking sound, and then looked down from the top of the tree.

"Are you stuck up there?" Gerald asked with a wild astonishment as he watched other animal heads peak out from nearby tree tops.

Animals that had been swept away in the rising waters had floated to the nearest trees where they hung on for dear life. Giraffes and alligators, bunnies and turtles sat on branches, gripping tightly, terrified of falling.

Gerald squinted his eyes more and then noticed squirrels, foxes, badgers and hippos all sitting on the tops of the mountains. Peacocks carefully perched on cliffs' edges, seemingly unwilling to fly to lower ground. All of the animals appeared afraid and confused.

Gerald realized they needed help - his help. He thought about painting ladders and bridges, but he didn't have his paints with him, and they needed help now.

He didn't think about himself or his rule. All he knew was that he needed to go inside and help his creatures. Without a second thought, Gerald stepped into the canvas.

Even with the destruction, his world was incredible. It was cooler and sweeter and prettier than his own world, times ten. No wonder everyone wanted to come inside.

This is paradise.

He ran up the pathway that led to where the animals were stranded. With the magic of his love, he helped the animals down. He built a bridge with loose debris, he bent nearby trees to create ramps, he climbed up the trees to help carry the turtles down and he taught the other animals what to do to help their friends.

He assisted as they rebuilt their homes. He brought them brush, swept away rocks and took away the trash. As they began gathering food he helped with collection. He had so much fun standing between an elephant, handing him a piece of fruit with its trunk, and turning to pass the fruit to a giraffe whose long neck lifted the fruit into the trees where a squirrel took it the rest of the way to a hole.

It was a soul-satisfying experience.

When the work was done, he stretched and looked around. The entire time he had been inside helping, his world had been recovering. Grass grew, plants flourished, flowers bloomed. At long last, he sat down and leaned up against a tree in the shade and closed his eyes to listen.

The birds were singing again. The stream trickled again. The flowers were blooming again. A cool breeze brushed against his face and the smell of freshly fallen rain and blossoms tickled his nose.

It was paradise.

He opened his eyes to take in the scene. The happier he felt, the more beautiful the world became. The tree leaves grew greener, the sky turned bluer. The colors of his world were simply radiant.

Curious animals approached Gerald, the one who helped them, the one who saved them. They sniffed his feet and carefully investigated his hair. A tiny white bunny hopped onto his lap, and with twitchy nose and soft bunny feet, stood up, and carefully placed a paw on his chest so he could sniff Gerald's face.

Bunny whiskers tickled Gerald's cheek and he giggled.

The peacock cried a vibrant tune. Deer and fox drew near. Turtles and frogs made their ways through the vegetation to approach him. They all were so inquisitive about their savior.

Gerald understood how special his world was. He knew this world needed to be saved, protected and cared for. It needed to be isolated from his outside world and the people in it.

"Never again will I let the people of my world come in and threaten my painted world here," he declared as the animals listened.

"Never again will I allow the waters of my world to destroy the beauty of my nature and wildlife."

He thought hard about it, and a conclusion, the most difficult conclusion he had ever imagined, came to him.

I have to hide this world.

CHAPTER 18

Gerald had concluded that to keep his world safe for all time - to keep it away from anyone who could ever do it harm, he'd have to put it somewhere no one could ever go. He'd have to paint a universe far, far away. A vast space that could support his world with its beauty and life. A colossal area that provided both day and night. A unique universe so isolated only he could find it. When the painting of that universe was done, he'd have to put his world, his painting, inside it. Once placed in its own cosmos, no one would ever be able to simply walk into it. It would be safe for all eternity.

But before he started, Gerald had to do one more thing. As he stood, surrounded by the animals of his world, he recognized that they needed a caretaker - someone to always be there for them. He knew it wasn't possible for him to remain inside, although he'd love nothing more than to stay in the painting forever. He had to come out. He had to leave this world in order to plant it into a protective universe. So, if he never came back, if he never again stepped foot inside this world, then it would need an inside protector. He'd need to paint someone to care for the animals. Someone to be their shepherd.

After finally stepping out of his painting, he gathered his supplies. He held his pallet and squirted small dollops of various color paints on it and pulled out his smallest detail paintbrush. Then he stood before his painting and collected his thoughts. Whoever he painted would have to appreciate the world, the beauty of his creation. They would have to love the animals like he did. To be there for them and help them. To tend to the plants, trim them and keep them watered. To help cultivate the vegetation and keep his perfect world flourishing.

So with tiny simple brush strokes, Gerald painted a likeness of himself. He spared no detail as he wanted this to be the most perfect depiction of love. He painted and painted, and when he brushed in the last stroke of hair on the young man's head, he stood back and watched him come to life.

The young man stared at Gerald.

"Hello," Gerald spoke kindly.

"Hello," he replied.

"This world is for you," Gerald explained. The likeness turned to gaze upon his world. He saw the beauty of the trees, the colors of the flowers, the movement of the leaves. The man crouched defensively, startled by the movement.

"Don't be afraid," Gerald calmed him.

The young man watched him and smiled. Gerald then explained what he needed to know about the world. He explained how the seeds grew plants, and the plants grew fruit and the fruit was food. He detailed everything the young man needed to know and when he was done, he watched as the young man turned around to gaze upon the world.

He was so small.

He was one small person in an enormous world, and Gerald felt sad for him. This young man would be lonely. To live in this world all by himself would provide peace. The animals would keep him company, but he would have no one to talk to. His loneliness would grow, as Gerald's had, and it would make his spirit sink.

A thought came to Gerald's mind.

This young man needs a friend. Someone he can talk to. Someone he could share his life with. Someone who would keep him company... Someone like Tiffany. Tiffany had shown Gerald what true friendship was. She understood him and truly cared for him and his feelings. She included him and made him feel cared for and accepted.

Pleased by his thought, Gerald began painting again.

Carefully, painstakingly, Gerald painted another person into his world. She held the likeness of Tiffany. Her hair was long and silky, her eyes bright and radiant and her smile as pretty as the stars and the moon when they shimmered on the still waters of his lake.

Finally, Gerald painted an additional feature. She would also contain the love of his mother - a woman who nurtured and encouraged him, who always knew when he needed a hug or a quiet, listening ear. She resembled everything that was good and kind in Gerald's life.

Gerald had painted someone who would ensure that this young man would never feel as isolated and alone as Gerald had felt in the past.

CHAPTER 19

With his painting now inhabited, Gerald knew he needed to get to work on the universe. He ran to Sam's house and asked if he could have one of her blank canvases. She didn't hesitate to offer him one and then attempted to console him about the destruction of his painting.

"I was so saddened to hear about what happened. Do you want to talk about it?"

Gerald smiled at her brightly. He was thrilled that she cared, but he had important work to do. It made him realize something important from the past, and that realization, he shared with her.

"When I helped you with your painting, suggesting the shadows, you got to work right away."

"That's right."

"You were so excited that it was coming together, you forgot about Tiffany and me – temporarily."

"I'm sorry-" she began.

"Don't be," Gerald interrupted. "I was upset at first; I didn't understand. But I get it now. I'm working on a project, a huge wonderful undertaking and I'm excited about it. I now understand that day with clarity." He gave her a hug. "I'm so sorry I did not understand before now."

She smiled as he ran off with his blank canvas. She was happy to know that he had found joy.

Gerald ran back to the greenhouse and propped the blank canvas on an easel. He grabbed his paintbrush and started painting a sun, a bright yellow ball that would be the center of his universe. He hoped that the people and animals of his world would look up at this sun and be reminded of him long after he was gone.

He then painted other worlds, simple worlds with much less detail than his own world of course, but a distraction that would help keep his world hidden and protected.

He painted stars to twinkle at night and a moon to light the night. He painted beauty into the universe, colors and infinite possibilities to represent the infinite potential of his world.

Then, when he had painted his last constellation, he put his paintbrush down and looked back at his world.

He was ready to release it – to let it go - when his father's words entered his thoughts.

"The instant you apply your name to your work, you declare it officially finished. Your signature identifies your art for all time as having been created, completed and approved of by you and you alone. You are the creator for now and all time."

Gerald realized his painting needed one more thing after all. It only had his initial on it. His first initial: a simple G. This G stood for Gerald but it could also symbolically stand for Good - the good Gerald had finally been able to understand. However, Gerald felt it needed more.

His painting needed his name: Gerald Oliver Delaney. It was a full and proud name, but there was a problem. The G took up every bit of space in that small unoccupied part of the ocean - right above the coral reef and below the school of fish. His whole name would never fit. He might be able to squeeze his initials into the space, but even they would look cramped.

If he wanted to add his O and his D he'd need to make them smaller, maybe even place them artistically inside his G.

So he did.

He dipped the tip of his tiniest detail paintbrush carefully into a dollop of white paint and kneeled down by the bottom right corner of his painting.

He carefully swished his initials inside of the G and put his paintbrush down.

"What is that?" his likeness inquired.

"That is my name. I put it there so you will always remember who created this world. So you will always remember to love me as much as I love you."

They both looked at it and smiled.

"It kind of resembles a face."

Gerald glanced down at it and smiled. He could kind of see that. How creative they were. "Then consider that a reminder of me. That I will always be watching over you."

After a short rest, Gerald drew a deep breath collecting his nerve. It was time. Time to let go of his world. Time to set it free. He knew he would miss it. He worried about it, floating in the universe all by itself. Could he really let it go?

The canvas's massive size overwhelmed him. He couldn't stretch his arms out and touch the sides of the canvas at the same time. He knew it was time for a little extra magic.

He willed the universe to open.

He willed this painting to shrink.

He willed a porthole to open and pull it in.

He was moments from letting it fall into place in its universe. The magic pulled on it. It stretched and blended the colors into a rainbow and pulled it like taffy.

But when he heard a small female voice speak from within the painting, he paused.

"What is he doing?"

"He's protecting us," his likeness answered her. "He's created a complete universe for us to live in so we will be safe forever."

"Wow. He must love us a whole bunch."

"His love for us is immeasurable. We can never fully comprehend how he feels about us."

Gerald smiled as he listened to his creations. He sensed their adoration and worship of him, for he knew what was in their hearts. He was certain he would never be separated from them. He would always be with them. They would always know him in their hearts.

He stopped and faced his painting and took in all of its beauty.

"All right. I think we're ready," he announced. They had not been told what to expect. They weren't sure what was going to happen, but they knew Gerald wouldn't do anything to harm them. They trusted him completely.

They held tight as Gerald carefully released his painting and set it free into the universe. He pushed it in place, between the other planets - third from the sun. When he got it just where he wanted it, he waved his hand to put the universe in motion.

He watched it for the longest time as it spun around the bright gold sun. The moon spun around it and the planets spiraled around them all. It was like a mystical dance, an energetic flow of perpetual energy that would always be in motion.

Gerald carefully framed his universe and hung it on his bedroom wall. He knew in his heart his world would now be safe. He would always be with it, watching over it, guiding it.

He would always hear the cries of his people, their hearts' desires. He would be a part of their lives, inspiring them to achieve.

He could hear them, feel them and care for them all from a distance – and yet, a part of him remained. His magic within had infused itself into every fiber of everyone's being. Symbols of his love could be found in every flowering bud, every blade of grass and every strand of hair.

No matter what might happen, no matter the situation, Gerald was with them. He'd will them to do the right thing, he'd feel them when they hurt and rejoice when they were happy.

He was a part of their lives as a part of him would always be there protecting them.

This was his masterpiece.

The perfect world.

A world he would love forever & always.

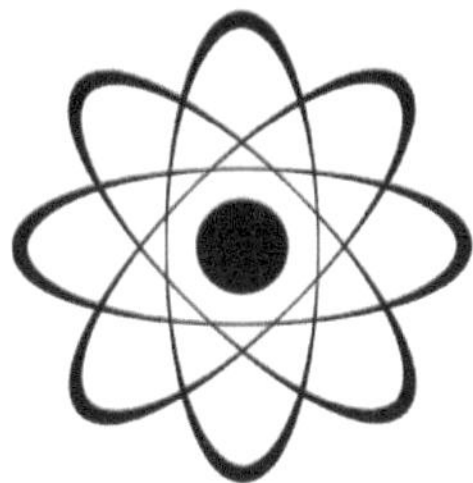

1 John 4:11-12 *Dear friends, since God so loved us, we also ought to love one another. No one has ever seen God; but if we love one another, God lives in us and his love is made complete in us*

The Painting 2

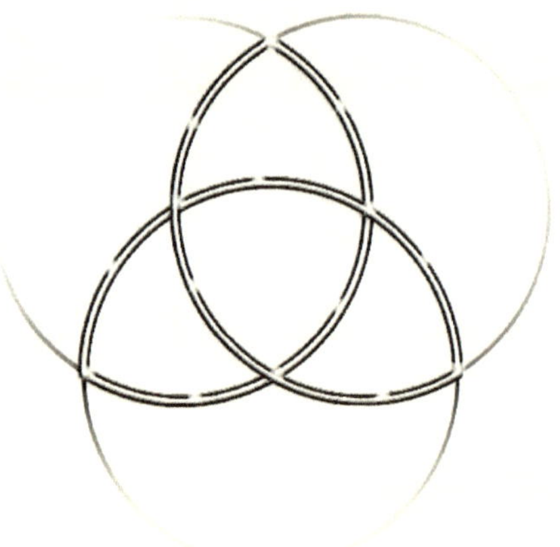

Introduction

Time changes all things...

There was a fun game that children used to play a long time ago… before technology changed the rules. It was called "Telephone."

The rules were simple. Gather a group of friends into a line. The first person in the line whispers something into the second person's ear. That person has to listen carefully because there are no repeats. They then have to turn to the third person in line and repeat what they heard.

As the story is whispered down the row, it changes. In a couple minutes time, depending on the difficulty of the first phrase, the subject, description or even the entirety of the sentence may change completely. It was quite funny to hear how something can morph and change in a few moments time.

Imagine what that story would turn into over the course of many, many generations. This is what happened in the Painting.

Gerald's story is quite unique though.

What he created defied nature and reality. It shouldn't have worked. He pulled and used a power from the depths of his soul that was not at all possible. Creating a real-live world from paint is something most people couldn't even begin to wrap their heads around. So Gerald's 'telephone' story changed and morphed to fit their beliefs and highly active imaginations.

Over time, over the years, through each generation, a story was told. The painter became the creator. His canvas became his world. The bucket of water that doused the fire became the great flood and his initials: G.O.D. that no one could find any longer in the depths of the ocean, became the spoken name; Geody *(Gee-Oh-Dee)*.

What follows is Gerald's 'telephone' story and how his son, Benjamin, visits the painting in hopes of correcting some of the misconstrued details of his father's greatest masterpiece.

CHAPTER 1

True Love is a feeling of complete peace.
It happens when you open yourself up to the possibility. It is a complete acceptance, an understanding. It is pure. It comes from the heart.
It is enchanting.

- K

Gerald wasn't alone any longer. He had found friendship. He was part of someone else's life. He had created his own world--a beautiful, enchanting world that was so magnificent and perfect, it needed to be protected. So he put everything he had left into the creation of a universe in which to protect his painting. His hopes and dreams still flowed from him into the Painting and the emotions still flowed from it into him. He could hear and feel the people within. He could feel their happiness, joys and pleasure, but he could also feel their hurts, sorrows and sadness. He wanted nothing more than for them to be happy and enjoy this world; find the peace within its perfection. But as *their* years passed by, things began to change.

Time worked very differently in the Painting. One day outside in Gerald's world was a year within the Painting. Every four minutes Gerald watched a day and a night go by. Every minute, more and more people were born into his world. Every few hours a generation expired. Every single day the story of what he created changed. By the time Gerald had become an adult, married and had a child of his own, the Painting's population had multiplied a thousand times. Two people became four. Four people became eight. Eight became sixteen, then thirty-two, sixty-four, and over one hundred. A hundred became a thousand, and a thousand soon turned into a million and the story of where 'we' came from? Well that seemed to be one of the first philosophical questions a curious child would ask as they gazed up into the night sky and tried to count the stars.

The twinkling of those tiny white dots that speckled the darkness of space enthralled the curious nature of a child whose favorite questions happened to begin with 'why?' "Why is the sky blue? Why's the grass green? Why do the birds sing? What else is out there?"

The answers, while ever changing intelligence, always tended to have a similar theme. "The sky is the blue that *he* painted. That shade of green is what *he* wanted. The birds sing because *he* thought it would be beautiful. The creator is out there. He watches over us through those twinkling stars. He smiles at us the way I smile at you," a parent would say as their child glanced up to see the twinkle in their eyes.

It was a beautiful life, a wonderful time to be alive - but there were some who didn't believe.

CHAPTER 2

"That's ridiculous!"

"But it's the truth."

"Says' who?"

"My grandfather told me. He told my mom who also told me. So it has to be true."

"Who told your grandfather?"

"His parents did. It's been a story that's been passed down over generations."

"That's the point," The person countering would grin, "it's a story. It's make-believe."

"That's not what I meant."

"It's a fairytale your family told you so you would go to sleep at night."

"That's not true!" Jeffrey felt the burning tears welling up in his eyes.

"It is. You are just too gullible." Franklin's lips spread into a cruel smile.

"I am not. My parents wouldn't lie to me. He IS the creator. He made everything and we should thank him for it."

"Well, until I meet him, I'm not going to believe it." Franklin turned and walked away with his head held a tad bit higher after winning this debate.

"One day you'll see." Jeffrey's voice cracked as a single tear slid down his cheek. He wiped it away with the back of his hand and turned to walk home. He believed so strongly and yet couldn't change one person's mind. As he walked, he wondered, is my acceptance of the Painter's creation strong enough?

He was deep in thought when a rustling in the trees to his left caught his attention. At first, he was startled. He thought to run home, but the trees rustled again and this time, his eyes focused on what was causing it.

"Hello big guy." Jeffrey spoke calmly as he slowly walked towards the deer. The large buck had gotten his antlers tangled in the branches of a downed tree. He pulled and yanked trying to free himself but was only getting himself more tangled and bringing attention to his plight.

Jeffrey lifted his hands and cooed a calm "Shhhh..." as he whispered in a low voice, "it'll be okay. Let me help you." He stepped closer, so very slowly, until he was right by the deer.

He could see the buck was terrified. Large animals could be very dangerous when they are scared, he knew this, but he also knew this guy needed his help. He slowly laid a hand on the deer's head. The frightened buck yanked back as hard as he could but the branches snagged his antlers and yanked him back in place.

Jeffery backed away just a step to give the buck a chance to catch his breath. His eyes were wide open; his breathing was heavy and staggered. Jeffrey could sense the deer's heart was racing.

He grabbed a tree branch near the buck's head and broke it. The loud snap startled the deer but again he couldn't escape. Jeffrey snapped another branch. After the third branch, broken and tossed to the side, the deer began to realize what was happening, he was getting helped by this young little boy.

He watched Jeffrey diligently as he worked. Some of the branches were too big to break. Some of them were too fresh to snap. Jeffrey worked hard to lift them and untangle them and move them to the side.

He had his hands on the buck's antlers. They were almost under him as he began maneuvering the sharp horns out of the tangled mess - this he knew was incredibly dangerous. If the buck gets free and lifts those pointy antlers quickly and forcefully, they could impale Jeffrey. He could be stabbed and left for dead!

Now, even Jeffrey's heart was racing. He pressed the antlers down and the branches up. The deer could sense the boy was helping him but his head and neck hurt. His antlers were heavy and they were being pushed and yanked on. He was tired and yet the adrenaline was keeping him energized.

Finally, Jeffrey got some air between the last antler and the brush. The buck yanked backwards and tumbled out of the trees. Jeffrey lost his footing and fell onto the pile. Quickly though, he turned to the buck who soon realized he was free.

The buck steadied his legs; he lifted his head up high. His antlers were much larger than they seemed when they were tangled in the brush. He looked at Jeffrey lying on the pile, then winked and walked away.

He walked away slowly and Jeffrey couldn't help but marvel at the beauty of this majestic beast. As the buck neared the edge of the grove of trees, he looked back at Jeffrey and just stared at him for a moment. Their eyes met and held for a long moment, a moment that filled Jeffrey with great satisfaction. Then the buck leapt out into the sunlight and galloped across the field.

Jeffrey felt like a hero. A pride filled within him as he had never saved a life before. He had heard stories of how the Painter wanted the people to tend to the animals, to take care of his creations. A smile spread across his face as he began to maneuver himself off of the pile of tree branches. Tumbling to the ground, he laughed.

A clumsy hero, but a hero nonetheless.

CHAPTER 3

Gerald Oliver Delaney truly enjoyed staring at the universe painting that hung on the wall in his den. It used to hang on his bedroom wall but he had grown up. It had been a long time since he moved out of his parents' home. He now had a home of his own. He married his best friend, Tiffany, and they even had a son.

Gerald's life had turned out much different than what he expected. Of course, he hadn't expected much at all growing up. He had always been so lonely, but now, he was happy.

As he leaned back in his recliner and watched the planets of his universe spiral around the sun, he let his memories take him back to the Painting, the original creation of his world. He'd get lost in his memories.

He could feel the sun warming his face, the cool breeze blowing against his cheeks. He could smell the flowers and salty sea air. He could hear the birds singing, the chipmunks chattering and the wolves howling.

He remembered how peaceful and beautiful it was, and how comforted and welcome he felt there. He fondly recalled the soft white paw of the bunny that had been so curious about him. How the bunny's nose twitched as it sniffed Gerald's face and how its whiskers tickled his nose.

He thought about the people he painted into his world, his likenesses. He thought about how small they were, how curious and brave. They trusted him with everything. They knew he would take care of them. They knew he would always watch over them.

Gerald heard them talking. He heard them as they lived their lives, as they became friends, as they fell in love, and as they had children.

He felt their joy as their first child was born, then their second. He rejoiced with them for every birthday and anniversary. He was with them as they worked the land, tended to the animals and built their lives.

He was a part of them as their children grew up, and their children had children. He witnessed the world evolve and change. He was a happy spectator beholding the growth of his magnificent world.

The population grew quickly. Towns were created. People spread out, built their homes outside of town. Some went so far away they started their own towns. More people ventured out that way. Those towns grew, so some went even further out.

Before long the entire planet had been occupied. Gerald found it amazing to observe the evolution of his world.

Some people lived up north where it snowed. They created warmer clothes, thicker walls to their homes and very creative ways to travel with the help of the animals that inhabited the land. Their skin was pale and very white because the cold temperatures tended to keep them inside and out of the sun. They almost blended in to their environment. They fished and shipped foods in from other places of the world.

Some people lived around the center of the planet where the sun shined longer and brighter. They were hot most of the time and wore much thinner clothes. Their skin tanned a golden brown, and their hair darkened. Their homes were made of thin thatched plants and they ate the fruit that grew plentifully on the trees surrounding them.

Some people lived much further south where the sun beat down upon the land. There was a lot of sand and very little trees. The animals of the land were larger and ferocious. They evolved to find ways to store water, to survive. The humans were much darker here. They were stronger and valiant. They hunted and herded the animals.

Each area of the planet created new and varied kinds of people. Each group lived differently and each group told their own individual stories of the creator.

Gerald giggled as he listened to the varying stories. He couldn't help but smile as the details changed. Each culture and civilization added their own unique flair to the story; some called him a painter, others a creator. Some described him as the grand designer, the architect of the universe, the author and even the inventor.

His painting, or his world, was formed of clay, constructed of love or established as the symbol of perfection. Each generation added their own style to the story, embellishing upon the legend until Gerald was a mysterious being whose enchantment held the glory of the moon and the stars.

Then there was the universe. The expansion of space and stars and planets, was almost more than most of the world could comprehend. To most, the story of him placing the Painting within the universe didn't make sense.

How could one person do this? A person can no less pick up a tree with his bare hands and move it. So how can an entire world be repositioned inside of a universe that one can't even touch?

Gerald's love was unexplainable, enchanting, and thrilling. Some found it inspiring while others found it terrifying. An omnificent being so powerful he could control the vastness of space? That fear, was what started the chaos.

As the people shared the story, their fears were added to it. "Geody could squash you like a bug if he so desired."

"Fear him, for it was his wrath that flooded the world."

These stories saddened Gerald. He wished he could go back and explain that it was an accident, a mistake. He was just trying to put out the fire, to help and protect the people. But he couldn't go back into the Painting, it was impossible, *now*.

However, he could will the people to listen to his heart. He could give them the desire to correct the story, or to instill a feeling of togetherness - that he did this for the good of everyone. But he couldn't force them to listen to him or believe it.

The arguments began.

The people would disagree with each other. It would cause separation between townsfolk and families. It was horrible.

CHAPTER 4

"What's wrong daddy?" Little Benjamin would ask his father, Gerald, as tenderly as only a four- year old could do.

"They don't understand, but you do, don't you son?" Gerald patted his lap, encouraging his son Benjamin to come sit with him.

Benjamin smiled at his father. He couldn't wait to come listen to another great story about his father's magnificent world.

"The canvas needed color and the color needed depth and the world needed life and the life needed love. This was how it began and that was how I painted it."

Benjamin curled into a small ball on his father's lap and listened with intent curious wonder. He loved hearing the stories. He heard them every day. Of a father's love, of a creator's will, of a painter's promise.

"Today a young boy saved a deer." Gerald smiled looking deep into his son's adoring eyes. "He risked his own safety to save the life of one of my animals. I felt the fear within him building. He was afraid he was going to get hurt but he knew he had to do this. He knew in his heart that someone had to save this massive beast, and so he did. And do you know what that deer did in return?"

"No." Benjamin hung on every word.

"When he was free, finally released from his captivity, instead of running away scared, he turned and thanked the young boy."

"He did?"

"A smile is the most powerful tool we are given. A smile and a wink, an adoring glance, can mean so much to one person. It tells that person, who may have been lost or alone, that he's loved. It shows you how we all have our gifts. That little boy felt the buck's appreciation and his heart swelled with happiness. Just moments earlier that little boy was sad. He was feeling lost and scared. After helping save a life, he walked away with a happy pride that only comes from doing good. This is what life is all about. One small act can mean so much. Just imagine what my Painting could be like if everyone did that."

"Your Painting sounds like a wonderful place, daddy. I so wish I could see it up close."

Gerald knew that his world was changing, though. Every minute that went by another fear was born. Every fear brought with it confusion and that confusion created disorder. Soon, Gerald worried, his world would be unrecognizable. The people would need more than he could provide. They needed clarity and understanding. They needed to know the truth, but there was only one way...

Sure, Gerald tried. When they cried to him, he would send tears from the clouds. When there was joy, there was also sunlight. When someone asked for a sign, he would send a butterfly and when they asked for help, he'd will someone to be available.

Sometimes they listened, sometimes they didn't. Sometimes, unlikely people felt the message and found themselves at the right moment, able to help. It gave them clarity. Satisfaction. For some, it gave them humility. For others though - arrogance was born.

"I was called! I was chosen by the creator to help others. Look at what I can do. See with your own eyes the magic I have. Believe in me and know the truth of it all. Give me everything you have and become one of the selected to do Geody's will."

Oh, how Gerald hated that; singling people out; the weak and the vulnerable. They all had the power, they just didn't know it. If only someone could explain the truth to them.

As the years passed, Gerald watched and shared each individual tale with his son. Benjamin grew up with the world. He was being molded into a very important person because he was being taught lessons no other could truly impart. His story was just as important as each story he heard, because his story was being written as well.

"Dad, I want to go to your world. I want to set them straight."

"You can't just walk into my world, Son."

"Dad, if you've taught me anything growing up, you've taught me there is always a way. Where there is a will there's a way; as we all have the power to find it. One of these days I will find a way to go to these people and tell them what a wonderful father you are."

Gerald smiled at his son with an adoration as large as his heart could create. His smile was bright on the outside, but what the world was becoming was giving him pain on the inside.

When his son was old enough to understand, Gerald would share with him some of the more horrible details of his world - the things that he was ashamed of.

He knew his son needed to fully understand good before he could share with him the bad. He knew his son's heart was strong and his desire to do good would prevail. He knew his son would be able to change everything and he knew it would happen sooner than he would be ready for.

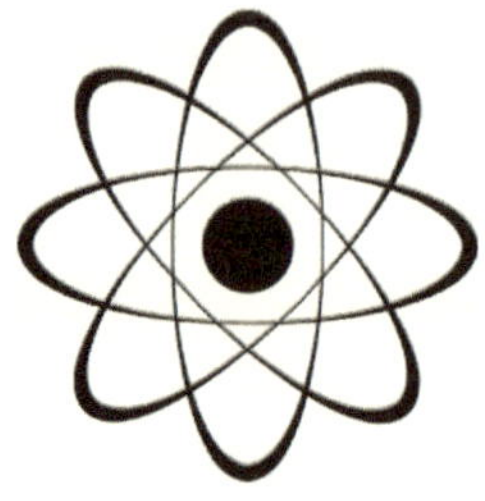

CHAPTER 5

"I don't believe!" The man stood at the top of the hilltop, screaming to the sky. "Show me your face! Prove to me you exist."

Gerald willed the clouds to roll in but then realized he was being goaded.

"Give me a sign or I will never believe. I demand you to show me something, anything."

He released his tension and a ray of sun peaked out from behind a cloud. Gerald took a deep breath, closed his eyes and willed the man's heart to change. The man paused for a moment and Gerald was hopeful that he had felt a twinge of love touch him... but the anger was stronger within him.

"The stories of the creator are impossible. Magic doesn't exist. This is all a fairytale meant to enchant young children."

Gerald wanted so badly to reach out and touch this man. To embrace him and show him 'I'm here.' He felt the man's words sting like a knife to the heart.

"There is nothing that can explain this, no one who can rationalize this story and truly accept these tales as fact. Anyone who claims they believe, must have some small bit of doubt within them, otherwise they would surely be considered crazy."

Was Gerald crazy? He created this world. He saved it. He watches over it still today and yet each day it made him more and more sad.

"Show me an adult who believes."

Gerald searched the world for anyone in the area to turn right and venture out towards this man. But the man continued screaming.

"Show me someone who has never done wrong. Whose good nature is all there is to him. Show me someone who can prove you exist, who has seen you, known you."

The sadness built within Gerald. This man refused to believe without proof and yet Gerald could sense how powerfully he wanted to believe. This man was crying for vindication. He wanted so desperately to be wrong that every fiber of his being was screaming out for it.

"Send a messenger. Communicate your will to us. Tell us what you want, or we will never know."

A tear slipped down Gerald's cheek. His heart ached in his chest. He knew what he had to do – he had always known what he had to do. He had hoped he would have more time, more time to prepare, but he could feel that it was time. He had always known that the Painting would let him know when it was time.

Just then, from the opposite side of his world, Gerald heard a newborn baby cry out for the first time. Its wail pierced the hole growing in his heart. With every bit of love he had inside of him Gerald spoke to the man. "You will get your proof. Go tell the world, that soon, you will get your proof."

"Son!" Gerald called out from inside his den. "Son, would you come in here, please?"

"Yes Father." Benjamin walked into the room. He was nearing adulthood, and so full of love. He was as perfect as Gerald's intentions had ever been. He had been taught his entire life what he was meant to do – without truly knowing, and now it was time.

"Tell me what is in your heart, Son," he spoke, motioning to a chair and watching his son come in and stand by it.

Benjamin thought carefully, then spoke. "I have been filled with love - nothing but love from you and mom. I understand this life better than most. I have an insight that no one else could ever have for I have received the fundamental lessons of life through your world. I have seen passion through your eyes, an understanding and patience stronger than any mountain. I have felt your hopes, been a part of your dreams, and desire nothing more than to share your legend with others."

Gerald smiled sadly. "My Painting I will always treasure. But you, Son, you are my masterpiece. I have spent my lifetime perfecting the perfect. Teaching you, developing my message. Today I have been enlightened. I can now see further than I ever dreamed, and what I see is magnificent."

"Tell me, Father, what's happened?"

Gerald sighed. "Son, please sit down." There was a darkness building within him that he was almost afraid of. "Life is precious, here as well as in my world. Life begins and it ends but the point of it – is that it exists." Gerald formed his words carefully in his head before he spoke them. "You would be loved by two, adored by many and hated by all."

"How can that be?" Benjamin questioned but was stopped by his father's raised hand.

"Can you be strong?"

"Of course."

"Can you be brave?"

"I think so."

"Can you be patient?"

"Father?" Benjamin's head cocked to the side a bit and his eyebrows furled.

"Benjamin, there is still so much to learn. No one who has not lived the life could ever truly understand it all. You must be a part of it, to grow with it."

He gazed at his father, examining the sweat on his brow. He was puzzled by his father's face. It was filled with thrill and yet his eyes held terror. Gerald stared at him and yet Benjamin felt as if his father were looking through him, to the Painting that hung on the wall behind him.

"You would retain my love, you would always be my son, but you would be the son of another." A single tear caught the light of his desk lamp but then was blinked away. "Your memories would be there for you when you need them. My will would be a part of your soul. You will learn how to use it with time. You will learn everything you need to. You will KNOW everything."

He stood, then immediately fell to his knees in front of his son. He took Benjamin's hands within his, the tears were flowing freely.

"But Son, there is so much pain. More pain than you could possibly imagine. It's blinding. Its torture endures forever. I cannot do this to you without you knowing - without you understanding completely."

He cradled his son in his arms. He hugged him tightly. He was full-grown and the apple of his father's eye. A replica of perfection as only a father would ever see.

"You've said that you wanted to go. You've voiced your request; suggested it time and time again, but you weren't ready. Even knowing how, I would have hesitated because it would have meant letting you go.

But I know you are ready. I know it. I just need to hear it from you. You must say it. But think hard about this. This decision cannot be made lightly and it will last forever...." Gerald looked up into the quizzical eyes of his son, took a deep breath and asked, "Do you still want to go into my world?"

Benjamin turned and stared at the Painting on the wall. The universe was magnificent, the way it moved; the colors of space, the shooting stars, the rays of light. Then there was the world - the original Painting. From this distance the green and blues glistened in the night. It sparkled like a gemstone, reflecting a multitude of colors.

He had NEVER seen it up close. He had always wondered what it was like inside of the Painting. It called to him.

He had spent his entire life dreaming about this moment. He had wanted to see his father's world since the very first bedtime story as he lay as an infant in his crib. He had worked hard, studied hard, and grown up with the willingness to do anything.

"Son, do you still want to visit my world?"

"Yes. Yes Father, I do."

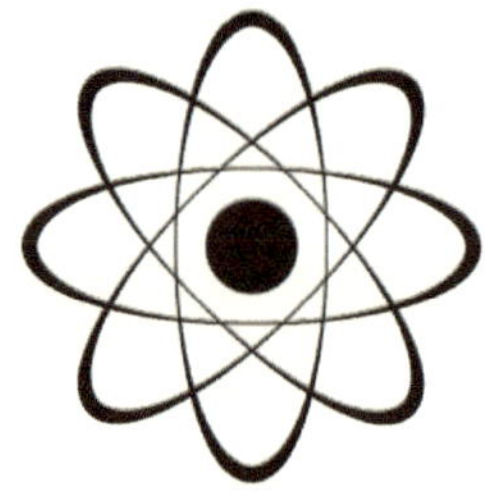

CHAPTER 6

"The Son is coming!"

Word of the creator's son spread across the land. The people rejoiced and the people rebelled. "Our creator is sending his son."

"Why?"

"To teach us. To rescue us."

"Rescue us from what?"

"Ourselves."

"I don't need rescuing."

"Everyone needs to be rescued."

Word spread like wildfires. It was impossible to understand and yet everyone knew. "He is coming."

People who believed, prepared. People who didn't believe, felt uncertainty. They didn't believe in the painter and yet, they feared the coming of his son. It was illogical to be afraid of something they didn't believe to be true, and yet their fears grew.

As some went about their days waiting with smiles and eager anticipation, others frowned and grumbled. They didn't know what to expect. They didn't want to be judged and they didn't want to be proven wrong.

The soon-to-be-parents were happily looking forward to the moment they would get to see their child, hold their newborn son in their arms and yet it wasn't *their* child. What would the creator's son be like? Would he look like them? Act like them? Talk like them? Would he grow up faster? Talk sooner? Walk quicker? Would he be as unique a phenomenon as the story of the painted world itself?

"Will he love us?"

"Of course he will." The soon-to-be mother sat down next to her husband, she held his hand. "Please don't be upset. Our love for him will be stronger, deeper than any other. He will be our baby. He will be raised by us. He will depend on us. He will be taught by us. He will grow up with his knowledge, but he will receive our values. What he will become will include what we teach him and if we do our job right..."

"He will love us as strong as any child who loves their parents." The husband kissed his wife on the forehead.

They were chosen. Why they were chosen of all of the couples in the entire world, they would never know. Were they the best choice? They couldn't be certain, but the creator, he was. The creator knew they were because they heard his call. They answered him.

"You will bring life to my Son. He will enter the painting through you and you will be responsible for raising him. You will teach him everything he needs to learn about your world. You will protect him until he is old enough to protect himself. He is my pride and joy. I will be watching over him. I will be watching over you all - as I always am."

Gerald walked into his son's room and noticed him standing outside of his closet staring in. The light was on, but he was just standing there.

"Son, is something wrong?"

"How do I pack for a trip like this?"

"You fill your heart to the top with all the love your mom and I can give."

Benjamin turned to look at his father. Gerald suddenly looked older. The worry lines were more visible. He smiled at his father, and then nodded.

"It is time."

Benjamin sat down on the side of his bed and exhaled. "Will it hurt?"

"No."

"How much time will pass by?"

"One day here is a year there. By the time you are seven a week will have passed. I imagine you will be gone for a little over a month."

"I will only live to be around 35?"

"You will live for as long as it takes for you to learn what you need to and teach what you are supposed to."

"What exactly is it that you want me to teach them?"

"You will know when the time is right. Once your message has been delivered, it will be the people who decide."

"What does that mean, Father?"

"You will figure it out, Son."

The mysteries of life were going to be a challenge to Benjamin, he knew, but he also looked forward to it. He hugged his mom goodbye, a long, drawn-out hug that would have to last for years. Then he lay down on the bed. Gerald kneeled down next to his son's bed side.

"Just close your eyes, Son. Breathe deeply and imagine my world; the Painting - the beauty within, the light, the sounds, the smells." Benjamin's breathing slowed – he was falling asleep. "Your journey will start in the dark, the unknown. You will understand but for a while, you will only be able to witness it. There will be much to learn, so much to discover. Your training will begin when the lights turn on."

Gerald had been holding his son's hand. He held it tight, as if he didn't want to let it go. His arm trembled as did his quivering voice. He inhaled deeply, then slowly, Gerald let go of his son's hand and all fell away.

"You are now in the dark. It is peaceful. Serene. You feel warm inside, and you can hear the beating of a heart as you are filled with love from within.

Your journey will begin when the cold hits you for the first time. When the light blinds you; when the pain of the world fills you; when this happens - you will be born."

CHAPTER 7

As the bitter cold air struck his bare skin for the first time, Benjamin trembled. It was a shocking, harsh change from where he had been moments ago. His body filled with desperate, excruciating emotions that were screaming to be released.

As he exhaled a cry into the wintry night, he didn't recognize his voice. It was small and frail and filled with despair. He was a baby.

He felt himself being swaddled, wrapped in a blanket that felt rough against his soft new skin. The roughness made him cry more. The sound of his screaming pierced his delicate ears. The smells surrounding him were confusing and sharp. His eyes wouldn't open. He felt heavier. It was harder to breathe. The tears were flowing freely and his cries became louder. He was confused and lost. He was miserable!

But then he felt someone hold him - pulled deep into the arms of someone warm. She kissed his head, rocked him calmly, and held him tight. She embraced him tenderly and calmed him from within. His fears started to subside. He stopped crying. His breathing slowed. The quiet of the night filled his ears and the silence was beautiful.

Gerald heard his son being born and sobbed quietly, listening. He knew for a while his son would be fine. He would be taught, then he would learn, then he would educate others. It would be good for quite a while. He rested on his recliner with his head back and his eyes closed, comforted in this knowledge.

It would be a long, long month - but the reason would be worth it. His purpose would be seen by everyone and it would be good. He knew this - HE KNEW - but still a part of his heart, the deepest darkest part of his heart, ached. There was a twinge of grief that was clawing at his soul and he had a feeling, this anguish would overwhelm him as the time neared. He feared it.

As the morning sun rose over the hills, Benjamin opened his eyes and took in its beauty. The rays of light illuminated the world in a way that nothing else ever could. The sky sparkled and glowed with a thousand similar colors. Red and violet, yellow and orange all combined to resemble a pallet, being mixed and blended to create the perfect color before the first paint stroke on a canvas of a brand-new day.

Yet the canvas was already painted. The hills of green transformed from dark to light. The grasses were various heights and colors. There was no way to count the number of greens that were used to paint a single blade and yet each piece of grass blended to form a hillside.

The trees and plants, displayed a depth of texture and color that was unlike any he had ever seen. As the light hit them, it showcased leaves of varying sizes, assorted shades of greens. It was almost overwhelming the detail that was put into every smudge.

The effect of seeing this beauty for the first time was overpowering. Benjamin stared at it until his eyes hurt, until the tears began to flow. Without being able to articulate the beauty he was taking in, all he could do was let the emotions out.

The cry woke Gerald. He looked into the painting and watched as his son was picked up for the first time this morning and cared for as any child would be, should be. He smiled brightly, a tear forming in the corner of his eye as a call pulled his attention elsewhere.

By the end of the day Gerald looked back in on the progress of his son. He had just pulled himself to his feet. His tiny unsteady legs trembled under the weight of his one-year-old body, but he did it - he was standing. His parents watched with proud smiles, holding each other when they saw his mouth open. They waited with excited anticipation as he inhaled – focusing on what he needed to do.

Watching, waiting, excited and expectant, Gerald listened as Benjamin looked up and closed his tiny eyes and then spoke his first ever words... "da da"

Each year, as Benjamin grew, so did his understanding of this world. He learned how to walk and talk, sing and dance. He played, made friends, went to school and read.

This world was full of unknown possibilities; the stories, the songs, the plays. The creativity inside each and every person was astounding. Each person was born with so much possibility. There was so much opportunity. The fact that they could become anything their heart desires astounded Benjamin.

His father had created the perfect world, so full of life with so many options. A single choice could open the door to an array of potential. They couldn't see it - not really, but they had so many opportunities to follow their dreams, their hearts desires, and so few of them did just that.

A young boy swung a bat at a ball and missed. He swung it with all of his might. If he would have hit that ball, he would have made a home run - all he needed was practice. But he gave up. He cried because he missed, threw the bat to the ground and gave up.

Benjamin saw how close he had come, he could see the fork in the road before this young boy. If he would have stood there and tried again, the next pitch would have been hit. He would have knocked it out of the park and started himself along the path of a great baseball player, but he threw it away.

As he sat in the crowd, contemplating what the boy had thrown away, he watched as the next opportunity came walking up to him. The coach's older son kneeled down in front of the boy. His arm was in a sling and even though he was only a teenager, his face held the wisdom of an adult.

He spoke to the boy. He showed him his shoulder, and explained how he had been following his dream of becoming a pro ball player, until he threw his shoulder out.

Benjamin saw how the boy listened, wiped a tear from his cheek and sat up a bit straighter in the dugout. He nodded and smiled and then stood up. He walked back out to the plate and picked up his bat. As he awaited the pitch, Benjamin returned his gaze to the coach's son who was watching and he saw his father's hand pat the teens back and then disappear. He knew this was his father giving him an "atta boy" and this made him feel very good inside.

Benjamin knew his father had opened another door for that young boy, and it was the coach's son who answered. As he heard the crack of the bat hit the ball, Benjamin returned his attention to the young boy who stood there in awe watching the ball fly farther and farther away. Everyone in the crowd stood and cheered and yelled at him to "Run! Run!"

The boy dropped the bat to the ground and began running to first base as quick as his little legs could take him. The smile that spread across his face was as big as his own father's smile as he watched from afar.

While this wasn't the first time Benjamin had witnessed his father's work here, it was one of the first times he saw his father truly intervene and suddenly, he understood.

Benjamin knew well how his father would watch over the Painting. He had witnessed his emotions skip around from happy from sad to angry to glad. He could easily be laughing and crying at the same time.

It always made him wonder, especially with the understanding of how time works here, how he could possibly hear and be a part of everybody's lives at every minute of every day, even when he slept.

But then Benjamin would witness his father sending love - so much love. A huge flowing wave of caring and hope would sweep into the Painting and blanket everything inside of it like a thick heavy coat of paint. He was sending the will and the way. He was giving everybody the chance to be the solution, to answer his call and help others by just listening and feeling. It was all about doing good deeds.

It excited Benjamin to learn how easy it was to do his father's work here. He gave everyone exactly what they needed to answer anyone's call at any time. Benjamin understood. He realized the simplicity of this complex situation and he valued that knowledge. The dilemma posed before him, was how to teach everyone else.

CHAPTER 8

As Benjamin grew up, he continued learning. With his mouth closed and his eyes and heart open, he witnessed the beauty of his father's plan in just about everything he looked at. Every person, plant and animal, every action, deed or phrase, gave an opportunity to be a part of a greater plan.

The problem he kept seeing was when someone turned the corner, many didn't follow through. He could sense that they felt it - even if it was just for a fraction of a second. They were given a decision: answer, or walk away. It was their decision as to what they would do.

Sometimes they would see someone who needed help and while their heartstrings tugged at the person to help, their brain reminded them they were running late. Maybe they saw danger, maybe they saw no need to help, maybe they thought someone else will do it – so why should they?

Yet as Benjamin continued to observe, he'd see that maybe it was the next person that came along that answered the call, or maybe the third. His father had answered that person's plea by providing not one, but many opportunities. Sometimes it took more than one. Sometimes, the potential would keep going down the line until it found the right person. Sometimes, the line was so long that the person awaiting an answer – gave up.

When Benjamin was about ten years old, he began sharing what he had been learning. Not as eloquently as he had wanted since his education on this planet was still in progress, but he was teaching his peers what he could.

"I am the painter's son. My father was the artist who painted this world."

While many joshed and laughed at the idea, some wanted to believe and others absolutely did. The ones that didn't believe didn't care to hear more. The ones that weren't sure if they could believe, well they asked for proof or watched from afar.

"I heard stories that the creator was sending his son but it was such a long time ago."

"I was born into this world. I was a baby. I had to grow up, just like you."

"How do you know YOU are the one they were talking about?"

"I just know. I was born knowing. I've seen my father at work here. I've heard him speak to me."

It took them a while to accept; the others who did, helped. But it was his lessons that validated his claims.

One afternoon three of his friends joined Benjamin for a walk. They walked out to a nearby pasture and gazed out at the field.

"What do you see?" Benjamin inquired.

"A field," Jacob spoke quick.

"A tree," Max added.

Benjamin smiled. "Tell me about that tree."

"It's a tree, what's there to tell?" Danny asked obviously confused as to the purpose of this talk.

Jacob described the tree. "Green leaves. Brown trunk."

"What else? Tell me about the importance of this tree." Benjamin looked at Jacob as they started to walk towards it.

Jacob shrugged his shoulders, so Benjamin began to describe the tree himself.

"That tree stands alone in this field. Its massive size towers over the grass. Its limbs stretch out so far, they almost bend down to the ground in search for rest. Its very existence reflects a bold symbol of solidarity - that anyone who stands up for their beliefs will prevail."

As they neared the tree, Benjamin started pointing out the details.

"The leaves are made up of many shades of green. Each leaf differs slightly from the next, from its color, to its shape. Some are small, some are large, some have been chewed on by bugs or torn by birds flying by. They are a lighter color green on the underside and darker on the top.

They have veins that feather out, getting smaller towards the ends."

The boys looked closely at the leaves as Benjamin redirected his attention to the tree's trunk. "The bark is coarse and textured. The trunk is not necessarily brown, but shades of brown and grey. Because of the texture, there is dimension; flat rough areas and deep cavernous gaps. Those crevasses provide pathways for ants and bugs to crawl up." The boys directed their attention to the bark and Danny poked at the ants. Benjamin continued.

"This tree provides shade for us. It's cooler under here than it was out there in the field."

"I'm thankful for that," Max spoke.

"This tree also provides shelter. It is a home for the animals. That squirrel has created a nest in the upper branches. That family of birds have built their nest in the lower branches. That woodpecker has drilled a hole for its home in the trunk."

The children looked and noticed all of the different homes that existed within the tree's limbs. Benjamin continued.

"Over here you can even see where a buck scraped his antlers against the lower limbs." Jacob rubbed his finger along the smoothly rubbed area.

"This tree produces acorns, which the squirrels and birds eat. It provides areas for the squirrels to store food for the winter. This tree does so much for so many."

"I never thought about it that way," Jacob spoke quietly.

"Guess trees are pretty important," Max declared. The boys took all of that in.

"But that's not all," Benjamin spoke. "We climb their branches and get exercise. When we look out over the canopy, we can see the world in a completely different way. We are taller and can look down at the world. We can see more, can expand our awareness."

"Wow," Jacob spoke, looking up at the light shining in through the leaves.

"Look, someone carved their initials into the trunk," Max added, starting to notice details.

"Good job." Benjamin smiled, "The tree is a way for someone to declare their love for someone else."

"I know of a girl who comes out here to read all of the time. She enjoys the quiet and the cool shade as she leans back against the tree trunk," Danny offered. Benjamin smiled and nodded.

"When I was younger, we used to hang a swing from the branches of a tree and it provided hours worth of entertainment."

"Oh yeah, we once had a tree next to a river and we hung a rope from it and swung out over the water and dropped in."

"The twigs that fall are collected to build campfires for keeping warm." Jacob added. "And woodworkers build furniture and tools."

"See," Benjamin smiled, "there is a lot to this tree. But there is even more than that."

He pointed to the roots as they stretched across the ground spanning up over and around the rocks. "These roots have had to work hard to grow. They're journey has been fraught with obstacles. Large rocks have blocked their pathway. They had to adapt and change in order to keep growing. What's important about that is that they need to be as wide as the widest branch to support its growth. This is very important - without a strong foundation the rest of the tree will topple over. If the roots would have stopped at the first obstacle, the growth of this massive tree would have been stunted. It never would have grown as tall and wide as it has. It would have been unable to give us shade, provide them shelter and supply us food."

Everybody sat down around the tree and thought about that for a few moments. "Obstacles are placed in our lives to help us grow, to become stronger." It was an insightful thing for a young boy to say.

A light breeze cooled the sweat from their brows, and Benjamin then asked another question. "Will this tree look the same in a couple months?"

Everyone thought about that and then Max answered. "No! Soon its leaves will turn red and orange and fall to the ground."

"I love jumping in piles of fall leaves."

"Me too!"

"What about a month after that? What will the tree look like then?"

"The leaves will be gone; it'll be bare."

"Right. It marks the seasons: fall and winter. A tree tells us time. It also mimics the stages of our life. We live in seasons and one season we will lose our leaves and leave nothing but a shell. However, the next season we will be reborn and become new. "

"Reborn anew?" Danny questioned but didn't think anyone heard.

"And did you know that the leaves of this tree generate oxygen? The air we breathe comes from the trees and plants around us."

Benjamin waited for all of that to sink in before he spoke again. "So what do you see here now? Just a tree?"

"No, there's so much more."

"And *that* is Father's design. Everything has been painstakingly painted for a reason. Everything has a purpose, multiple purposes. Every single thing in the Painting has THAT kind of detail and purpose - including us. It's when we slow down, take a long look at what's in front of us, that we begin to see."

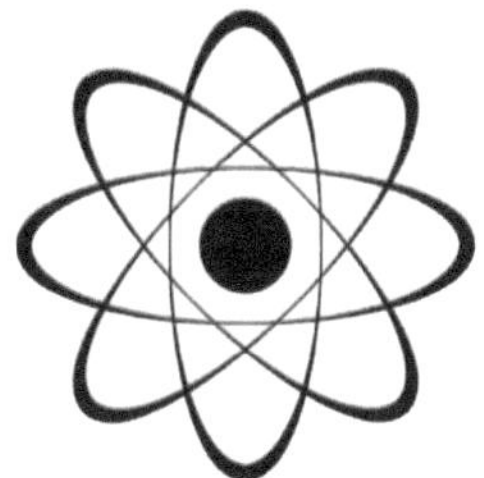

CHAPTER 9

As the four boys rested, they watched a couple other children enter the field throwing a ball back and forth. They watched for a while, until Jacob stood up and began looking around the tree. He wanted to refocus his attention on the masterpiece before him when he noticed something that seemed to confuse him.

"Benjamin, what about this?"

Benjamin, Max and Jacob all stood and walked around to the opposite side of the tree. There they saw a burnt limb that had been split down the middle and sat dead on the ground.

"Can you explain this?"

"It was struck by lightning," Max spoke, certain as to what had happened.

"Right, but why would your father strike down and kill a part of a tree that has so much symbolism, importance and meaning?"

"Yeah?" Max and Danny spoke in unison.

Benjamin smiled. "Look closer. Look inside that burnt out crevice and see what's inside." Max leaned in and saw a colony of milky white worm-looking things crawling around.

"What are they?"

Jacob took a peek. "Termites."

"They are eating the wood. This tree limb is providing sustenance," Benjamin offered.

"Yeah, but when it's gone, they'll move on to this amazing tree."

"If they do?"

"They'll kill it. We can't let that happen," Jacob voiced his concern.

"We don't have to. It is our will to do something about it."

Max tilted his head curiously. "What do you mean Benjamin?"

With a smile, "You've seen a problem and my father has given you the will and ability to do something about that problem. It is up to you to decide whether you are going to listen. Will you ignore the problem and let the termites live another day to eat this tree? Will you kill the termites, solving the problem but ending a civilization? Will you move the tree limb to another part of the field, so they can live?"

"I choose the latter," Danny spoke.

"Why?"

"Because," Danny grinned "it sounds like the right thing to do."

"What if the termites venture back over here?" Benjamin suggested.

"What?" Danny spoke, confused. He had been certain that his answer was the right one.

"What if you move the termites over there and they finish off the dead tree limb, then come back over here later and start in on the tree?"

"So we should kill the termites now?" Max spoke ready to start stomping on them.

Benjamin stopped him. "I'm not saying you should kill them, and I'm not saying you shouldn't. What I'm asking, is for you to follow the pathway that has already been set. Danny has already decided to move the limb. Consider the fact that the task is done, the limb has been moved, the termites have eaten it and are ready to move on. What happens next?"

Jacob sat up. "Well I know that Danny moved the limb, maybe now I go and check on the termites to see what they're doing."

"Good. But what if two days from now you've forgotten about the termites?"

"Then I'll go," Max added.

"That's my father at work. That's how simple and hard life is." Benjamin sat up. He looked up at a distant storm cloud rolling in. We could decide to do something, we could decide not to do something, or that storm cloud could bring with it rain that may wash the termites away and the tree will still be safe."

Now I'm starting to get confused again," Jacob admitted.

Benjamin realized he may have been throwing too much at his friends at once but he had already begun. "Jacob could move the termites. Max could stomp on them, or those boys playing ball in the field out there could pick up this stick and bring it home not even knowing about the termites.

The termites may be washed away from the tree by the coming rains or the storm may bring another bolt of lightning to strike another tree limb down to continue feeding them. Each day, each moment brings with it an unlimited amount of possibilities. Everyone and everything in this world has the opportunity to bring change. Each prospect of modifying the world brings with it more chances and variations.

The possibilities to do good are endless, as is the odds of doing something bad. It's how we deal with those actions that define who we are and how we will grow."

Benjamin looked at his three friends who were staring at him with their mouths open.

"Too much?" He asked.

The three nodded in unison.

"Sorry." Benjamin sat there letting his friends take all of that in.

Danny looked out over the field to the other kids playing. "Nobody else thinks about things the way you do, Benjamin." The others followed his gaze to the field. The three of them, and the kids playing in the field, were all the same age, but suddenly Jacob, Danny and Max felt older and wiser.

"It almost doesn't seem fair – knowing as much as you do. Having all of this awareness..." Jacob trailed off.

Benjamin looked at him curiously. He could sense Jacob's thought process was almost overwhelmed. He finally turned to Benjamin and asked, "Can you ever just be a child?"

"What do you mean?"

"I've never seen you just go out there and play. You're always sitting somewhere watching others."

"He's played before," Max offered, "I saw him throw a ball up in the air and catch it."

Jacob nodded, "But were you just playing for fun, or were you looking at the ball, judging the speed it was going to fall, testing the wind, feeling the leather wrapped around it?"

"What do you think?" Benjamin asked with a smile.

"I think you know more about that baseball than I can possibly fathom. I think you know more about it than a pro-ball player could understand."

"And?" Benjamin was curious where Jacob was going with this.

"And, I think it's sad that you know as much as you do. You can't just be a child and have fun and live with no worries or responsibilities for just a while. My father is always telling me to stop worrying, that my job is to be a kid because this is the only time we get. But Benjamin, you don't get even this time, do you?"

The look on Benjamin's face changed. His eyes lowered and his brow furled. He knew he was different, but it had never been put so bluntly before.

"Don't you listen to him," Max interrupted. "I think the fact that you know so much is exhilarating. Imagine all of the things you can do with what you know."

"But he just said that he can't control it, everyone has the ability to do whatever they want. He can't change anything no matter what he says or does."

"That's not what he said, he said his father will make sure what needs to happen, happens."

"No, his father can only watch and hope for the best. Bad things happen. That's why he's here. To teach us. Right?" Danny asked noticing how conflicted Benjamin was looking.

"I think everything you all are saying is interesting. I'm trying to teach you about my father's world and you are looking out for me. You are worried about my well-being and I appreciate that."

The four of them looked out at the others playing when they all heard a loud thunder clap. It made them shudder as the other boys took off running towards home.

"Guess they've got the right idea. Apparently, this tree is prone to lightning strikes." Max stood and stretched.

"Good point," Danny added as he scrambled to his feet. The two of them helped Jacob and Benjamin off the ground and they began walking home.

As they walked away from the tree, Jacob looked back at it. He saw the storm clouds rolling in and it made him shiver. Thinking about everything they had just learned and the knowledge Benjamin had instilled, was still spiraling around in his head.

He knew he would never look at another tree the same way again and he began to wonder what else Benjamin would teach them that would change the way they saw the world?

CHAPTER 10

Sitting in class listening to the teacher describe today's assignment, Benjamin began to wonder what his father would teach him about the Painting today. He looked out the window and noticed the clouds drifting by in the sky. He noticed how they would at times block the sun's light, but then as they moved and parted, bright rays of light would beam through the openings and shine down on the world. It was as if his father was putting a spotlight on small patches of land. Benjamin sat up straight and craned his neck to see where the light was pointing and saw a pond shimmering off in the distance.

The way the water moved with the wind made the sunlight refracting off of it look like glitter. With imagination combined with what he could see, Benjamin found himself standing along the shoreline. He watched ducks swimming across the water. He witnessed turtles ducking under the water after a quick breath of air and then he heard birds singing in nearby trees.

Benjamin realized he had let his mind wonder completely out of the classroom. He hadn't heard the teacher and wasn't even worried about it until a loud alarm rang out. Not knowing what was going on, he returned his attention to the class and the teacher announcing this was a fire drill. The teacher instructed the students to line up single file and walk out of the school building.

The alarm was deafening. It hurt Benjamin's ears and he began to wonder quietly what the animals and birds felt when they heard this loud, high-pitched squawk. He could cover his ears with his hands, they couldn't.

Standing outside, even amongst the commotion of the students, teachers and reverberation of the alarm, Benjamin felt happy. He always found himself most comfortable within the natural world his father painted. After a while, the okay came to reenter the school, and the students began to walk back to the building. As they neared, Benjamin heard a loud thump. The sound attracted everyone's attention and many of the startled students began to vocally express their shock over the scene unfolding before them. Just a few feet in front of Benjamin was a bird lying motionless on the ground. He stepped up to the bird, kneeled down and picked it up.

"Is it dead?" One of the children asked.

"What happened?" Came another inquiry.

Benjamin held the bird's lifeless body in the palm of his hand and cupped his other hand over it. The pain he felt in his heart for this poor little bird grew. It was the alarm that interfered with his flight. His direction was obstructed by the sound. It was their fault for this small bird's collision and he felt so strongly about fixing the situation; he willed the bird to get better. He wanted so much for this bird to shake it off, stretch his wings out and lift off of his hands and fly away, that at that moment, he believed it would happen.

With eyes closed, and a tear streaking down his face, he opened his hands. That's when he felt the bird press its feet against his palm and leap into the sky. Benjamin heard everyone gasp in amazement as they watched the bird fly away. When he opened his eyes and saw the bird flying higher, higher up, he smiled and whispered a thank you to his father.

As he rose back to his feet, he felt his father speak to him. "That was all you, Son. You are a part of me, and thus you have the power."

Moments later in the hallway Danny and Jacob came running up to Benjamin. "Someone said you brought a bird back to life."

Benjamin said nothing.

"Another moment later Max came running up, "Hey, I heard you were taking credit for bringing a bird back to life, but it had just been stunned."

Jacob turned to Max. "The bird was dead, he saved it."

"Were you there? Did you see it?"

"No, I don't need to, I believe Benjamin."

"Believe him?" Danny interjected, "He hasn't said a word."

"Sure he did. He saved the bird's life."

"No he didn't." Danny spoke matter-of-factly. The three looked at Benjamin, who stood there looking back with his mouth shut.

"The bird had been stunned and you woke it. Right?" Max asked.

"The bird was dead and you saved it. Right?" Jacob countered.

"Benjamin, tell us what happened," Danny begged, not wanting to jump to conclusions.

Benjamin looked at them sadly. "Something happened with the bird. People know what they saw. They said what they saw and they all saw something different. The only person who asked to know the truth was Danny - and you only asked because the confusion has made you uneasy."

"So which is it?" Jacob asked. "Was the bird dead or stunned?"

"Does it matter?" Benjamin countered.

The three looked at each other then back to Benjamin. "Of course it matters."

"You could have done a miracle!"

"Would you only respect me if I had?"

"No," they replied

"Would you think less of me if the bird had been stunned and I comforted it until it was able to fly away?"

"Of course not."

"Is that what happened?" Max asked.

"I can't tell you what happened," he admitted. *Benjamin didn't know what happened, not really.* And within minutes of him having done whatever it was, he had two conflicting stories floating around.

"Liar," A tall girl spoke, as she walked by Benjamin with a glare on her face.

Danny was shocked. "What did you lie about?" He looked at Benjamin with worry.

"I haven't said a word," Benjamin admitted. "I can no more control their thoughts as you can. They are free to take what they saw or hear and form their own opinions. It is the way of this world, and all I can do is be me--who my father made me to be."

"Yeah, but did you?" Danny asked again.

Jacob tagged him on the shoulder, "Dude! It doesn't matter!" He spoke, with exasperation.

"Can you show us some magic?" Two girls ran up to Benjamin. They were star struck with the idea that he had saved the bird's life and wanted to see more for themselves.

"Doesn't it?" Danny looked back at Jacob, who was just as lost.

The three boys realized the truth of what Benjamin had said, through the actions of his deed and what hadn't been said. Their hearts hurt for Benjamin as the various looks of thrill, anger, fear and confusion turned towards him.

Benjamin seemed to know that this uncertainty, the misunderstandings of others, was going to be a new constant in his life. The perplexity of his goal within this Painting was going to cause turmoil and chaos and it would carry through for the rest of his life.

This must have been why his father had looked so worried that day. He knew what was going to happen and there was no way to prepare his son for it. It just had to happen.

CHAPTER 11

As the years progressed, so did Benjamin's studies. With an opportunity to take an elective, he chose art, and this is when he was able to realize his true gift. He learned about a way to revolutionize the way he delivered his message.

Learning how to draw and paint helped to enhance Benjamin's expressive abilities. As situations between friends or strangers arose, his keen insights as to what could be, inspired the desire to doodle. He began drawing scenes, not the way they were, but how he saw they *could be*. It was when he shared those scenes that he began enacting change - change for the better. His capabilities were growing as he followed the footsteps of his father.

One morning, while sitting on a bench in town, Benjamin watched the people as they went along the pathway of their day. As he found himself staring at them, taking in the details of their lives, he was also sketching.

A young girl walking hand in hand with her grandmother caught Benjamin's attention. She looked so bored as she shuffled her feet. As they walked down the sidewalk, the young girl stared longingly at the clothes in the storeroom windows. As they walked past Benjamin, he ripped a page out of his notebook and handed it to her. She didn't look at it at that moment. Her grandmother was pulling her along and she needed to keep up.

Hours later she sat in the back of a room listening to sewing machines buzzing away. Her grandmothers quilting class was busy creating a new quilt design when one of the ladies walked up to her. She looked at the paper lying next to the girl on the table and spoke.

"That's a beautiful sketch, why don't you see what you can do with some of these scraps of material?"

The young girl looked up at the lady inquisitively then down at the paper Benjamin had given her. She stared at it for the longest moment, and then glanced over to the pile of material. Suddenly a creative spark ignited within her. She took a piece of the colored cloth in her hand and draped it over her doll. Then she grabbed another piece and wrapped it around the doll’s hips.

"What a beautiful dress you've started," another lady spoke as she walked by.

Suddenly, the little girl realized how important this day was going to be. While she had hated the idea of spending her afternoon here with her grandmother’s old friends, this opportunity helped her realize a dream. She loved fashion and design. She loved clothes and this was an opportunity to start designing her own clothes.

If Benjamin hadn't been there this morning, if he hadn't handed her that sheet of paper, if her grandmother's friend hadn't noticed, she may have let this day go by without realizing her desires. How easy it would have been to continue to sit here moping. Bored. Focused on the negative instead of making the best out of the opportunity ahead of her.

That afternoon as she and her grand-mother walked back the other way across town, she saw Benjamin sitting on the bench. She ran up to him and showed him her doll's new dress. "I made this today because of what you drew. Thank you!"

Benjamin understood and smiled. This young girl was one of many lives Benjamin changed with his doodles today alone. He started being more adamant about his sketches. He'd finish them as quickly as he could so he could share them with those who inspired them. Before long, Benjamin found that people were searching for him, lining up to receive a sketch of what their future was going to be like. Of course, it didn't really work that way, but how could Benjamin explain that if he couldn't explain how he had this ability.

Some doodles never got ripped out of his sketchpad and shared. He wondered if they would ever have a chance to change lives or if these were missed opportunities. He began wishing he knew more people so he could find the intended recipients of these drawings. Maybe he should start traveling?

Sammy and Franklin were known as the town's biggest troublemakers. Sammy loved to incite anger and cause problems. He'd key cars, graffiti storefronts, break windows, and steal from local establishments. While no one really knew it was him causing all of the trouble because he was never caught, they all had their ideas. Franklin never really wanted to do these things, but he joined Sammy because he was his friend. He was also slightly afraid *not* to do it. Tonight, as they kicked cans around a back-alley way, Sammy got another wicked smile on his face. He looked at Franklin with this wry, evil look and then glanced at a rather large window.

"Ah, you don't want to do that, do you?" Franklin began, hoping he could talk his friend out of more vandalism.

"Want to? I have to! That guy kicked me out of his store today for no apparent reason."

"You've stolen from him many times in the past," Franklin reprimanded.

"Yeah, but he doesn't know that."

"But, what if..."

"What if what?" Sammy countered the hunched-over Franklin, trying desperately to find a way to get his friend to stop misbehaving. "What if I just let them mistreat me, us? What if I just sit back and let these people walk all over us? What kind of friend would I be if I didn't look out after you?"

"But they didn't kick *me* out," Franklin offered, trying to help.

"So it's okay they kicked *me* out?" Sammy growled angrily. "It's okay they mistreat me so long as they don't mistreat you?"

"No. No it's not okay," Franklin sighed and acknowledged reluctantly.

"Are you sticking up for them? Are they your new friends?"

"No, Sammy, they're not."

"Then why don't you do the honors?" Sammy smirked as he kicked the can over towards Franklin's feet.

Franklin looked at the can.

"Do it," Sammy insisted. He watched Franklin look at the can and hesitate. The anger was building within him.

It was dusk, Benjamin had drawn all day. His sketch pad was almost empty. The only pages left were doodles that he didn't finish in time to hand out. He was walking home alone when he heard the sound of glass shattering off in the distance. He stopped and turned to face the sound, curious as to what had happened when he saw two boys racing around the corner laughing. As they ran towards Benjamin, Sammy closed in and when he was within distance, he knocked Benjamin's sketchbook out of his hands. As the book slammed to the ground and flipped open, Benjamin watched as Sammy continued running, laughing hysterically.

Franklin, however, felt a twinge of guilt. He didn't run as fast as Sammy so he was trailing behind at quite a distance. He was also slightly overweight and already out of breath. When he saw Benjamin turn back and look at Sammy, Franklin slowed to a stop. For some reason he stopped directly in front of Benjamin. Their eyes caught. The two of them faced each other, and Franklin didn't know why. It was awkward, and yet, calming. He was able to catch his breath and as he exhaled, he saw Benjamin's eyes glace down to his sketch-book.

When Franklin realized Benjamin was starting to bend down to get his book he spoke, "Wait, let me get that for you." He quickly squatted down and picked the book up into his hands. It was open and as he stood back up, he glanced at the picture the book had opened to. It was a picture of someone handing another person a book. He stared at the picture a bit longer. It was dark. There was pencil shading all around the two figures, as if it took place near nighttime. But then Franklin recognized the figures in the book. This was a sketch of him, handing the book to Benjamin - exactly as he was doing now.

With a pang of reluctance, he did exactly as the sketch had shown. He handed the book to Benjamin, who took it. He watched as Benjamin glanced down at the picture and then back up at Franklin. He then ripped the page from the sketchbook, and handed it to the boy.

"You have a good night," Benjamin spoke as he walked away.

Franklin stood there, dumbfounded for a few moments, until he finally glanced back down at the paper in his hand. When he saw the pencil sketch of the act that he had just done--a sketch that had been drawn much earlier in the day and long before he had ever dreamed of running down this street--he cried. Franklin had only heard stories about the Painter's son. He had never met him... until tonight.

CHAPTER 12

Franklin stood there alone on the side-walk for the longest time. The knowledge of what had just taken place was spiraling around in his head. He felt as if his eyes had been opened and he was seeing clearly, as if the light was brighter than the night sky.

"I thought I lost you!" Sammy yelled down the street when he saw Franklin from afar.

Snapping out of his daze, Franklin looked at Sammy strolling towards him and quickly folded the drawing in his palms and tucked it into his back pocket.

"Where did you go? I thought you were right behind me."

Franklin shrugged, knowing better than mentioning any of this to his friend. Sammy was the only person in town who seemed to give any notice to Franklin. Being slightly chubby and quite too shy to start his own conversations, Franklin had always been alone.

When Sammy found Franklin, way back when, he had attempted to cause trouble and pick on him. But when Franklin stood up and his heft and weight towered over the boy, Sammy instead, became quite scared.

He almost backed away, but with a need to keep his tough-guy routine, he half-laughed and joked it off. With Sammy chuckling about the situation, Franklin didn't realize how afraid he looked. Without much knowledge of social interactions, he believed Sammy's laugh was an attempt at camaraderie and misconstrued it as friendship.

Franklin really liked having someone to hang out with and talk to, albeit he didn't do much talking. He did do a lot of listening. Sammy, on the other hand, really liked the idea of having this large guy being near him. It made him look even tougher. He became aware that they would make a good team. Sammy could do whatever he wanted, and no one would be able to stop him for fear of being pummeled. It seemed like a perfect match.

"I'm glad I found you, I thought you got picked up by the cops."

"You were worried about me?" Franklin smiled adoringly at his friend.

Sammy frowned, "No, of course not. It's just more fun to make trouble with someone else around."

As the two of them walked off, Sammy told Franklin everything that had entered his mind since shattering the glass window, and when he was done with that, he began talking about their next caper and what he was thinking they would do next.

It was a long night. They finally settled down in their favorite hangout, an abandoned garage just outside of town. Franklin was grateful for the rest and, when he leaned back in a chair and stretched out his legs and feet, he exhaled as if he had walked miles.

"You should really get in shape, Sammy spoke with the intention of pointing out how much larger Franklin had gotten since they met.

"And you care about my health."

Sammy's brow furled, "It's not easy to break in new friends."

"It's cool that you care," Franklin smiled, not catching the sarcasm that was rolling off of Sammy's tongue.

Franklin shifted in his chair and felt the crunch of the folded paper in his back pocket. He rolled to his side with two attempts and yanked the wad out. He unfolded it and looked at it again. He began to remember how unique that moment felt, how light and simple the world seemed at that moment. He was lost in thought about that, when Sammy snatched the paper from his hand.

"What's this?" Sammy spoke as he peered at the drawing.

"Nothing."

"Nothing? It looks like you."

"I think it is me."

"You think?"

"I think that was Benjamin, the Painter's son who you passed and smacked his book from his hands. I stopped and picked up his book and when I handed it back to him, he gave me this."

Sammy was stunned and yet felt an agitation build within him. "Why would you pick up his book for him?"

"It felt like the right thing to do."

"When do we *ever* do the right thing?"

Franklin shrugged his shoulders.

Sammy looked at the paper again, and a shiver went down his spine. A moment later he crumpled it into a ball in his hand and tossed it over his shoulder. "It's just a stupid drawing. You're just too good for your own good."

"But don't you think that looked like me? How do you think he drew that moment before it happened?"

"It's all part of the scam, Franklin. That's why I'm here; to make sure you don't get manipulated."

"But..."

"Forget about it. I'm your friend. I'm the one who looks out after you."

"I know you are," Franklin agreed quickly realizing Sammy was getting angry. He didn't like it when Sammy got mad. He would say and do very mean things and so Franklin always went out of his way to keep those moments from happening.

CHAPTER 13

It had been nearly a week since that chance encounter on the sidewalk where Benjamin handed Franklin the sketch that opened his eyes. Franklin was terrified of upsetting Sammy by talking about it, but ever since that night, Franklin couldn't get it out of his head. He wanted to do something more with his life. It wasn't until this afternoon, while Sammy was preoccupied with another group, that Franklin found himself walking through the park and spotted Benjamin on a bench sketching. He approached.

"What are you working on?"

"Just doodling."

"Who is that?" Franklin asked pointing to the drawing.

Benjamin glanced at it and then up to Franklin and smirked, "I don't know."

"What do you mean you don't know? I thought you knew everything."

"Sometimes scenes and pictures of people come to me and I sketch them as I see them. They weren't brought on by someone as they walked past me, they were just there."

"Does that happen a lot?"

"Kind of."

"And you sketch them all?"

"I try. There's a reason I see them."

"But if you don't know who the sketches are of, how will you get them to the people who need to see them?"

Benjamin looked at Franklin, a smile spread across his face. "Maybe that's why you are here."

"Me?"

"Maybe you are meant to find these people and deliver my pictures to them."

"But I can't..."

"What? You can't walk? You can't see the faces of the people who are out and about in town? You can't recognize their facial features and walk up and hand them something without saying a word or even so much as interrupting their path?"

"Well, I can do that, I just thought you would do it."

"I'm in charge of drawing, maybe you're in charge of delivering those drawings. Maybe it's my father's plan."

"You don't know if it's the plan?"

"There are many plans, Franklin. Many opportunities within this life. Each pathway that falls before you has an alternate road. It's up to you to choose the route you want to take."

"What if I choose a different road?"

"That is your will. It is one of the many gifts my father has bestowed upon you."

"Even if I don't do what he wants me to?"

"My father wants you to be happy. That is all. He painted for you a world of beauty and perfection and he gave you the choice to experience it in any way you desire."

"Wow," Franklin spoke as his thoughts swirled within his head.

Benjamin returned to his sketchpad. He put the final touches on his picture and then closed his book. He then handed it to Franklin.

"What are you doing?"

"Giving you my sketchpad."

"Why?"

"So you can deliver my pictures to the people who need them."

"I never said I was going to do it."

"You didn't need to. It is now yours. You can do with it what you want."

"What if I throw it away?"

"That's your choice."

"But you put a lot of hard work into it. Wouldn't you be upset?"

"I couldn't be upset at you for doing whatever you want with your book."

"But it's yours."

"Not anymore. I gave it to you." Benjamin stood from the bench. "Have fun, Franklin. Enjoy your life. Fill it with moments that you can look back on and smile about."

Over the course of many years, Benjamin received the rewards of his wish; to be able to share his sketches and message with more people. He began traveling, walking along the country side, visiting town after town.

Word spread across the glossy canvas of this world. The Painter's son was telling futures, performing enchantments and sharing insights about their planet. Many people liked it and sought him out. Many didn't. Those that wanted to learn more, who wanted to meet the son of the Painter, traveled long distances to find him.

Benjamin's closest friends had to get creative so as to find some quiet time and a safe place for Benjamin to rest. He was almost always surrounded by crowds. It took a lot out of him. He longed for the days he could sit around and not have nearly as many demands expected of him, and yet, he was always energized when he was able to share his father's plan with huge crowds.

One day, as Benjamin rose to the sound of singing birds and a bright sunny day, he announced to his friends a detour. He wanted to have some time to be closer to his father and so he decided that instead of going around the mountain, they would climb over it.

"Are you serious Benjamin?"

"Yes, of course."

"It won't save us any time. It may even take more time for us to go all the way up to the top and back down again."

"I realize that. But this is what I need."

His friends shrugged their shoulders. They packed their food and belongings and prepared for their trek. As they began ascending the mountain, they could see a spark ignite within Benjamin. He was looking more rejuvenated with every step he took. He'd look up – up the mountain, up to the sky.

"I feel like I am closer to my father, that I get closer to him with every step I take."

When word spread that Benjamin had gone up into the mountain, many people who had trekked long distances to meet the Painter's son grew agitated. They didn't want to climb a mountain. Instead, they decided they would catch up with Benjamin on the other side. Everyone began to journey through the valley, crossing rivers and caverns for the chance to be there at the foot of the mountain when Benjamin returned.

Jeffery was one of the travelers. He was a much older man, had lived a very long life. He had attempted to do good deeds throughout his entire life. It had taken him a while to find the time to escape his life in order for him to learn more. From the first time he had heard about Benjamin, he had been unable to get his mind off of him. He was curious as to how much more he could learn from this amazing man.

As he approached the opposite side of the mountain, he was taken aback by the amount of people who had collected. Thousands of people were camped out at the base of the mountain waiting. It invigorated him to know that so many people had also felt this desire to find Benjamin and learn more about the painter.

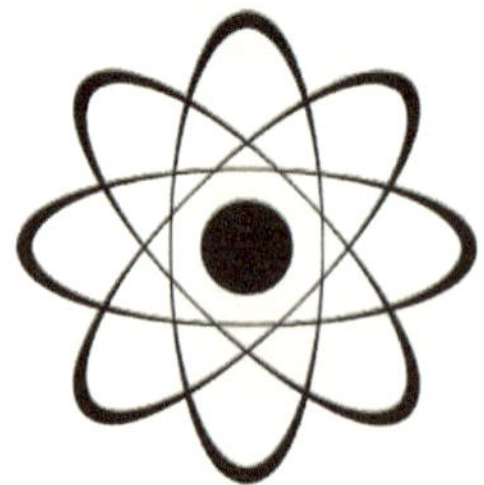

CHAPTER 14

As Benjamin and his friends descended the mountain, they could see the gathering from afar. Danny was stunned. "How did they know you would be here?"

"Hopefulness, I guess," Benjamin smiled. Throughout his journey he had become inspired again. The mountain had helped clear his head, give him a new perspective to come up with a new message.

As he entered the crowd, Jacob, Danny and Max did their best to shield Benjamin from so many who just wanted to touch Benjamin. Who cried out for guidance, who wanted their futures told or health situations healed, or to see some sort of enchantment that only he could do?

Everything they had heard, every story about Benjamin had geared them up, primed them. They all stood there prepared to hear something amazing from the son of the Painter and Benjamin knew exactly what it was they needed to hear.

"Let us all gather for a feast!"

Danny turned to Benjamin and informed quickly in a hushed voice. "We don't have enough food to feed this many people."

Benjamin smiled and then announced to the crowd, "Could you believe that after everyone's journey, after everyone here has gathered, that my father wouldn't have found a way to feed us?"

There were murmurs in the crowd. They looked around and shrugged their shoulders.

"Does anyone have a large basket we could use so to pass out food to the crowd?"

A traveling basket maker stepped forward. "I do." He then crawled into the back of his truck and pulled out the largest basket he had ever made.

Max and Jacob gathered all of the food they still had with them and placed it in the basket. Then Benjamin stepped up to it.

"My father created this world from the need for perfection. He wanted a place that would always make him, and those within it, happy. From the rich soil, luscious plants, and the sky that rains and helps those plants grow and produce fruit, he created a world that provides for all.

While the people of his world, my other world, struggle and fight, work hard and go without, this world, the Painting, wasn't meant to be that way. I guess it wasn't until the people of our world invaded the Painting that their ideals tainted it.

Your currency wasn't meant to exist. You were supposed to collect your food, build your homes and tend to the animals. If you had too many bushels of apples you were supposed to share with neighbors. If you had a talent for building you were supposed to help those who didn't possess that skill. If you had a way with animals you were designed to assist those who couldn't care for my father's nature. And if your desire was to travel and never stay in one place, it was hoped that you would travel with extra surplus and spread the wealth of my father's bounty with those in areas that couldn't get it.

It's not about money, wealth or greed. It's about helping one another, being a part of something bigger. So, as I send this rather large basket through the crowd, full of all of the food we have left, I want you to take what you want. Feed yourself; feed the person standing next to you, and pass that basket on. I fully expect this food will fill everyone's belly here and then we can settle down with full bellies and readied ears to hear my message."

Jacob and Max glanced at each other, and then looked back at the basket they were holding. There was not much food in it. Definitely not enough to feed this crowd. The looks on their faces spoke this to Danny: "I trust that Benjamin knows what he's doing. The three of them carried the basket down to the crowd and handed it to the first person. It didn't take long until that large basket was encapsulated by the masses and no longer visible to them.

Benjamin sat down on a nearby rock and took a drink from his water canister. Danny and Jacob sat next to him as Max stood still attempting to catch a glance of the basket that had long disappeared. After a significant amount of time had passed, he saw the majority of the front of the crowd sitting on the ground eating and the crowd off in the distance was slowly, one by one, settling down for dinner themselves.

Max wanted to be amazed and awe-struck at how such a small amount of food could go so far. He finally returned to Benjamin and the others and sat down to join them.

"You are confused, aren't you?" Benjamin looked at Max knowingly.

"I trusted it would work..." he hesitated, "but don't know how."

"Do you need me to tell you what the people of the crowd figured out on their own?"

Max didn't want to admit it. He looked over at Danny and Jacob and could tell they already understood how it worked. How did they figure it out and he didn't?

"Some people in the crowd, I am certain, are in the same situation as you. They don't know how it happened; they just accepted it since they got fed. Others in the crowd KNOW how it happened because they helped to make it happen. Can you guess how?"

Max sat there in thought for a moment, when fragments of the story Benjamin had told earlier popped into his head. "They added to the basket?"

Benjamin nodded. "Sharing. Contributing your excess to those less fortunate, those who need it... We were designed, painted into this canvas to first and foremost be caretakers of my father's work. To nurture the animals, tend to the plants, and cultivate their bounty. It was a given with this task in mind, that we would care for our fellow man as well.

After dinner was over and the entire crowd's bellies were full, the basket maker's basket found its way back to him. When he looked inside, he still saw some food, and was just amazed at the phenomenal act that had happened today. How had Benjamin done it? How had he fed so many people with such a small amount of food?

He turned to someone sitting next to him. "Did you get enough to eat?"

"Sure did. Isn't Benjamin amazing?"

"You pulled your food from the basket?"

"Yes of course."

The basket maker turned to the person sitting next to the other stranger who had been listening. "You full, too?"

"Yes, and I got it from the basket. Aren't you full?"

"Well yes... but when the basket passed me by there wasn't much food in it. In fact, I'm almost sure that there's more food now, than there was earlier."

"Well there you go," replied the stranger.

The night sky was dark and clear. There were no clouds, no lights from nearby cities. As Benjamin looked up, he could see every star in the galaxy. As he stared at it, it reminded him of the view from his father's den. Of course, this view didn't include the Painting he always strained to see.

Straining now to look at each star individually, even the ones furthest away, Benjamin began to wonder if his father was looking at him from his chair. Could he see his son, this tiny speck on that tiny blue speck within that massive black canvas surrounded by millions of tiny white specks? The universe his father painted to protect the

Painting was enormous. Benjamin could just barely comprehend how large it truly was. From this small spot that he sat on, after traveling for so long and hardly making it very far at all compared to the mass of this colossal canvas, Benjamin's mind spun like the galaxy his father designed.

He was lost in his thoughts for who knows how long, when the crowd hushed. The silence attracted his attention and he looked out upon the massive group. They were all looking at him, as he stared up towards the sky. They were certain he was receiving a message; so they expectantly awaited him to say something.

With a deep breath, Benjamin stood and began to speak. "From my father's chair I can see this world, but it seems so far away. It's a tiny blue and green speck surrounded by so many white dots that I could never finish counting, and trust me I've tried on many occasions.

Look up at the sky. What do you see? Stars. Thousands of tiny shimmering stars completely surrounding us in the vastness of space. Can you count them? Has anyone ever tried? Has anyone ever traveled completely around the globe? It took us an entire day of walking to get here, and from my father's perspective, we hardly moved at all.

Did you know that what my father sees is very much like what we see when we look up at the night sky? We see stars that are bigger than others and some are smaller. Some are bright, some are dim, some are so small and so far away we can hardly see them, but we know they are there.

My father sees the stars we can't see. He sees the stars on the other side of the planet. He sees the stars that are so far away from us that we can hardly see them and yet, those stars are the biggest for him to see. The biggest stars to us, are the smallest stars for him.

The difference with what he sees, the biggest difference, is that from his chair, he also sees us. He sees this planet spinning around the sun, followed by planets that were designed to separate the Painting from the rest.

This world is the only world in that Painting that has these colors. The various hues of the blues, the large specks of green that dot across the curvature of the canvas, the browns of the land and the whites of the clouds that move along the outskirt, making a unique halo around the globe. It's a glow that helps this Painting pop off the canvas.

I mention this not to make you feel isolated and alone, but to help you realize how incredibly special you are. There are no other worlds as perfect, as purposely thought out and planned, as this one. My father put almost everything he had into this canvas to create us and then he used everything else to protect us.

When you think about it this way, when you consider life and you contemplate your purpose or speculate what might be out there, I want you to know in your heart how important you are. I want you to look up at the night sky in astonishment and admiration that my father, your painter, designed everything around us, including us.

We're all part of his plan. We are all exceptional and unique. We are loved more than we, as mere humans, can possibly fathom. Even with my knowledge, even with everything I have learned and taught, even with my own connection as being raised by your creator, I am still awestruck by his design.

CHAPTER 15

Over the course of many years, Benjamin traveled and shared his father's love with anyone who would listen. His three friends, Danny, Jacob and Max joined him. Their journey was the longest, hardest and most tiring excursion they could have ever dreamed, and yet, it was the most rewarding as well. The three of them learned more about Benjamin's father than they could ever retell. As the four of them turned the corner to the road leading to their home town, they felt the excitement begin to build. Seeing the outskirts, knowing they were almost home, lifted their spirits. As they crossed the threshold of the town, they began getting recognized and word spread like wildfire.

"They're home!"

"Benjamin is home."

"The Painter's son has returned!

As they made their way down Main Street everyone emerged from their businesses and homes. They filled the streets and applauded and cheered. It was a wonderfully uplifting feeling. They were being inundated with questions from every direction.

"Where have you been?"

"What did you see?"

"What magical acts have you performed?"

Benjamin was almost too tired to answer. He smiled and waved, and when he felt as if his answers weren't going to be heard, he simply responded with, "Later."

A number of business owners sent their employees or their own children to the homes of the returnee's family. Before long, word got out to Benjamin's parents and they came running to see their son.

"My Son!" His mother, Miriam, exclaimed when she saw Benjamin standing on the street surrounded by the masses.

The crowds seemed to part to make way for Benjamin and he gladly ran to his mother. As they hugged, his father, Christopher, joined in. It was a wonderful reunion.

"I'm so glad you are home!"

"It's good to be home," Benjamin smiled.

"You must come for dinner tonight! A celebration of your return."

"And of course, bring your friends," his father added.

Franklin had been standing nearby in a dark alleyway. He chose to stay in the shadows and out of sight as the town crowded the street. When he saw Benjamin, his heart sank. Before Benjamin left for his journey, he gave Franklin his sketchbook with the hope that he'd deliver the pictures within.

Franklin never told Sammy about the sketch-book. He knew Sammy would not understand. He'd find a reason to belittle Franklin for thinking he was someone important. Or he'd put Benjamin down and take away and destroy the book, like he destroyed the picture Benjamin had given him the first night they met.

Although Franklin had tried, he had been unsuccessful in finding a single person from the sketchbook. He hadn't been able to deliver a single picture and it worried him that Benjamin would be disappointed. Yet, it wasn't for a lack of trying.

Franklin studied the pictures. He looked at the sketches every single night, memorizing the people, the facial features, the clothes. He didn't know them. He didn't recognize anyone, but he didn't ever want to come across them and not give them their picture. He put every picture to memory. Every sad face, every group, every loved one hugging one another. He saw dirty tear stained faces, and some had torn clothes. He always wondered if these people were homeless, but when he'd venture down to the homeless shelters, he never saw them.

That was another thing he never told Sammy. So he could get near the homeless people in hopes of finding those images from the pictures, he offered to volunteer. He handed out food in the soup kitchen, greeted people as they walked in the door and handed out clean blankets to those staying on cold nights.

Sammy never would have understood why Franklin was doing it. Franklin didn't even fully understand why he was doing it – but he knew it made him happy. He enjoyed helping others, but there was always a twinge of disappointment each night when he left and he hadn't handed out a single sketch.

Sammy sat fuming in the garage. He was watching sports and drinking but he was angry, a bitter fury was continuing to build within him each hour Franklin wasn't there.

Franklin wouldn't tell him where he spent his time. Sammy was certain Franklin had made other friends, although he hadn't any proof. He resented the idea that Franklin was going to move on with his life and leave him.

That night when Franklin walked in Sammy ignored him at first. The irritation he felt kept him from even acknowledging his friend's presence.

"Sammy, I'm here."

"What do you want? A medal?"

"I didn't think you heard me enter."

"Where were you today?"

"Running errands."

"What kind of errands?"

"Boring errands," Franklin lied, although with very little believability.

Sammy looked at him angrily.

"If you are going to lie to me, then leave. I don't need to see your ugly, fat face."

Franklin started to protest, but he stopped. He didn't like it when Sammy acted this way and he realized there was no reason to put up with it. Especially not tonight, when all he really wanted to do, was see Benjamin, even if he wasn't invited to the celebration dinner.

Franklin stood there looking at his friend for a long moment and suddenly realized, he didn't need to stay. He lowered his head, exhaled a brave breath, and then turned to leave. As the door closed behind him and he never heard his friend utter another word, he left feeling he had made the right decision.

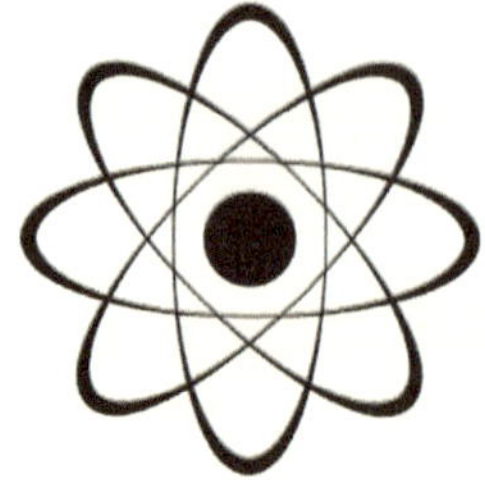

CHAPTER 16

As Benjamin walked the pathway to his parent's house, he thought about all of the wonderful accomplishments he had made. He felt he had taught the people so much. He knew there were still tons of stories to tell, so much more information he could impart. So many opportunities awaited him right around the corner.

The sun was starting to set but it shined out brightly. The wind was whistling softly through the leaves of nearby trees and nightingales were singing. The day had turned out to be wonderful and tonight was going to be grand.

He was on his way to a celebration, a dinner meant for a king and he looked forward to just relaxing, hanging out with his friends and celebrating into the morning hours. What a great life he had.

"Son." A voice reverberated within his chest and nearly knocked him from his feet. "Son, please hear me."

"Father?" Benjamin spoke kneeling on the ground and looking up towards the sky. The sun was setting and yet it seemed to shine directly over Benjamin. The shadows surrounded him and he felt like a spotlight was shining on him.

"Son, heed my warning."

"I hear you Father."

"Heed my warning and know that the time has come and danger is on its way."

"Danger?"

"The end is drawing near. Something bad is coming and you need to be prepared."

"What do you mean Father?"

"I see and hear everything. Like the day I watched the inchworm, I can look down and see your pathway and the obstacles that are coming and I can't do anything to change it."

"What's going to happen?"

"What they do will be linked to what you do. You must follow the path that will be set before you and you must see it through to the very end."

"See what through? What's going on?"

"There are those who fear the unknown. Those that don't understand your gifts. They don't believe you are my son."

"They have free will, they don't need to." Benjamin spoke feeling as if something was off about his father.

"Yet they spend their efforts turning others against you. They're planning something horrible."

"I'll stop them. What should I do?"

"I can't tell you what to do Son. You must seek the answers on your own."

"But you know what is going to happen. Why can't you just tell me?"

"Because my worries for you will remove your ability to choose your own path."

“I'm not sure what I’m supposed to do.”

“Be brave my dear son. You’ll be coming home soon.”

Benjamin shivered. I'll be coming home soon? He wondered as the silence filled his heart. *What did his father mean by that? Was he about to die? Was someone going to kill him? Why? Could he do something to stop this from happening? Should he?*

He watched the sun continue to dip down behind the hilltop and he witnessed the sky turn blood red. A terrifying fear swept through him as he kneeled onto the pathway and called to his father again.

As his adrenaline spiked his heart rate sped up. He found himself trembling. He had never felt this scared. Was this his father's doing, or was it fear of the unknown that terrified him? Nothing in his life had ever caused him to feel like this.

With no answer, Benjamin turned his heart outward to collect any will his father may have been sending. He felt the warmth of the day escape the land and he felt the bitter cold of the wind chill him to the bone.

He opened his eyes, worried, terrified, wishing he knew exactly what was coming, wanting to know how to prepare, how to stop it, how to fix it. He started to cry, when a bunny emerged from the tall grasses beside him.

He looked at the small white rabbit and smiled at it. It was curious about him. Its whiskers twitched but still it took tiny hops towards Benjamin and approached cautiously.

Benjamin recalled the story his father told him about the day he went into the Painting. He remembered the scene of the bunny that climbed onto his father's lap and tickled his nose with its whiskers.

He always loved that story. It reminded him of peaceful times, of simplicity, of love. It was reminiscent of how wonderful and enchanting the Painting was. How it fixed itself with rebirth and fresh life. It was as if he were being told that everything would be okay. That even the aftermath of a great flood that destroyed so much could still bring life and joy.

Benjamin realized that the warning wasn't meant to stop him or frighten him, but to prepare him. To face what was about to come with dignity because it was going to be in this moment, his last moment, that would last for all eternity in the minds of those he loved.

Benjamin stood and continued walking towards his friend's house. He knew that a celebration was coming, they all needed it, and he knew that this would be his last chance to teach them one final lesson.

As he approached the door, the words were still forming in his head. The door opened and arms reached out to grab him. They pulled him into the house, and the music and laughter began.

CHAPTER 17

Franklin may not have been invited, but he desperately wanted to hear what Benjamin may say. He sneaked in the back yard, climbed up the trellis, and squeezed his way in through the attic window.

As he slowly crawled out onto the rafters of the ceiling, he looked down upon the crowd gathered below. It was dark where he was, dusty, and felt far away. He looked down to a well-lit room, at a crowd of happy people, and smelled the aroma of the food waft up to him.

"To the man of the hour!"

Jacob held up a glass as everyone joined in. "To Benjamin! My best friend and the son of the Painter!"

Benjamin joined as everyone toasted, then all settled down in their seats. The words were still forming in his head but he knew he needed to get some of them out while he still could.

"May I have everyone's attention?" He tapped the side of his glass with a fork. "I have something to say."

Everyone quieted and looked over with adoration towards their friend. No one knew the fear he was feeling in his heart.

Benjamin took a deep breath. "You will have to bear with me; there is so much I want to say and so little time."

"Yes, we don't want the food to get cold," Jacob laughed with many others. Benjamin smiled, yet his facial expression showed the group that he had something important that needed to be said. They quieted again to listen.

"I have one last thing I need to teach you."

"One *last* thing?" Jacob asked aloud. "Are you going somewhere?"

Benjamin shrugged with a half-hearted smile. He didn't answer the question, but he did continue his thought.

"This is something very important to me. It is my desire that you may know my father as well as I know him - that these words may comfort you in times of sorrow."

"Sorrow? This night is for celebration!" A voice called out from across the room. Yet the majority of the room remained quiet. Something important was going on.

"This night will end soon and what comes next, no one can prepare for."

Someone coughed, but otherwise it was so quiet you could've heard a mouse squeak.

"Today was perfect, tonight will be great, but tomorrow isn't promised and we must take heart in remembering why."

Everyone knew Benjamin was letting on that something was coming. They began to wonder what he wasn't telling them.

Franklin, still straddling the rafters above, squirmed a bit closer so he could hear what Benjamin was about to say.

"My father, the artist of this universe - Geody he's been named. He painted this world and willed it to life. He made us all in his image."

Just then everyone heard a loud crack from above. They looked up and scrambled as Franklin fell from the rafters on the floor behind the table. Many of the men stood and ran to him. "Intruder!" They grabbed his arms and yanked him to his feet.

While Benjamin had been caught off guard by the intrusion, he recognized Franklin. He understood why the man wanted to be here and he felt sad for him that he didn't feel wanted enough to come in through the front door.

"Let him go," Benjamin pled.

"But Benjamin he snuck in, he could mean you harm."

"He's trespassing." The angry words filled the room.

"He should hear what I have to say too," Benjamin declared. "We should forgive those who interfere or impose upon us. They know not what we are facing in our lives. All they know is what is important in their lives. How would you feel, if you wanted to be included, if you crashed someone's party because you were so desperate to belong, and you were judged and kicked out? We are all one family in my father's eyes. You are all his children just as much as I am. He made you out of love and wants you all to love one another."

The men looked amongst each other, then hesitantly, released Franklin's arms. Franklin dusted himself off as one of the ladies grabbed a spare chair for him. As everyone sat back down at the table, Benjamin collected his thoughts.

"My father sent me here to teach you his will. He desires good from everyone but knows you each will be tempted towards evil. It is our will to choose our path. It is up to us to make the right choices, to do what is best for us, but also what will make my father proud.

What I want to remind you about is my father's love. It was his love that created this world. It was his love that brought you to life. And it was his love that sent me to you. He wants nothing but happiness for each and every single person on this world. If you just consider my father's will, if you stop to think about what is right and wrong, he will open your heart to doing the right thing. He is the king of all creation. He has the power to bring life. He is the glory, for now and forever. Remember this, all of you."

Benjamin sat down and bowed his head. With eyes closed and hands clenched together, fingers intertwined, he whispered just loud enough for all who strained to hear.

"Thank you, my father, for this food we are about to eat. May our lives bring you joy as we hold you in our hearts."

Benjamin looked up to the ceiling and closed his eyes. He listened to his father's silence, absorbed whatever it was his father wanted him to have and then looked back at the gathering of people at the table before him.

"What's going on Benjamin?" Jacob asked with worry in his voice.

"What's going on is we're about to have a meal together. Please pass the bread."

CHAPTER 18

The thanks of blessing was a first for anyone. It set the mood for an interesting evening. Dinner was incredible. The time with friends was a blessing to Benjamin. He even allowed himself to let go his worries long enough to enjoy the time they all had together.

Benjamin watched the hours tick by faster than a woodpecker's beak. Before he knew it many of their guests had left and he sat alone on the living room couch with his thoughts.

His father's warning repeated itself in his mind. Knowing the end was near terrified him. Not knowing what to expect or how to prepare left Benjamin's mind swirling with thoughts.

The room was dark, but there was enough light for Jacob to notice Benjamin sitting alone.

"Benjamin?" Jacob spoke low not wanting to startle him.

"Jacob, please sit with me. There is something I should tell you."

On the other side of town Franklin was making his way back home. Having heard what he had heard and witnessed the love of this family of friends, Franklin felt conflicted. He was angry he wasn't invited, but happy he was allowed to stay. He was lost in thought; his pace slowed.

"Where were you tonight?" Sammy stepped out of the shadows.

Franklin looked at him and felt a fear surge through his body.

"Don't bother trying to lie because I already know."

"Then why ask?"

Sammy stalked up to him, towering over him like a monster. "Did he mention where he was going tomorrow?"

This was one of those moments that tested what you were made of. Franklin knew Benjamin was acting weird tonight. The words he had said, his actions all reflected a person who knew something was coming. Had he known?

"I'm waiting," Sammy growled reminding Franklin his patience was running thin.

"There's a ballgame tomorrow afternoon."

During dinner Jacob presented Benjamin with a set of tickets to see the ball game tomorrow. Everyone was excited about this game. It was going to be the biggest most important game of the season. Most everyone in town was planning on attending.

The excitement throughout the streets was wild. Benjamin even began feeling the excitement himself. He wanted to experience this joyous event, this gathering of so many of his father's people. It felt like a happy place, a safe place. He even half-hoped that the warning his father gave him about tomorrow had been wrong and that tomorrow would be fine.

The entire town had gathered in the overly packed stadium. There was food and cheering, talking and excitement. The game was close; the score was tied most of the time. One team would score, then the other team would score. The crowd was on the edge of their seat. No one knew about the evil scheme Sammy had put forth.

After the halftime break, Sammy made Franklin go in and chain up all of the exit doors. While Franklin was preoccupied with his task, Sammy initiated phase two. Franklin didn't know much of Sammy's plan. They still hung out together, but since Franklin's time with Benjamin, Sammy began keeping secrets. He was angry a lot, but kept

Franklin close. It was an odd feeling, being needed but not knowing why.

After Franklin had locked the last door, he made his way back over to where he had left Sammy and was shocked by what he found.

"You can't do that!"

"Oh yes I can" Sammy scowled as he connected the last wire to the bomb.

"But you'll hurt people, kill people!"

"That's what I want to do."

"But why?"

"Why?" Sammy barked angrily. "How can you ask me why? They all treat us like scum. They hate us, judge us, want to lock us up and throw away the key."

Franklin was terrified. He didn't know what to do. He knew he couldn't let this happen. He lunged towards Sammy right as Sammy switched the power on.

Franklin knocked Sammy to the ground and held him there. "I won't let you do this. I'll turn you in myself."

"And I thought you were my friend!" Sammy struggled beneath the large man. "Well, you're too late." Sammy's face filled with an evil grin as he caught the panic in Franklin's eyes.

Franklin turned around to look at the bomb and saw the timer ticking down. He shook Sammy, "Turn it off!"

"No!" Sammy kicked Franklin off of him and jumped to his feet. "And now I know where your loyalties lie." Sammy towered over Franklin on the floor. "Now you'll suffer the same fate as all of them!" He kicked Franklin in the gut, then turned and ran towards the last remaining unlocked door.

Franklin struggled to get to his feet. He was fairly certain Sammy had just broken one of his ribs, but there was no time to check his wounds. He ran to the door to chase after Sammy but when he tried to pull it open, he felt it tug back and heard the rattle of chains. Sammy had locked him in.

Franklin turned back to the bomb and ran to it. He looked at all of the wires, a cluster of colors he couldn't even dream of deciphering. He didn't know how to turn it off and he was terrified if he tried, he'd trigger it.

The only thing he could think to do now was run to get help. He ran towards the first opening he could find into the stadium. He ran to the edge of the railing and over an enormous crowd talking, laughing and cheering. He yelled at the top of his lungs, "Where is Benjamin?"

People near him turned to look at him, some shrugged, some looked around.

"Benjamin, I need your help!" He yelled again, his voice cracking with terror.

"I'm here," came a voice from a seat a number of rows up. Benjamin stood so Franklin could see him. Franklin was holding his side. He was visibly wounded and the look on his face was far worse than any fear Benjamin had ever seen. "The time – it's counting down!"

The word time echoed in Benjamin's head. His father's warning repeated and his stomach filled with butterflies.

"What's going on?" Benjamin inquired as the cameraman panned the view to Benjamin in the crowd and displayed him on the big screen.

"A bomb!

The people nearest to Franklin began to scream, while others a bit further, started to ask, "What did he say?"

"He said there was a bomb!"

"A bomb?" another screamed.

Benjamin realized within a fraction of a second that the entire stadium was going to fill with panic. He had to do something; he looked at the cameraman so his eyes were looking out at the entire stadium from the big screen and he spoke as calmly as he could.

"Everyone please stay calm. Cautiously make your way out to the exits. Do not push each other."

"They can't!" Franklin yelled. The camera-man spun the camera down to Franklin so everyone could hear and see. "All of the exits have been locked."

Women and children screamed. Panic was already taking over.

Benjamin called out as loudly as he could, the cameraman swung the shot back up to him. "I need the strongest men to be let through. Every man strong enough to break down a door, get to the closest exit and help the people escape."

CHAPTER 19

As everyone began moving, tears, cries of fear and panic filled the stadium. Benjamin quickly pushed his way down the stairs to Franklin and Franklin led him to the bomb.

They ran up to it, past panicked people waiting in terror for the larger men at the closest exit to do their job. Some were heaving their shoulders into the door to loosen it, while others were trying to find something to break it down. A woman broke an emergency fire case and pulled out an axe. It was hastily handed through the crowd to the men at the door, while another man grabbed a large metal trash can and began banging it against the exit lever, hoping it would break.

The people were working together to free themselves. If Benjamin would have been able to praise them, he would have, but he was looking at the bomb and feeling completely lost.

As doors opened and the light of the day shone into the dark crowded hallways, Benjamin started to rejoice. He turned to Franklin and demanded of him, "Help them out. Make sure everyone gets to safety."

"What about you?"

"Go! Save them!!" Benjamin demanded.

Franklin did what he was told. He turned to help the crowd. He helped up those who were smaller and weaker, who had gotten pushed out of the way or knocked over. He lifted many people off of the ground and got them to their feet again. He ran down the hall making sure everyone was getting help, and finding their way out.

Danny, Max and Jacob finally found their way through the crowd to Benjamin. They had no idea where he had gone, but knew in their hearts they needed to find him. As they ran up, Benjamin was fast at work disconnecting wires from barrels.

"How can we help?"

"Make sure everyone gets to safety!"

"We aren't going to leave you, Benjamin," Jacob declared.

"We're running out of time. These barrels are close together. If I can't disassemble all of them there will be a domino effect. The stadium is going to go down, and if it does, it will take everyone in it. You must help the people escape!"

Max and Danny both glanced at each other. They realized Benjamin was right. They each turned and ran separate directions back into the stadium to make sure no one had been left behind. Jacob however stayed with Benjamin. He watched what Benjamin did to withdraw a wire and ran to another barrel to do the same.

He looked at the barrel and was immediately overwhelmed. He couldn't recall which wire it was Benjamin had grabbed. He was flustered and couldn't make a decision. His hand hovered over each wire, he was reaching for one, any one to pull, when Benjamin took his hand in his.

"We've got to go!"

Hearing the words 'we' come out of Benjamin's mouth and being dragged towards the exit, Jacob felt relief. They ran towards the exit. It was a rectangular opening filled with light and two large metal doors lying haphazardly on the ground next to it.

Jacob and Benjamin were running at full speed, faster than Jacob had ever run his entire life and as he neared the light, he felt Benjamin's hand let go. Before he knew it Benjamin pushed him through the exit and then turned back towards the bomb.

With the speed Jacob was rushed through the door, it took him more than twenty feet to slow to a stop. By the time he was able to turn and try to find Benjamin with his eyes, all he saw was the dark shadow of his friend racing back towards the bomb with a large metal door width way in front of him.

As he started to take his first step back towards the stadium, the reddish orange flames came shooting towards him and the aftershock of the explosion threw him backwards another twenty feet.

He hit the pavement so hard his elbows, back and head felt as if he had been hit by a train. He looked up towards the opening and watched helplessly as concrete and metal came tumbling down into a pile.

"Benjamin!" he yelled, scrambling to get to his feet. He ran to the fallen rubble and began pulling away loose rocks.

"What's going on?" A couple of men approached.

"Benjamin was still inside."

They, too, immediately began helping to pull away the debris.

Others came up, they, too, joined in the task of removing debris. When there was an opening just large enough for Jacob to crawl through, he did. The others kept at their duty.

Jacob crawled over large chunks of fallen concrete and twisted metal support beams. "Benjamin," he called out, as he made his way to the last location he remembered seeing his friend.

When he saw the metal door, he slid to his knees and began to lift it. As he slid it away from his friend's body, he cried, "No, no, no, no, no! You can't be dead! You can't!"

Jacob kept removing debris off of his friend until he came to a mottled steel beam pressing his friend down. He tried with every fiber of his being to lift it and when it budged, Benjamin coughed.

"Thank Geody you're okay!"

Benjamin slowly opened his eyes and watched as his friend helplessly attempted to lift the metal beam but failed.

"Jacob..." Benjamin voiced through pained breathing.

Jacob kept trying to move the beam. He didn't want to give up although he knew in his brain there was no way he could lift this monstrous girder.

"My friend..."

"I've got to get this off of you."

"Jacob, you won't. I've not long left in this world."

The tears burned Jacob's eyes and he tried again to lift the metal beam.

"Jacob, please stop."

Jacob stopped, but continued to look down at the beam, terrified to look at his friend, horrified that he was going to watch his friend die. "I can't move it."

"You aren't meant to."

The tears flowed down Jacob's face.

"My time has come…"

"No, Benjamin. You're going to be okay." Jacob cried as he turned to face his friend. "Others are coming, we'll get you out."

"I must tell you something."

Danny and Max had joined those removing debris until they, too, were able to get in. They crawled through the debris and called out for Jacob and Benjamin.

"We're over here," Jacob cried out.

They followed the sound to their friend and paused when they saw the scene. Max smacked Danny on the arm and he snapped out of it. They both ran to the metal beam and with both of their strength they attempted to lift it. It moved, slightly, but when it did, the sound of creaking metal and large boulders shifting filled the cavernous tomb. They paused.

"It's too late," they heard Jacob whisper.

They carefully released the metal beam and looked at Benjamin's lifeless body. His eyes were closed. He wasn't moving. All of the muscles in his face had relaxed. It almost didn't look like him.

Danny and Max fell to their knees next to Jacob. They wailed.

Two other large men came into the stadium and grabbed the boys by their arms. They lifted them to their feet and pulled them to the exit.

"We can't leave him!" Danny cried.

"The stadium is coming down. We've got to get you out of here."

"We can't leave him," Max echoed.

"He's already gone." Jacob stood and solemnly walked towards the exit; the others followed. Danny looked back and saw his best friend's body lying under the debris. He suddenly felt as if half of his heart was still there – that it might always be there.

As they crawled through the narrow opening of collapsed debris, everyone heard a snap. Then they heard a crackle.

"It's going to come down!" Someone nearby yelled.

The people outside grabbed the men's arms and with adrenaline pumping through their veins, they hauled the guys through the opening.

As everyone cleared the exit and ran, the final snap sounded from a structural beam collapsing, and the remainder of the stadium came tumbling down.

Chapter 20

Everyone screamed as the shockwave hit them and knocked them over. The dust cloud from all of the ground up dirt and crumbling concrete knocked them over. It took a fair amount of time for the dust to clear. There was silence as everyone stared at what used to be the stadium, was now a large pile of rubble.

A woman nearby Jacob was the first to speak. "Where is Benjamin?"

Jacob looked at the woman solemnly, feeling the eyes of everyone nearby turn to look at him. He shook his head sadly and with a shaky whisper, about all the voice that he could muster he spoke.

"Benjamin is dead."

The woman gasped and screamed, then covered her mouth as her husband took her into his arms. Cries and screams and shocked people inquiring and repeating what they heard spread deeper into the crowd of people.

"What did he say?"

"Benjamin is dead."

"Benjamin, the Painters' son? He's dead?"

"That's what he said."

"Was he in the stadium?"

"Was he trapped?"

Jacob felt he needed to add more to the dialogue, "He saved us. He used his own body to block the blast."

"He saved us."

"He blocked the blast."

"He got us to safety."

"He's a hero."

"He's our savior."

"He just walked past? Where?"

As word spread down the line through the mouths of emotionally distraught on-lookers. Weeping and crying filled the parking lot.

The conversations and murmurs grew louder. The sobbing and disbelief increased. No one wanted to believe it. Some adamantly refused to believe it while others threw in their own ideas.

"He's not dead. His father, the creator of our entire world, wouldn't have let his son die!"

"He's not dead?"

"I heard that Jacob said he was gone."

"Gone? His body's disappeared?"

"I'm sure it's still there."

"What is?"

"His body, I heard he's walking around."

"Where? Where's the Painter's son?"

"He's gone."

"He's somewhere."

"Have you seen him?"

"I heard he was just here."

"He's around here somewhere."

"Benjamin is all around us now!"

Just then a low rumble filled the sky and the town quieted. A light rain shower blanketed them and moistened the ground.

"It's his father, crying…"

Jacob heard the people talking, their fears and confusion, their questions and answers. He felt he needed to correct them, to try to speak to them, but he was so devastated. The last scene of Benjamin's life kept repeating over and over again in Jacob's head. Jacob sat on his knees holding Benjamin's hand. He watched helplessly as Benjamin slowed his breathing and closed his eyes. With his last breath he spoke three last words.

"It is done."

As Benjamin's last breath escaped his body, Jacob felt it go through him. It filled him with hope and faith. It was as if Benjamin's being touched his soul. And yet, as it escaped, it also filled him with an ever-growing anxiety that he was now alone. That the world was never going to hear another insightful message from the painter's son again.

As the crowd accepted the news, people just held each other. Their faces looked so sad. They hugged one another and held hands. It was a quiet, somber time. As Franklin looked out amongst the crowd, he felt so guilty. He hadn't planned it, but he had helped make it happen, unknowingly. He scolded himself silently for not asking more questions, for trusting Sammy. At first, he didn't make eye contact with the crowd. He hoped he wouldn't get in trouble or that the crowd wouldn't punish him for Sammy's acts, but he fully expected it to happen, and he knew he'd accept his punishment like a man. But then a little girl approached him.

"Sir, are you okay?"

Franklin looked down at her. She looked so concerned. He knelt down to her height and spoke, "Are *you* okay?"

"I am. I was just concerned about you. Your head is bleeding." She reached towards his head as he, too, placed his palm on the side of his face that he hadn't realized was throbbing, until now. When her little fingers touched his hand, a flutter tickled his heart. He looked at the girl carefully and then all of a sudden, he recognized something.

"I think I have something for you," Franklin said calmly, except inside him, the excitement was about to burst. He swung his backpack around to his front and opened it. He pulled out Benjamin's sketchpad and flipped to the page he recognized. It was a scene of a small girl reaching over to a man kneeling before her. He never realized in all of this time that the man in the picture was himself. He tore the picture out of the sketchbook and handed it to the girl. She took it and stared at it, as her mother approached and looked at it as well. Her father joined them, and held his wife and they both looked at the girl as she turned to show them her picture. When the parents recognized the picture was one of Benjamin's sketches, the mother gasped. She began crying and calling out thanks to Benjamin.

"Thank you, Benjamin. Thank you for being a part of our lives."

Other's nearby heard her, and in hearing Benjamin's name, approached hoping that he was there, that the news of his demise was inaccurate. Franklin watched as the people gathered. A small group approached the woman and with hand gestures they asked where Benjamin was. They pointed towards the stadium as another couple hugged. Franklin recognized this scene as well and as he flipped to that page in the sketchbook and found it, he ripped it out and handed it to the person who initially asked about Benjamin.

"Benjamin is still blessing us with his gifts!" Someone exclaimed.

A restaurant owner walked up to Franklin. He had been watching the young man and was quite proud at what he was doing for the people. He gave Franklin a hug.

"Why?" Franklin asked, feeling the emotions whelping up within him.

"Because you listened to the message."

CHAPTER 21

The cries and screams of the people lifted up from the crowd like a chorus filling the skies. The sound trailed off farther and farther until it escaped the planet, the universe, and then, the Painting.

From a distance, Benjamin could hear the crying of the people and slowly opened his eyes. He looked around the room and felt confusion. He didn't seem to recognize where he was.

"My son..."

"Father?" Benjamin questioned as he looked over at his father sitting on a chair across from him. But it wasn't the father he had grown accustomed to seeing, it was his real father. When the confused look on his face morphed into a tired smile, his father spoke.

"Welcome home, Son."

Benjamin looked at the room, the familiar furnishings that he knew of more than a lifetime ago. It reminded him of his childhood, his first childhood; of hearing about the Painting and always wanting to go into it, to experience life within it. Then he remembered his life inside. His friends, his family, what had just happened; he suddenly began to cry.

"What is wrong, Son?"

"I failed you."

"Failed me? Son, you didn't fail me."

"I didn't accomplish my task. I wasn't able to fix things. I wasn't able to turn everyone's hearts towards you."

"Son, you could never fail me."

"What do you mean? They killed me, Father. They refused to listen."

"Many heard you Son. Many continue to hear your word and spread your message."

"I need to go back!" He sat up in bed.

"Why?"

"I should explain more. There's more to say, more information I could give. I shouldn't have left them like that, the way I did. They are heartbroken and lost. Can't you hear them?"

"I hear them, Son. Do you?"

"Of course I do. They are crying, wailing. They are lost and confused. Their hearts hurt..."

"Is that all you hear?" Gerald inquired.

"What else is there?"

A sly smile glimpsed Gerald's face. "Find Franklin's voice."

Benjamin quieted his mind to search for one voice within many. It took him a few moments of really focusing his attention but then he heard it.

"You will pay for what you did," Franklin growled angrily at Sammy.

"What I did? You were just as much a part of it as I was," Sammy came back.

"You didn't have to kill him."

"That was the only way to stop him. Now they will cry and move on and forget about him, we can all finally move on."

"Forget about me?" Benjamin's heart broke. "I worked so hard. I spent so much time with them. How could they forget?" Benjamin wanted to cry.

"Keep listening," his father spoke calmly.

Time speeds by much faster within the Painting. By the time Benjamin found Franklin's voice again another day had passed.

"I may not have known what Sammy was planning but I take responsibility for being a part of it. I locked the doors to keep everyone in so I need to be punished for my part."

"You can't!" Someone from the crowd cried out. "He's Benjamin's messenger. He shared Benjamin's sketches with the crowd. He helped to change so many lives."

"He also helped to hurt so many people."

"But everyone got out. No one died! It was a miracle."

"It was because Benjamin saved everyone. He's the hero, the savior, not Franklin."

Benjamin closed his eyes. His heart pained for Franklin. He could feel the man's guilt overwhelm him. He could also feel how much Franklin just wanted to do the right thing. He just wanted to be a good person. He had always wanted to do the right thing, but he was weak and just needed a good leader.

Benjamin didn't want this one act, this trust in a friend who didn't deserve it, to ruin a man who could do so much good in his life. He wished so hard that he could be there, that he could do something to help, that he could say something on behalf of Franklin... then before he knew it, he was standing in the Painting.

On-lookers gasped.

"Benjamin? Is this you?"

Benjamin looked at the crowd and smiled. He took Franklin's hand and then gazed at the on-lookers. "Love one another."

"What if we can't?"

"Forgive him," he continued.

"How can we?"

"It is what I want."

The people looked at Franklin whose eyes were as wide and filled with light and hope as any had ever seen. When they turned back to Benjamin, he was gone.

When Benjamin opened his eyes, he was back at home. His father was smiling at him.

"You are an amazing young man," he spoke proudly to his son.

Benjamin listened as a small group of his friends continued to tell the story about him. Over time their numbers grew. Those people told others. The word of Geody and his son blanketed the land. The creator is out there, watching over us, loving us." He accomplished what he came here for.

It took many, many generations, but the word stretched over the land. More and more people found a love for Geody and his son, Benjamin. Yes, there were still others who were against him, doubters, but the numbers who wanted the life Benjamin spoke of, continued to grow.

"One day Son you may need to go back. One day you may need to give them hope again. But since you've already been there, since you were born into the Painting, you will always have the power to go back. You can go back whenever you want to. You have the power now. They talk of you as much as, if not more than, they talk of me. In fact, many of them consider us one."

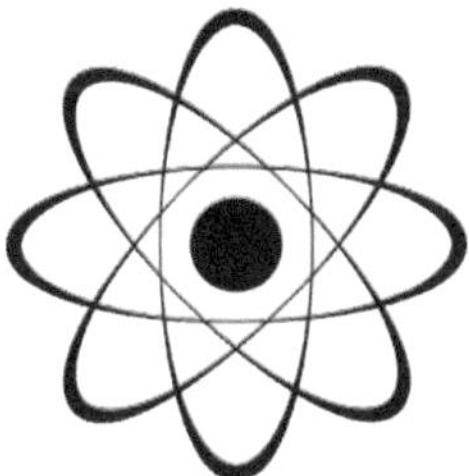

Ephesians 2:10 *God has made us what we are and... he has created us for a life of good deeds, which he has already prepared us to do.*

The Painting 3

Introduction

Imagination is key...

The human brain is capable of the most complex manifestations of intelligence ever imaginable. Not only is the brain responsible for every single action, movement, breath or step we make, it is also credited with every innovation humankind has ever created.

When there is a need, the brain discovers a way. With our imagination we are able to produce and simulate complex thoughts and memories into our senses and form an understanding in our mind. This can turn past experiences and lessons into more, by completely inventing new and ingenious ways to solve problems.

We take the basic training our lives have given us to open up possibilities to better our situations or the lives of those around us. It was the imagination that honed electricity, designed the car, and discovered a way to record our stories onto film. The imagination brought us the understanding of fire and the warmth it gave, the intelligence to sow the seeds of the foods we wanted to grow and the knowledge of medical advancements that can cure the sick and vaccinate us from diseases.

Every great innovation through time came from a spark of imagination. The inventor saw a need, realized a solution and created a way to make it happen. Imagination is the spirit and tenacity that leads to progress.

We were born with a brain capable of learning, growing and expanding our understanding so we could imagine greatness, to interpret the world around us and envision ways to make it better.

Our imagination is our greatest gift, the most important aspect of humanity. It must be cultivated, cherished and encouraged – so we can further ourselves and each other.

Chapter 1

Desire is a sense of longing, a hope for a better outcome. It is a thought that flows out of one person and becomes something real. Desire is what makes plans succeed. It comes from the heart. Desire takes faith.

The Painting was flourishing as were its people. Gerald had painted a perfect world, a masterpiece so awesome, it came to life. A world so amazing, he had to perform the miraculous to protect it. Then, when it was time, he sent his son, Benjamin, into the Painting in order to teach the people about his father, the one who painted them. You would have thought the story was complete, but Gerald knew there was one more thing needed.

When Benjamin returned home, he experienced conflicting emotions. He had lived two lives – one growing up with his father, the painter of a universe. A life that taught him about the joys of doing good, the perils of bad and the incredible opportunities his father granted for those people within the Painting.

His second life was designed so he would utilize the knowledge his father had bestowed upon him growing up, in order to share it with the inhabitants of the Painting. He was born there, grew up and lived within the Painting. He died in the Painting. His second life was enchanting, beautiful and traumatic. He witnessed first-hand the miracles of his father's world, his influences and how wonderful life could be, if only they would let it. He had an understanding greater than any could possibly comprehend, and a message that was so valiant it strengthened fear within those who couldn't understand.

When he returned, he, too, heard the people of the Painting, just like his father. He heard their joy, laughter and excitement. He also heard their cries, conflicts and sadness. He felt the pain they felt, and the hurt it left in his heart was powerful. It took him quite a long time to adapt to the changes in his life – but adapt he did. With the overwhelming assortment of emotions barraging him day-in and day-out, he decided he had to go to his father for help.

"Father, I've seen you, and watched you for years. I know you hear and feel this, and I've seen what it can do to you. But I've also seen you at peace. I've seen you where the accumulation of cries didn't overwhelm you. Father, I need to know how you do it."

"You need to find your own inner joy, son. You need to discover something in your life that brings you peace and tranquility."

With some soul searching, Benjamin realized his dream of painting – to be like his father. He would paint scenes from his father's world, like beautiful pastures of flowing green grasses swaying in the breeze and colorful sunsets shimmering into still waters, mirroring the beauty and doubling the majesty of the scene.

He'd paint flowers and birds, so many landscapes, an array of settings that had brought him joy. Seascapes of crashing waves on shimmering rocks, a multitude of blues and greens mixed with pristine whites that according to the hues of paint shouldn't be possible.

His father adored his son's work, but he knew that painting wasn't the only thing his son needed in order to find peace. He encouraged his son to venture out, to explore the world he had long forgotten *their* world.

So Benjamin did. He ventured out into their world and discovered all that he had been missing. Of course, compared to the Painting, Benjamin found himself unimpressed. Within the Painting he had seen anger, confusion, hate and mistrust – but he had also experienced love, friendship, and compassion. As he ventured throughout his world he found increasing disappointment, loneliness. He felt as if he didn't belong here.

"Father, I'm suffering. I feel so alone and lost. I want to go back, but I'm afraid. I want to stay here but I feel unwelcome. I don't know what to do with these emotions."

"Find someone to share them with."

Benjamin walked away feeling conflicted. That's what he had tried to do with his father, and he was dismissed. Why? He was sitting on a bench mulling this over when a woman sat down beside him. Why she sat down next to him wasn't important, why she decided to strike up a conversation with him wasn't the point. The fact that she listened, cared and heard him, that's what mattered.

She understood him. They discovered commonality, they melded and became friends. This friend, with her bright smile and keen intellect, her appreciation of his talents, who devoted herself to him, also became his wife. And after some time, he was gifted with a child of his very own. The day he presented his newborn daughter to his father was one of the happiest and joyous of Benjamin's life.

"Her name is Nevaeh." *(Neh-Vay-Uh)*

"A perfect name for a truly perfect being." Gerald smiled knowingly. "I am so happy for you, my son."

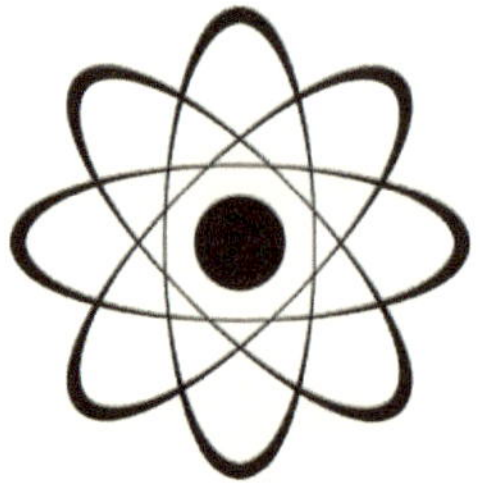

CHAPTER 2

Now that Benjamin was a father, he developed so much more appreciation for what his own father had done for him. He understood the pride and fear of being wholly responsible for this tiny soul. He worried for her, protected her, and would do anything for her. He wanted for nothing but her happiness, for her to be safe, and then it occurred to him what his father must have gone through with him.

Letting him go into the Painting must have been the most terrifying decision he had ever made. Knowing what was going to happen, letting go of his hold, his protection of his son. Benjamin thought about his own daughter and how devastating it would be to his heart to see her hurt, even for a minute. But then he realized why. The Painting was his legacy. His father's creation was his undertaking. His assignment was to share love. It was the same expression as the love he felt for his own daughter.

Raising this precious life showed him how frail we all are. Benjamin realized how closely related the emotion of love and fear are. He understood how easily the conflict could escalate, how quickly the emotions could flip. He had seen and shared the beauty of his father's design, but he hadn't understood the passion until now.

Benjamin had been sure he had shared his father's love with the Painting, but now he wondered had he really? He knew there were many who declared Geody's love, who shared with others the beauty of what they had learned, but there was still division. There were still people who were afraid, angry, confused. It was they who had expelled Benjamin from the Painting with their fears, their anger, their absence of connection, and their lack of love.

Benjamin realized he had failed them. Had he failed his father, too?

Sitting with him in his study, Benjamin watched his father stare at the Universe Painting. His eyes glistened as he followed the stars spiral around the sun. He heard the laughter and cries of the people within, his heart ached for them.

"Father, I think I failed you."

Gerald turned to his son in confusion, "How could you think that?"

"I only touched half of the people. There is such division, so much conflict and confusion scattered throughout your Painting."

"You know you did everything I wanted of you, and then some. I am so proud of the work you did. Don't ever think I'm not."

"I thought I knew everything about life. I thought I had learned everything there was to learn. I have literally lived two lives, how could I have not known?" Benjamin declared.

"Because there is more to life than simply living." Gerald spoke as he stood from his chair. "Take a look at this Painting, what do you see?"

Benjamin stood and looked, but before he could come up with an answer, his father spoke.

"I see infinite possibilities for everyone, and an inexhaustible array of opportunities for an immeasurable amount of people. And every single one of those options are connected to the life experiences of that particular person at that precise moment in their existence. The same exact advantage for one could be a dilemma for another. It's all about perspective. Your perspective was that of a son, there was absolutely nothing wrong with what you did, just like no one in the Painting could make the wrong choice, if their heart's choice is pure."

"So how can we change the hearts of those who don't understand?"

"That opportunity will come in time. I didn't paint this canvas in a day, so you can't expect the answer to evolve overnight."

Benjamin nodded and they both stood in silence for a long moment.

"Dada, what are you and Grampa doing?"

They both turned to see little Nevaeh standing at the door. They smiled at her and then glanced at each other.

"Come here, Sweetheart. Do you want to see something neat?" She walked over to them, and Benjamin lifted her into his arms. He braced her on his hip and pointed her attention to the Painting. "Your Grandfather painted this."

Nevaeh gazed at the Painting and realized it was moving. Her eyes widened as she marveled at the canvas.

She touched it, the rough canvas, feeling the texture on her finger tips and yet the landscape moved. She followed the stars as they spun around the sun. And she giggled as she traced her finger following the motion of the planets.

The three of them sat down and regaled the young girl with fascinating stories of a Painting come to life, and a world of magical hope and of a beauty unlike any she had ever seen. The stories fascinated Nevaeh, her mind reeled with questions, a desire to hear more stories, and so they shared until she couldn't keep her eyes open any longer.

From then on, whenever they'd visit her grandfather, Gerald, he would show her the majesty of the universe Painting and enthrall her with stories of the original Painting within. He'd tell her all about how he could step inside of the Painting, as if walking through a door. He told her about the fluffy white bunny whose whiskers tickled his nose, and how the sunset would paint the sky in the most beautiful colors imaginable.

Then when she'd go home, she'd ask her father, Benjamin, to tell her more stories about his growing up within the Painting. He showed her his artwork, all of the beautiful scenes he had painted from memory, and she loved them.

Yet, while Nevaeh loved the stories, she was filled with confusion. All she ever saw was the stars. She watched how the stars and planets spiraled around the sun in an awe-inspiring display of color and energy, but she couldn't seem to understand how this dark canvas of white specs spinning like a top, held within it such an amazing world. Until she understood, she was determined to watch it.

As a toddler, Nevaeh's eyes would glisten as she stared at the dazzling painting hanging on the wall in her grandfather's study. She'd lie in his lap and simply stare at it while he rocked her to sleep. Then she would dream about seeing all of the sights she heard about.

As she grew, she began exploring, walking and choosing which rooms she wanted to visit. Time and time again she'd return to her grandfather's study where they'd later find her sitting on the floor staring up at the Painting. They declared that they had been looking for her, and she'd sweetly turn to them with a smile and ask, "Where else would I be?"

When she turned old enough, Gerald did something Benjamin couldn't even comprehend – he gave Nevaeh the Painting.

"What?" Benjamin nearly collapsed from the shock. "You are giving her the Painting?"

"I am."

Benjamin's head was reeling. His father had always had the Painting. It hung on the wall of his study his entire life. Why now, after all of this time, after everything this painting meant to him and to Benjamin, would he give it to a young girl?

"Nevaeh has heard the stories. We've both shared with her the enchantment of a world she can't see, and she's been taught by the most amazing father I have ever met." Gerald smiled at Benjamin. "My son, it is nearing her time. It is time for this Painting to hang on her wall, so she can marvel at it as you did growing up."

Benjamin looked quizzically at his father, then at the Painting. "I remember growing up, sitting in this den watching the Painting for hours. I remember asking you questions about it, questions that occurred to me after long stents of time wondering about it curiously."

"And that, my son, is why she should have it on her wall - in *your* house."

"But why our house? How could you part with something so precious?"

"What could be more precious than you?"

"Won't you miss it?"

"I could never miss anything that stays with me, heart and soul."

Maybe we should hang it in our living room, or my studio?"

"How much time does she spend in those rooms, son? Would she get the full benefit of viewing it there?"

"No, I guess not." Benjamin hummed, "But Father, I wouldn't want it to get ruined. What if she spills something on it, or draws on it?"

Gerald smiled. "What could she do to a universe so dense and black that wouldn't make it become something better?"

Benjamin shrugged his shoulders. By the end of the day Nevaeh was sitting on the edge of her bed staring at the most magnificent Painting in the cosmos. While Benjamin worried a little bit, he trusted his father.

CHAPTER 3

It had been a week of Nevaeh asking many questions, some of which caught Benjamin completely by surprise. He was quite impressed with his inquisitive little girl. He was talking with his wife about her latest question when he heard Nevaeh calling them from upstairs. "Daddy, Daddy, come see!" They ran up the stairs and into her room to witness what Benjamin feared most.

"Father, you need to come over, now." Benjamin spoke into the phone.

"Why? What's going on?"

"I can't tell you over the phone. This is something you need to see in person."

"Okay Son, I'll be over in a bit."

About twenty minutes later Gerald arrived. He was walked upstairs in silence.

"What's going on? Why all the secrecy?"

"There you go." Benjamin spoke low as he pointed to the Painting hanging on the wall in Nevaeh's room.

"Isn't it amazing?" Nevaeh smiled as bright as the sun shining in the Painting. She leapt on her bed joyfully.

Gerald peered over at the Painting and smirked with delight. "It truly is."

"Father, you can't be serious!" Benjamin croaked. But Gerald held up a finger.

Benjamin watched as his father the creator of this universe, approached the Painting hanging on the wall and carefully examined the newly added splotches.

"May I make one little alteration?" Gerald asked of Nevaeh who was so proud of her vibrantly colorful watercolor addition. She nodded her head.

"Come closer." He spoke as he pulled out a chair from under her desk. Nevaeh hopped down off her bed, skipped over to her grandfather, and climbed onto the chair.

"Watch this." He spoke whimsically as he pressed his palm over one of the splotches, closed his eyes, and pressed on it as if he were pushing something heavy through a tiny hole.

When he removed his hand, Nevaeh clapped proudly as she took in the most amazing magical feat she had ever seen. Gerald had taken her splotch of orange and blue watercolor and pressed it into the Painting. It suddenly seemed so far away as it moved with the stars of the universe. What would someday be known as a nebula, a colorful cloud in a distant part of the universe, had been added by a child, and brought to life by Gerald.

"It looks like a giant eye ball!" Nevaeh screeched gleefully as she pointed at the now distant, spiraling splotch within the Painting.

"That is the blue part of the eyeball…"

"The Iris" Gerald assisted.

"And that looks like the skin around it."

Benjamin walked up closer to see. He was mystified – although he should have known better than to doubt his father, he still found himself astounded.

Just then Nevaeh leapt off of the chair, grabbed her watercolors and hopped back on the chair. She slapped her tiny palm into the colors and smeared some bluish purple in the bottom corner of the canvas. Then she smeared some orange-ish red to the right of the blue-green and made it look like it was swirling.

Then she wiped her hands on her apron and dabbed it in some pink. Tip-toeing on the chair, she reached up high and spread a wavy line across the top of the Painting. Then she grabbed her paintbrush and smeared a bit of light green just above it – it was a bold and stark contrast to the black space with white specs.

Looking at the lower corner she smeared a cloud of blue, then topped it with a swish of her paintbrush. Gerald stepped back and watched as Nevaeh embellished his masterpiece with her creative style, with her joy of colors, with her youthful innocence, and he marveled at it. He was so proud of her when she turned to him and exclaimed – "Now, do it again!"

Gerald stepped up to her, cupped his palm over a blob of color and pressed it into the painting. When he removed his hand and Nevaeh saw what he had done she squealed with delight. "Again!"

Gerald did it again, and again, pressing all of the unique blotches, splashes, splotches, dabs and blots into the universe and setting them in motion around the sun. The colors followed the stars. They swirled and mixed within the universe until there was an expanse of colorful reminders that something bigger and better was out there.

"What a splendid imagination you have, Nevaeh. How did you realize that this Painting would benefit from a splash of color?"

"Color is the most precious gift we have. There are so many kinds of colors - so many reds and yellows and greens and purples that there is almost no way that you can mix a palette and ever get the same exact color twice."

"That's very true." Benjamin chimed in, marveling at his daughter's insight.

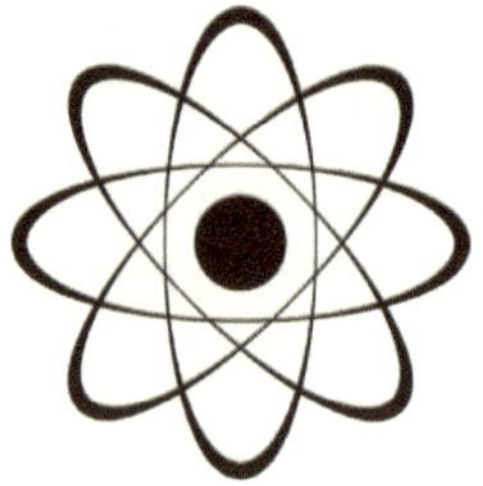

CHAPTER 4

"That looks like a butterfly. And that looks like a beach!" Nevaeh was saying as she pointed out the colorful blotches as they spiraled around the sun. "Aren't those the prettiest reds and pinks you've ever seen? Look how they sparkle!" She squealed with delight.

"And those purples and blues really help to brighten up that darker corner of space, don't you think?" Benjamin spoke, as his father and he stood at the doorway marveling at the newly revised masterpiece.

"Wait!" Nevaeh spoke as she leaped off her bed. She ran to the Painting and pointed at a spot that was coming around the sun that didn't have enough color. We need something there."

"Are you sure?" Gerald asked as he stepped up to the Painting to inspect the empty black area.

"Yeah, but it spins around so fast I'll never get to paint it, and have you press it inside, in time – what do we do?"

"I'll teach you how to do it, yourself."

"You will?" Excitement gleamed in her eyes.

"Of course. Did you not know that you have the gift?" He smiled.

"The gift?"

"Yes ma'am. I painted it. Your father was born into it, and you have the gift to see inside of it anytime you want."

"Really?" Her eyes sparkled with wonder and fascination.

"You have the ability to enact change. Whenever you want to do something for the good of it, you will be able to do it."

"Wow! How does it work?" Nevaeh clapped while jumping up and down, gleefully.

"It will take a while to learn, of course, but I can show you this one little trick right now. Would you like to learn?"

"Yes! Yes Grampa, I would!" Nevaeh squealed with delight as Benjamin glanced over to his wife, whose inquisitive look spoke volumes.

She had heard about Benjamin's adventure. She had a hard time truly believing it, but she acknowledged it as truth. Then, after she saw the Painting, the universe moving within a textured canvas, she accepted it even more. But she had also experienced Benjamin's mood swings, his sadness, his pain. She had seen residual memories attack him while he slept at night, awaking in fear. She knew how he died in the Painting, so hearing Gerald speak of Nevaeh's ability, made her panic inside.

"Okay," he clapped, "go get your paints." He watched her run to her desk, pick up her paints and paintbrush and then look up at him adoringly, awaiting instruction.

"Now paint the shape and color you want to create, on the palm of your hand."

She did so, carefully working out splotchy details, and then proudly held up her palm to show her grandfather.

"Oh, that is going to look nice." He turned back to the Painting, "Now, come here."

She leaped onto her chair and spotted the area she wanted to color. "Right there."

"Right here?" Gerald asked, making sure.

"Yes!"

"Okay. Hover your palm just above the canvas in that exact spot that you want this paint to appear." She did. "Now, think about it being right there, inside the Painting. Imagine the universe full of color in that exact spot. Imagine how beautiful it would be, as you watch it spin around the universe, and then desire it."

"Desire? What's that?"

"Desire is having a feeling, a want, so strong, that you will do anything to make it happen. When YOU desire something, your sense of seeing your desire happen is excited by the enjoyment that you expect to feel when that item or person decides to take actions to obtain your goal. All you need to do is want it to happen strong enough, and it will happen. Can you do that?"

"I think so."

"Now visualize your splotch of color floating like a cloud in that dark, empty spot of space. See it spiraling around the sun, shimmering with the stars and becoming real. And when you have that vision, that desire in your mind, press your palm onto the Painting and push that paint right through the canvas."

Nevaeh looked at the Painting one more time. She spotted that dark spot one more time, then she closed her eyes envisioning that spot filling with the spiral colors on her hand. She saw them in her mind forming the nebula. When she had the perfect feeling of it, she pressed her palm onto the Painting, held it there for a few moments, willing it to work, and then pulled her hand away.

Benjamin was in awe. It had worked. When Nevaeh's eyes opened and she saw what she had done, she squealed in pure merriment.

"I did it! I did it! I did it!"

"Yes, you did." Gerald took the happy young girl into his arms and hugged her. "You can do anything YOU put your mind to!"

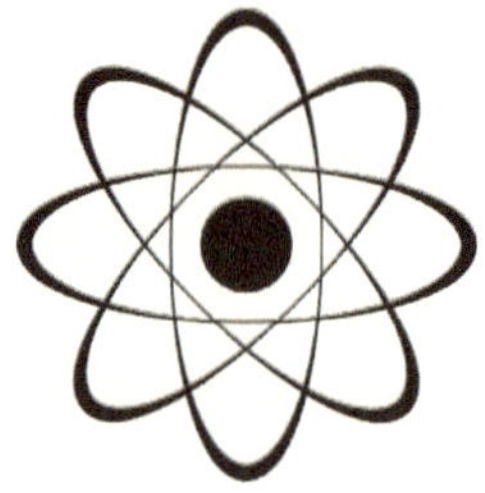

CHAPTER 5

That evening after dinner, after her grandparents left, Nevaeh returned back to her room to watch the Painting. A few hours later, Benjamin went upstairs to check on her and tuck her into bed.

"Daddy, tell me about the Painting?"

"What do you want to know?"

"Everything!"

"I've told you so much already..."

"But now, now I want every single detail."

So Benjamin refreshed her memory on how the Painting came to be. How her grandfather, Gerald, painted the world that came to life. How later he realized he needed to protect that world with everything he had in him, so he painted the universe. Then he explained how the Painting was pressed inside the universe, just like she pressed the colors inside today. Then he started it spinning around the brilliant, bright sun.

"And then you went into the Painting."

"That's correct. I was born into it. I grew up seeing so many fascinating, magnificent creations. The Painting is a marvelous place. The trees are exquisite, with so much detail you can hardly imagine. The flowers - you love colors – there are so many colors of flowers that dot the landscape. And the sunsets... to see a sunset again, to sit there and watch it dip down below the horizon, letting that explosion of color paint the sky with such beauty...." Benjamin trailed off simply reminiscing about it.

"I want to see it someday."

Benjamin pulled back from his memory and looked at his precious daughter sitting beside him, staring longingly at the Painting. He suddenly thought about his last day there, the explosion, the pain. He couldn't fathom a single thought of his daughter feeling that.

"I've painted them." He reminded her, "You've seen my paintings in my study."

"I have." She smiled.

If you ever want to see anything, I can always try to paint it for you."

That evening as Nevaeh lay in her bed, head on her pillow, she watched the Painting. The stars within shimmered like tiny diamonds. The new colors glowed with a radiance that entranced her senses. As her eyelids became heavy, she thought about flying into the Painting. She wondered how small she would be as she soared into each nebula. She wondered if the paint of the nebula would still be wet or if it would have dried by now. She wondered how close she could get to the stars. Could she touch them? Would they be cold or hot, smooth or sharp? And as her eyes closed, her mind drifted into the Painting. When she awoke the next morning she was exhilarated. She leaped from her bed and ran downstairs. "Guess what!"

"What?" Her mother and Benjamin asked.

"I saw the stars!"

"That's nice dear." Her mother cooed.

"I saw the stars and they were huge! They were much bigger than I could have ever imagined. The nebulas were made of so many colors, and they were like massive clouds. I could soar through them but not really touch them. I was floating inside them, but not getting covered in paint. It was the most amazing adventure I've ever had!"

"That sounds like a wonderful dream, Sweetheart." Benjamin heard his wife say, but he grew ever more curious. When it came to his father's artwork, anything was possible.

"You should tell your grandfather about that! He would love to hear about it."

Later that day, Nevaeh relayed her experience all over again to Gerald. She held her arms out to the side and danced around her room, showing him how she flew through the colorful clouds in the dark black sky. She described how the stars drummed, and how she could hear them pulsate. Benjamin hadn't heard that part, where did that come from?

Gerald sat down with her and began asking so many questions. "How far did you go? What else did you see?"

"I flew for hours. I saw tiny planets and large planets. I saw one so big I couldn't see the entire thing with my eyes. But I was so far away from the sun."

"Was it cold?"

"I didn't feel cold."

"Did you smell anything?"

"No."

"Taste anything?"

"No." Nevaeh looked at him curiously.

"You just saw and heard the sights and sounds," he confirmed. Nevaeh nodded her head. "Wonderful." Gerald grinned.

"How is that wonderful?" Benjamin asked hanging on his father's every word.

"It's exactly how I imagined it would be." He paused forming his next words carefully. "Nevaeh, did you know that each time you fly into the Painting you can fly faster?"

"How do you mean?"

"Well, everything you've seen, you can soar past faster, if you want to. That way you can see what you haven't seen yet."

"I can go farther? Towards the sun?"

"Towards my Painting." Gerald declared. "That blue and green spinning spec, right there." He pointed to the twirling ball rotating around the sun, the marble that shimmered like an emerald.

"Oh, I want to go there!"

"Why?" Benjamin found the word escape his mouth before thinking.

"So I can see the world that my daddy lived in!" Nevaeh answered with adoration. "I want to see the trees and flowers. I want to watch the sunsets and hear the rain..."

Benjamin looked worried. His father took his hand and let Nevaeh finish her speech.

"I want to see the ocean and feel the fluffy white bunny tickle my nose with its whiskers!"

"Now that part can't happen." Gerald confirmed, intriguing even his son.

"Why?" Nevaeh asked with a tear forming in her eye. The disappointment apparent.

"Because you'd only be there in spirit."

"What does that mean?"

"It means you won't be able to touch anything. You won't feel cold or hot..."

Benjamin watched the excitement lift from his daughter's face, so he spoke up. "So you won't get burned or hurt."

"That's right." Gerald added. "You can't get pricked by a rose's thorn, scraped if you fall, or harmed in any way."

"That's good." Nevaeh smiled, but then the smile faded. "But I won't be able to feel the soft bunny's fur, or pet a deer..."

"True," Gerald acknowledged, then added, "but you'll be able to talk to them!"

"I will?" Her eyes beamed brightly.

"The animals of my world will be able to sense you. There are so many animals, so many species. Some will be able to feel your presence, you may catch them turn and look at you, maybe even look through you, as if they know you are there but can't see you. Others will be able to hear and see you. They may or may not interact with you, as some of my animals can be quite afraid of humans, but they may hear you. Wouldn't that be nice?"

"That really would be neat!" Nevaeh expressed with the brightest smile Benjamin had ever seen. "I can't wait to go there!"

Benjamin interjected. "But there is so much to see before you get there. I've seen some of it."

"I'll bet just looking at the Painting, your grandfather's world from above it in space would be amazing."

"I'll bet it would."

"You should spend plenty of time just experiencing all of the beautiful nature your grandfather has painted when you get there."

"Like what?"

"Like the plants, the trees, the ocean. There is so much to see, it may take you years!"

"Wow!" Nevaeh cooed.

"Spend as much time as you can seeing the world, the land, the seas, the mountains…"

"I will, Daddy."

Gerald glanced over sadly at his son. He understood Benjamin's worry, he knew of his son's fear, but he was certain Nevaeh would be safe. He just wished he could confirm that with his son. Time would tell.

CHAPTER 6

Over the course of many weeks Nevaeh explored the universe. She flew farther - farther into the Painting, seeing sights no one had ever imagined. As she neared the original Painting, Gerald's world, she couldn't help but stop and hover above it. It was the most outstanding sight she had ever seen, and up until now, she had seen some pretty amazing sights!

The simplicity of the clouds, flowing around the planet, the fluffy white, the heavy grey, and the lightning... the lightning alone was magnificent! The wiry lines, jagged rays of light spider webbing across the sky, like fireworks, exploding across a horizontal canvas and the way it lit up the stratosphere. The colorful glowing of the clouds that resembled the nebulas she had painted, but in a more spectacular pageantry that danced across the top of the planet. It was a display of colors and lights that dazzled her senses. Nevaeh couldn't help but marvel at it.

If what she was going to see when she entered Gerald's world was anything as wonderful as this, she knew she'd be in for a treat. The one thing though, that she knew for certain, was this world was big! The closer she flew towards it, the more details she saw. She saw the pointed white caps of mountain ranges that so often poked the clouds in the sky.

She witnessed so many shades of blue circling around the land masses. She saw beige lands, green lands, bright white lands, and at night she saw lights, so many lights. They speckled across those lands, long lines that merged and accumulated largely in specific circular areas, and some lights that dotted areas so far away that they seemed lost.

Nevaeh just sat there hovering above the planet, watching it spin for days. She watched those lights move, grow, dim. She watched fires start and fade. She watched as small lights soared up into the sky, traveled long distances across the clouds, and then land elsewhere on the planet.

Each night Nevaeh returned to the planet. Each night she flew closer, just a little bit closer. It was so beautiful to see from this distance. But more impressive – the closer she flew, the more she heard!

She heard noise at first, a lot of noise. A barrage of machines, talking, and thunder. But each night, she focused on one sound. Thunder took her from lightning to cities full of people, sitting in their houses awaiting the storms to end. Those cities took her to people and talking. That talking took her to mass conversations, people expressing thoughts, desires...

Then she heard voices turn into song, music, the most delightful music. So many types of melodies, from vocals to instrumentals – she was amazed at how many sounds they could make. There were slow songs and fast songs, songs with a twang, and songs with a beat. There were loud, electric songs and soft, acoustic songs. Drums of all sorts, loud, leather, metal... she was entranced just listening to it all.

When Nevaeh finally decided she wanted to venture into the world her heart fluttered. What was she going to see first? The oceans? The mountains? The prairies? Which animals would she meet first? Where would she find soft, fluffy, white bunnies?

"How is Nevaeh doing?" Gerald asked one day of his son, Benjamin.

"She's good. She's been telling us all about her adventures; the sights, and sounds."

"Has she met the people yet?"

"Oddly enough, she's been taking it slowly." Benjamin admitted with relief. "I fully expected her to zoom right in there, but she hasn't yet."

"I had hoped she'd take it all in." Gerald admitted. "I told her the story about how you were born into the Painting. The reason I did it that way was so that you could grow up in the world, learning it; that there is so much to experience and know, so many joys and so many dangers."

"Dangers. What did you tell her about the dangers?" Benjamin's breathing quickened.

"You know she will be safe, right? No one can hurt her. No one can touch her. No buildings can fall on her."

"I know you've told me this, but she's my little girl, how can I not worry?"

"Of course you will worry – as I did, when my only son was born into that world. But the difference was that you were there in the flesh. Your skin could bleed, your eyes could burn. Every pain you felt, I too felt. But you did so much good! You must remember that."

Benjamin nodded and lowered his head, "Just tell me she will be okay."

"She will be better than okay."

The day Nevaeh touched down on the ground was still many weeks after she had decided to do so. The closer she got to the ground, the more she saw. She explored hills and valleys, flew through dark caves, seeing crystallized formations. She discovered a vast underground world of caves that took her to depths even her own father had never seen.

Last week, at one point, Benjamin suggested she explore the oceans before she touched down on ground. He told her all about his love of the water. How he used to fish and swim on hot days to cool off. Then he told her about how his human body held limitations, like how he couldn't stay under the water because he couldn't hold his breath that long.

"You don't have to hold your breath. You can swim down into the depths of the oceans and see sea life and creatures no one has ever seen – except for my father who painted them."

So she did.

She described these creatures to him, sea-faring dragons, eight legged ghostly octopods, fish with glowing heads and tentacles, an array of creepy crawlies, and so much more.

She explored the multitudes of colorful corals, followed underwater rivers to worlds much like the one she hovered above. She saw lava flowing through channels and caverns even farther below the surface of the water. And when she was ready to go to land, Benjamin described to her the wonders of the forests.

He knew he was prolonging the inevitable, but he also knew that as soon as she met the humans, as soon as their lives started playing out before her – she'd lose sight of the wonders of the planet. So he told her about the trees, how tall they were, how their limbs provided housing for so many animals. He told her about the day he described the tree to his friends. He gave her the speech he had given, and she hung on to every word.

So she explored the forests. She walked the pathways through the canopy of leaves. She heard trickling streams, as water flowed over smooth pebbles. She heard bird songs, insects chirping, and she watched spiders build intricate webs that sparkled in the morning dew.

She witnessed the complexities of the natural world, watching the birth of plants and animals, flowers blooming for the first time, moss spreading across stones, and mushrooms peeking through fallen leaves.

She learned about reptiles, water and land venturing creatures, and frogs that were born as tadpoles but grew to hop on land. Turtles with their thick hard shells, snakes that slithered and snails that moved incredibly slow were special learning experiences.

She met birds of all colors, shapes and sizes. Each type of bird had their own song, their own unique features. Some cawed while others chirped. Some whistled while others hooted. Some were so massive they could have almost been scary, especially when she saw others that were so small and fast, their wings fluttered faster than her eyes could see.

She met monkeys, of all shapes and sizes. She watched them use their hands to solve intricate puzzles, like how to break into coconuts to retrieve food. Some of the creatures blended so well into their environment that she could have missed them, except for their ooh-ooh-ah-ah calls. There were flying squirrels and other tree-going creatures; some were quick, some were slow. But each and every creature she laid her eyes on was unique in its own way.

She spent weeks exploring forests and jungles all over the planet. She witnessed how different each tree was, from the large leaves to the small. She saw trees that were so tall they could have touched the sky and she witnessed saplings just emerging from their seeds within the dirt, only to begin their struggle of growing.

And then she saw a beauty like no other. She observed the sun's rays streaking through the open patches of leaves, illuminating pathways. The golden white light was mystifying as it speckled the ground with shadows. And as she looked up at it, she was drawn towards it. She emerged from the edge of the forest and was struck by the brightness of the day light.

When her eyes set on the scene ahead of her, the road that led into a town, she realized, it was now time to meet the people.

CHAPTER 7

When Nevaeh stepped into the town she was taken aback by the hustle and bustle. Everyone was busy. And everyone was unique.

Each person looked different. They had distinctive hair colors, altering lengths, designs and shapes. Their body structure and contours varied, some were tall, some short while others round or thin. Each person wore something specific to their own style, a diverse mix of clothes in an array of styles, colors, shapes. There were short shoes and tall shoes, and all of those shoes were moving!

Some of the people were carrying bags of goods, others were walking across the street, entering stores. Some were working, sweeping, washing windows, while others fed livestock. There was a person handing out papers, one was running and sweating, while yet another was sitting on the sidewalk holding out a cup watching people go by. It was overwhelming to Nevaeh to see so much motion at once.

She sat on a nearby bench just watching the people. It was easier to watch them when she was sitting still, but all she witnessed was short blurbs of everybody's life. She was only able to see the people as they walked from one section of town to the next. When they turned a corner, went into a building, or moved far enough away, she'd lose sight of them. She began to wonder if she should pick someone and follow them, but then she began wondering who? How could she pick just one person when everyone was so fascinating?

As she sat there pondering, a sound caught her attention. It was a small high pitched cry that seemed scared and sad. She followed the sound to a drainage culvert and looked in. There she saw a tiny kitten stuck at the bottom. It couldn't climb out and there was no way for it to squeeze through the bars and venture further into the drain. It was trapped.

Without thinking, Nevaeh reached in to pick up the kitten, but she watched her hands flow right through it. She tried a couple of times before she realized that she couldn't touch the poor animal. She stood, turned to the first person walking by her and spoke, "Can you help the kitten?"

The person didn't acknowledge her, they just kept walking. She tried the next person, "Excuse me, Sir..." He kept moving. "Ma'am, would you mind..." The woman kept going.

Nevaeh tried over and over again to attract someone's attention to no avail. She looked back down at the kitten. It was dirty, hungry, thirsty and tired. Nevaeh knew that kitten needed help, and soon, or it would die. Just then, she saw a young girl, about the same age as she, walking up. She was dragging her feet, looking in the windows, slowing down her mother's stride.

Suddenly, Nevaeh had a good feeling about this little girl. She ran to her and spoke as they walked down the sidewalk. "There's a kitten up ahead in a drainage culvert. It's hungry and thirsty. I think that kitten has been trapped there for a long time. I need you to help that kitten. Would you please help that kitten?"

The girl didn't respond. She didn't even look towards Nevaeh. Knowing she had to try again, Nevaeh gathered all of her hope for this kitten and barked, "You have to help the kitten!"

The girl stopped and looked around. A moment later, her mother pulled her back towards her to get her walking again.

That kind of worked, Nevaeh thought to herself, I need to believe it more, I have to desire it... like Grampa said. The girl was quickly getting away from her, and they were just a few feet away from the culvert. Another few steps and they'd walk past the kitten. Panic filled Nevaeh's heart. It was now or never.

Pulling every hope and desire she had for saving the kitten, letting it fill her heart, she ran. She ran towards the girl so fast, with no other thought than the kitten and before she could even think, she accidentally ran through the girl. As Nevaeh skid to a stop to turn to the girl and face her, she noticed the girl had come to an abrupt stop. She looked around, as if someone had tapped her shoulder and disappeared. Her mother pulled at her arm, but she refused to move. She kept looking around, and then, she looked down.

"Momma, look!"

"What is it?" The mother demanded. The little girl kneeled down by the culvert to get a better look.

"What are you doing down there?" the mother inquired with annoyance.

"Momma, there's a kitten in there!"

The mother leaned over and looked. Suddenly the kitten, the frail, skinny kitten who barely had any energy left at all –meowed the most pitiful yowl.

"Oh, the poor little baby!" she cried. She kneeled down and reached into the culvert, but her arms were too short. Realizing she needed help, she looked up at a tall man walking by. "Sir, would you please help me?"

He looked at the woman and girl on their knees and peered into the drain. Spotting the kitten, he inquired, "Is that yours?"

"No, but it needs help. I can't reach it."

He looked at it again and then at the arms of his suit. He had no intention of getting his suit jacket dirty. He stood there, mulling over the problem for a moment, when another man walked up to them.

"What's going on?"

The woman and child explained the situation. This man seemed more amicable towards helping so the other man in the suit just walked away. Nevaeh watched him leave for a moment and shook her head with disappointment. She couldn't understand how anyone would see this predicament and NOT help. The thought was really bothering her when the scene grabbed her attention and redirected her back to the kitten.

The second man kneeled down next to the two ladies. He reached in and grabbed the kitten, scooping up the tiny fur ball in his large, warm hands. When he pulled the kitten out, into the daylight, the little girl reached for it.

The man relinquished the cat to the young girl who thanked him.

Cradling the kitten in her arms she noticed how skinny it was. "Momma, it's gotta be hungry. You can see his ribcage."

Just then a little boy and his father walked up. "What's that?" The little boy asked.

"It's a kitten we just rescued."

The little boy reached to pet the kitten, then looked up at his dad. "Hey Pop, we were just heading to the pet store to get a kitten, why not just take this one home?"

"Son, look how scrawny and dirty it is. It probably won't make it."

"But Dad, we'll never know if we don't try. Please?" The little boy pleaded.

When the father finally let in, the little girl relinquished the kitten into the boy's arms and looked back up at her mom. "We did a really good thing just now, didn't we?"

"We surly did, Sweetheart. We surly did!"

CHAPTER 8

When Nevaeh woke the next morning she leapt from her bed, raced downstairs and ran up to her father. "Daddy, Daddy, I have to talk to Grampa right now!"

"It's a bit early to call him," Benjamin glanced at the time. "Can you wait?"

"No."

A few minutes later Nevaeh was reporting her uplifting tale about saving the kitten to her grandfather over the phone. She described how she talked one child into saving it and how the kitten even found a home. Her grandfather, as well as her father (who was listening in) was quite pleased.

"That is a wonderful story." he exclaimed happily. "I am so glad you shared it with me."

"But Grampa, I have questions."

"Okay, what are your questions?"

"Why can no one see me? Why do my hands go through things? Why didn't the adults hear me? Why did the other girl only hear me when I went through her? Why did the tall guy in the suit not help? And why..."

"Whoa, Sweetie, one question at a time," Gerald stopped her. "The first two questions we discussed before. You are only there in spirit. You will only be able to see and hear. You won't be able to talk with or touch the people."

Gerald then added, "Why didn't the adults hear you? It could have been a multitude of reasons. Maybe they don't normally listen to children. Maybe they were too busy or preoccupied to hear you..."

"The little girl looked like she may have heard me, but it wasn't until I accidently ran through her that she looked down and saw the kitten. Why?"

Gerald smiled. "Think about the wind. You can't see it. You can't touch it, but you can feel it. You can sense that it is there because whatever it does: going through the leaves of trees, moving wind chimes or swooshing around a big building, it makes itself known. The wind itself isn't visible, the wind by itself doesn't make a noise - but its presence does."

"So I am like the wind. I can be felt if I..."

"Make waves." Benjamin added.

"All you have to do is be a strong enough presence to be felt, and you'll be able to do some miraculous feats!"

Later that day Benjamin looked outside the window to see Nevaeh sitting in the field looking up into the sky.

Every time the wind blew she'd raise her arms to feel it move around her. He was entranced watching her study it. He was curious as to what deep thoughts were going through his little girl's head, but he let her be. She needed this time to study.

That evening she excused herself to go to bed early. "Are you sure? We were going to play a family game."

"Please, Daddy? I want to go practice what I learned today in the Painting."

"Alright." Benjamin conceded. He smiled as he watched her race upstairs.

The next morning Nevaeh was not nearly as excited as the morning before. Benjamin could see it in her face that she was not at all happy. "What's wrong, Sweetheart?"

"It didn't work!"

"What didn't work?"

"Nothing! Nothing worked! And I just don't understand it at all!"

"Start from the beginning and tell me everything." Benjamin sat down at the table and readied himself for a long tale.

Nevaeh told him how she flew into the town and began trying to knock people's hats from their heads, like the wind does, how she tried to slam doors closed like the wind. She tried to jostle unsuspecting horses. She tried to stop a ball in mid-air, and how she tried to pick a flower. "I just don't understand why none of it worked!"

Benjamin sat there stunned. He couldn't believe his sweet, innocent daughter could try all of those troublesome things. He sat there for a moment trying to pull from his father's many teachings, how best to approach this situation.

"Do you remember what Grampa Gerald told you about his Painting? About how he designed it?" Nevaeh shrugged her shoulders. "Do you remember us telling you about good deeds? About how he coated the world with aspirations of goodness..."

Nevaeh interrupted, "I remember when you said 'One small act can mean so much'."

"Exactly." He scowled at her lovingly. "Your grandfather painted that world so anyone who had the will, the desire to do *Good*, will have a way to do it. He gave everybody the chance to be the solution, to answer his call and help others by just listening and feeling. Everything within the Painting, everything he intended for it to be, is all about doing good deeds. Making the world a better place."

Nevaeh smiled as she remembered.

"Now, do you know why everything you tried to do last night, didn't work?"

Nevaeh thought about it for a bit and then spoke. "I wasn't trying to do good things."

"That's right. The things you were trying to do either wasn't nice or was self-serving. You weren't trying to do good for others. You didn't have the desire to help people, you just wanted to play. That is not the reason you were given the gift to enter the Painting, was it?"

"No Sir."

"I think you should excuse yourself and think about this conversation. You get to go to this amazing world and watch the most phenomenal things take place and you – if you want it bad enough – can make this place, this wondrous world so much better, simply by wanting it. You've been given a gift, an extraordinary gift, and all you have to do is make sure that everything you do is always with the purest intentions.

"Yes, Daddy."

As Nevaeh sulked away slowly, Benjamin smiled as he recalled all of the important life lessons his father shared with him growing up. He remembered feeling confused like Nevaeh felt just now, and being overwhelmed with the knowledge he was gaining. He remembered growing up inside the Painting. He was trying so hard to live his life with the purest intentions, when the playfulness of just being a child would overwhelm his senses.

He also remembered the day that his best friends talked about feeling sorry for him for not being able to just be a child, for knowing so much and having so much weight on his small shoulders. It made him sad for just a moment, knowing that his friends worried about him, but then it encouraged him because he was more grown up than even the grown-ups sometimes.

Knowledge is power. The more he learned, the more he taught, the better he felt. The easier it became for him to face any challenges life threw at him.

Benjamin suddenly had an overwhelming urge to call his father.

CHAPTER 9

The next night when Nevaeh flew back into the Painting she flew to the town she had grown so accustomed to and walked around.

She actually found being here kind of boring. The people were always so busy doing their daily tasks. Working, cleaning, cooking, sleeping, they hardly ever played or relaxed. Plus, there was so many of them. To her it was like watching the chaos of a disturbed ant bed. Everyone had their own individual tasks but if you didn't know what each task was you'd lose them in the shuffle.

As she walked around, trying to keep up with one person, someone more interesting would grab her attention. She'd turn to follow that person until someone else caught her attention. She was crisscrossing all over the town having only glimpsed a fraction of its people and she was growing exhausted. She hadn't learned anything about the people, except that they never stopped to appreciate their beautiful world.

As she sat down on a nearby bench she looked around at the nature around her. It was beautiful and colorful. The animals knew how to appreciate the world. The birds would sing, the turtles would sun bathe, the flowers would bloom brightly showing such joy to simply be alive. Why couldn't the people do the same?

Maybe that was how she could help, Nevaeh thought. Maybe it was her task to help the people learn how to enjoy themselves, and to appreciate the simple things in life. She walked up to a mother who was busy trying to keep her children in tow. She had a baby on one hip, a toddler holding her hand, and an older sibling trudging along slowly behind her, causing her to constantly turn and harp on him to "keep up." This reminded her about her own mother, and suddenly a plan came to her.

She approached the first person nearest the mother and spoke, "Give her a flower." The person kept walking, but Nevaeh was not deterred. She walked with the woman and kept speaking out loud enough for anyone nearby to hear her, "Someone, please give this woman a flower! Look how hard she is working. Look how tired she is. I know that when I give my mommy a flower, it makes her pause and smile. So would someone please, give this nice woman a flower?"

Just then a man bent down to tie his shoe. While crouched down a bird dropped a daisy on the ground in front of him. Curiously he picked it up and returned to a standing position. He looked around and saw the mother coming up the sidewalk. Something inside him made him want to give her this flower, so as she neared he approached her.

"I want to give this to you."

She stopped and looked at the man, then at the flower in his hand. A tear started to form in her eyes as she looked up into the man's face and asked, "Why?"

"I remember how hard my own mother worked to raise my brothers and me. I just felt the desire to give this to you."

"Mom?" The toddler looked up at the flower curiously. "Is that for Jenny?"

The mother burst out crying.

"I'm so sorry ma'am." The man backed away slightly. "I didn't mean to upset you."

"Oh, no, I'm sorry, sir! I should explain."

"You don't have to."

"Please let me." She placed her hand on the man's hand. "Jenny was my oldest daughter, she loved daisies. She would draw them all of the time."

"Might I inquire as to why it seems you are talking about her in the past tense?"

"She passed away one year ago today. I've been going all over town looking for a daisy to take to her grave site but they are out of season. I was just about to give up."

He placed the daisy in her hand. "Then this daisy is for your daughter, Jenny."

"But sir, how did you know?"

"I didn't. I just had a feeling that you needed it. I guess the only thing I could say, is thanks to Geody."

"Thanks to Geody!"

The next day Gerald stopped by to check on Nevaeh. She was sitting at the table eating breakfast when she saw him walk in. With a full mouth and holding her spoon in the air, she burst out with a question that had been bugging her all morning. "Grampa who is Geody?"

"Are they still using that name?" Gerald smiled as he pulled out a chair and sat down next to her at the table. "How funny."

"Are *you* Geody?"

"I guess I am." He smiled. "You see, my father, your great grandfather was insistent that after I finished painting the world that I sign my creation. He once told me that signing your art is an important part of the creative process. The instant you apply your name to your work, you declare it officially finished and ready to be seen by the world. No matter what your signature looks like, what form it takes or where you put it, no work of art will ever be complete without one. Your signature identifies your art for all time as having been created, completed and approved of by you and you alone. You are the creator for now and all time."

"Wow," Nevaeh cooed but interrupted her grandfather's deep thoughts. "But why do they call you Geody?"

"Because that was what they saw." He laughed out loud. He reached for a pen and paper and started to draw. "My first thought, because my name is so long, Gerald Oliver Delaney, was that I would just put my initials." He drew his G.

"But then I realized that the G took up every bit of space that I had in that small unoccupied part of the ocean. If I wanted to add my O and D I'd need to make them smaller, maybe even place them artistically inside my G. So I did." Gerald drew his initials just like he had painted them on the Painting so many years before.

"Over the years, people stopped referring to my initials as G. O. D. and instead lost the pauses and spelled out the letters. That's how I started getting called Geody."

"That's funny." Nevaeh smiled as she looked at her grandfather's drawing. "You know, it kind of looks like a face."

Gerald glanced at it and smiled. "I can see that." He looked at Nevaeh who was deep in thought.

"Maybe that's why everyone says that you are always watching over them. Because you drew your face right into the Painting."

Chapter 10

After her meal, Nevaeh returned her thoughts back to the Painting and last night's activities. She told her grandfather how the daisy made the mother so happy that she cried and the reason why she cried. "Grampa, how did the man get the daisy?"

"Well, you said a bird dropped it."

"Yeah, but how did the bird know?"

"I painted them to know. The animals are more in tune to the happenings of the world than the humans could ever grasp. They know when something is coming, like a storm or earthquake. They know when someone is feeling sad or angry. They know how to care for the people, if they're allowed to, and they know what needs to happen when the desire is there."

"But how could the bird know that the flower I asked for needed to be a daisy. I didn't know it should have been a daisy, so how could the bird know?"

"How did you know the mother needed a flower in the first place?"

"I didn't. I just thought it would make her happy, like my mommy."

"So you knew she was sad?"

"No…" Nevaeh thought, "I don't think so."

"But something in you made you want to give that specific woman a flower, right?"

"Right."

"That is how my Painting works." Gerald smiled. "Everything is connected. Every little thing, every big thing, every plant, animal and human. You simply helped to reinforce what needed to happen with your desire to get the task done for her."

"So when I wanted to give the woman a flower, the Painting knew exactly which flower and told the bird to find a daisy and give it to the man to give to the woman."

"That's right."

"But wait," Nevaeh realized, "Why didn't the bird just drop the flower by the mother?"

"You said she had a baby on her hip, a toddler in her hand and that she kept looking back at the older child, right?"

"Yes."

"Do you think with all that she had going on, that she would look down as she walked and see a daisy laying on the ground?"

"Probably not." Nevaeh agreed, but then she thought of something else. "The bird could have landed on her to give her the flower."

"True." Gerald agreed, then added his own question for Nevaeh. "But, wouldn't that have startled her?"

"Maybe."

"And if she would have been startled, she might have dropped the child."

"I didn't think of that."

"Besides," Gerald added, "no one else would have known why that daisy was so important, not even you. The man that helped wouldn't have become an instrument of good. He wouldn't have heard her story or learned how easy it was to do something nice for somebody else. He wouldn't have walked away feeling good about himself, or to tell anyone else how great it made him feel."

Gerald observed Nevaeh's smile stretch across her face, then heard something he decided to add to his story. "Additionally, a few days have passed on the Painting as of now. I just heard the man bump into that mother on the street again. They struck up a conversation and he's going to see her again tonight."

"He is?"

"It seems the father of those children passed away as well."

"He did?" Sadness flushed across Nevaeh's face.

"But I have a good feeling that your single act of kindness, is going to become a future for those people."

"Really?" Nevaeh's eyes brightened. "How?"

"I can see things flowing. He's going to check in on that lady and her family, and to be available for them if they need him. Eventually, they all will become closer. Friendship will turn to more and at some point, if all goes well, who knows? Maybe those children will get another father figure in their lives."

"Wow." Nevaeh took that in thoughtfully. "It's like a ripple," she concluded.

"What's like a ripple?" Benjamin spoke as he walked into the room. Seeing his father and daughter sitting at the table, he pulled out a chair and sat with them.

"The good deed I did. It's like an ever expanding ripple in the water. It keeps spreading outward, until it changes the course of the lives it touches."

Benjamin smiled knowingly. "A simple act of caring creates an endless ripple."

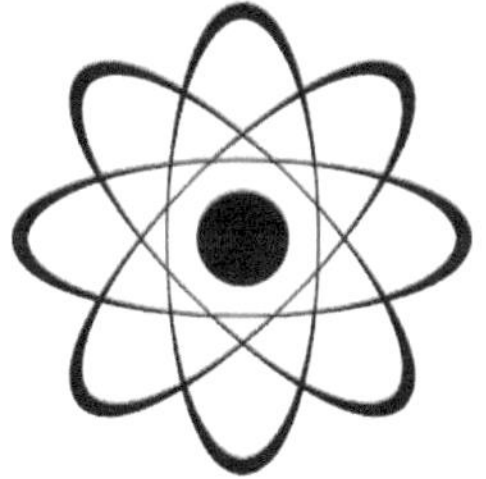

CHAPTER 11

When Nevaeh returned to the Painting she made a point to check in on the mother and her children. She watched how the man would check in on them from time to time. Over the course of many visits, or in the timeline of the Painting, many years, Nevaeh watched that couple grow closer, get married and flourish.

Every once in a while they'd thank Geody for bringing them together. They'd tell friends about the day they met. How Geody made it happen. How it was like his spirit pushed him to offer this woman a flower and how miraculous it was that a daisy just happened to land in front of him. Nevaeh found the entire story to be quite inspiring. Especially because she saw herself as the spirit that helped it happen.

In the meantime, Nevaeh had done quite a few good deeds throughout the Painting. She had encouraged unsuspecting people to feed the hungry, water the thirsty, and help the elderly.

One day not so long ago, Nevaeh was sitting on the bench watching the hustle and bustle of the people. She saw what she would learn to be a blind man slowly making his way down the sidewalk. He used a stick to find obstacles before he tripped. He used it to approximate distance like when the curb dropped down.

People avoided him as he walked, so they wouldn't get in his way, or accidentally trip him, which Nevaeh found good, but when the bag he was carrying developed a hole and an apple fell out, Nevaeh jumped into action.

The blind man had stopped walking. He was using his stick to sweep the walkway searching for his lost apple, but accidentally tapping people's feet as they walked by. Some of the pedestrians grimaced or groaned as they attempted to avoid the man. Another bumped into him and feigned a fake apology as he kept walking by. The jostling though, shifted another apple from the blind man's bag.

Nevaeh heard the man let out a rather dismayed, "ohhh..." and she could hear in his voice that he was flustered as to what to do.

"Hey, did you see that?" Nevaeh addressed the crowd. "He's losing items from his bag. He can't see where they fell, but you can! Someone please help him." Nevaeh stood between the man who couldn't see and the apple that fell from his bag and she willed the bystanders to do something. As another apple rolled through the hole in his bag, she pressed harder for someone to help. "There goes another apple. Would someone please help this man? He can't see where they are."

Just then a woman noticed the apple on the ground, and another apple ahead of her. She looked around to see whom it may have belonged to and saw the blind man looking overwhelmed and confused. She hastily picked up both apples and rushed up to the man. She called to him just as another apple slipped through the hole.

"Sir, your apples are dropping from a hole in your bag." He reached for the hole in his bag when she placed the two apples in his free hand. He fumbled to hold them as she retrieved the third apple on the ground. As she attempted to hand him the third apple, he clasped both of his hands together and dropped his walking stick.

A fellow bystander picked up his stick and realized the dilemma. He pulled his sandwich from the bag he was carrying it in and offered the bag to the lady. "It's not very big, but will this help?"

"Yes, it will." She smiled as she dropped an apple in it and then took it from his hand. She took the other two apples from the blind man's hands and placed them in, as the bystander returned the walking stick.

"You two are very kind to help me." The man spoke softly. "May Geody bless you."

Once the two of them had resolved the issue of the falling apples, the blind man thanked the both of them and started on his way. The two looked at each other and smiled.

"That was a very nice thing you did, to help that man." The bystander spoke with an inner delight.

"I couldn't have done it without your lunch bag." She smiled back. "He was right, that was such a kind thing to do."

"Kindness is something the deaf can hear and the blind can see."

"That's a beautiful phrase, she spoke as she looked towards the blind man almost fully across the street.

"Grampa, it was a good feeling to help that man, but why was he blind?" Nevaeh asked after talking with Gerald about the good deed she helped make happen that night.

"That is a good question, one with which I've heard many times. So let me answer your question with a question. Would the man have needed help finding his apples if he could have seen them?"

"Probably not."

"The other two people, would they have received the benefit of those feel-good emotions if he didn't need the assistance?"

"I guess not."

"And finally, is it not true that everyone in the Painting is different in a multitude of ways? Size, shape, color and affliction?"

"That's true."

"So why shouldn't this man be blind if his presence helps others and good things can come of it?"

Nevaeh thought about that for a moment and then she countered her grandfather's question. "Okay Grampa, but what about the fact that he can't see all of the beauty of your world?"

"When I take one sense, I make sure the other senses develop stronger skills. That man may not be able to see a sunset but he can hear the quietest bird chirp, the hushed rustling of leaves in a slight breeze, and he can feel more through a stick than most people notice with perfect vision. He's got abilities others can't even imagine, so why would I want to deprive him of such a unique experience?"

Each time she visited the Painting, Nevaeh continued doing good deeds. She got better at sharing her heartfelt desires with others and enacting change in small ways.

She helped people do things that they struggled with by sending passersby to help. She encouraged those with plenty to share with those who were hungry, either with extra food or their time. She opened the heart of an affluent man who helped a young girl just wanting to get an education and paid for her tuition. With every good deed and act of kindness Nevaeh was able to enact, they received a delight within. She witnessed happiness, reached a deeper understanding of life, and made the world a bit more beautiful.

CHAPTER 12

It had been a number of weeks, for Nevaeh, which in the Painting was about 15 years. So much had changed, the people had aged, the trees had grown taller and the buildings had been torn down and replaced with bigger, better buildings.

Nevaeh was sitting on her favorite bench, watching the hustle and bustle, wondering what she was going to do today, when a piece of paper, floating on the wind, landed on the bench beside her. She read it, to discover that a brand new veterinarian practice was opening in town, and she became curious enough to check it out.

As she watched the young man work on his advertising, handing out flyers and meeting his clients, something kept tugging at her heart. There was something familiar about this man, but she knew she had never seen him before. It wasn't until a couple brought in a kitten they found, and the man started regaling them with a story from his past, that Nevaeh realized why she was drawn to him.

"When I was a boy, my father and I were walking down the sidewalk in town when we met a young girl who needed help rescuing a trapped kitten in a storm drain. After one man rescued the cat, I got to take it home and care for it. That was the most magical day for me, because that was the day I decided to dedicate my life towards helping animals.

You see, nursing the kitten back to health, bottle feeding it, helping it to walk, to grow, was more rewarding than I would have ever imagined. Learning how easy it was to save a life opened my eyes to possibilities I had never dreamed of. I started rescuing all sorts of critters as I grew up. I nursed multiple baby squirrels who fell from their nests. I mended bird's broken wings, helped turtles heal broken shells, and I can't even begin to tell you how many cats and dogs I helped nurse back to health from bite wounds, broken legs, chipped teeth and more.

For me, that one simple act opened doors I didn't even know existed. I realized I would grow up to become a veterinarian and I've been sharing my story to help others realize their potential ever since."

"That's a wonderful story." The client spoke as the Vet peered into the kitten's mouth.

Just then a woman walked in, "Sorry to bother you, but your ten o clock just arrived."

"Thank you. I'll be right out."

After she closed the door, the client watched the vet check the kitten's ears and temperature and then spoke again. "I wonder what happened to the young girl who originally discovered the trapped kitten?"

"Funny you'd ask..." he smiled as he looked up at the client. "That was she just now."

"Really?"

"That little girl came by to check on the kitten often after I took it home. We became friends. She helped me with many of my critter-saving ventures and eventually, we got married."

The client smiled brightly. "Wow, Geody sure does work in mysterious ways."

"That he does."

Nevaeh learned that it was her desire, her push for someone to help that kitten that day, that made the action take place. But now, she beamed brightly, realizing that her one simple act of kindness had trickled down the line and had done so much good. That her will to help that one kitten had also willed these two souls together, to become friends and then chose to go into the field of helping other unfortunate animals... the knowledge was overwhelming and beautiful.

When she awoke that morning she called her Grampa Gerald to tell him about it. She just couldn't keep the thrill inside and not share it with others.

CHAPTER 13

Over time, Nevaeh explored many towns and cities. She ventured into small country communities and large bustling metropolises. She found the big cities to be overwhelming, but beautiful. She was inspired how the people could build such intricate communities and thrive living so close to one another. But she also found it noisy.

The people, the traffic, the vehicles and workers – everything was so close together, all of the noises blended together. And yet, it was those people who enjoyed the noises. They would talk about it as if it were a song, an orchestra of sounds all working together to make a wondrous place. Crying babies, car horns honking, and jack hammers breaking up concrete completely drowned out any nature in the area. She couldn't hear the birds, she couldn't focus on the plants and she missed the flowers. Sure there were stores that sold flowers, all sorts of beautiful flowers brought in from all over the world. But they had been cut and kept cold to preserve their beauty, and because they had been refrigerated, they had lost what smell they used to have.

Granted Nevaeh couldn't smell them, but she could see the people as they'd walk by and stop to smell the flowers and simply shrug their shoulders and move on. It was completely different than what she had seen before in smaller communities. There flowers grew along the sides of the road and apparently smelled so good, they'd breathe deeply of the aromas and bask in the scent over a long few moments. The flowers also attracted bees and butterflies and hummingbirds.

She realized she would never get bored here in the big city, where there was something going on everywhere. There was dancing in the street, artwork on the building walls, music from the subways, singing from the upper windows of nearby buildings. People all over were finding ways to share their creativity with the world, and yet, so few people truly noticed them. However, the people who did notice the talents that were being shared, well, they were truly the blessed ones.

Nevaeh would then travel to smaller communities, towns that were so small there was only a couple of small stores. There people would travel more than an hour to get their needs met in nearby cities, because they thrived in the small country living their lives offered. They were so close to nature, and to the animals. They rode horses, milked cows and spent long Saturdays fishing. It was so quiet you could hear the crickets chirping, the wind whistling, and the neighbors hunting. They held rodeos to show off their talents and skills, and they had dances and social gatherings to get together and catch up with each other's lives. They walked slower, talked slower, and took their time because all they had was time. And yet, when their children were old enough to decide what they wanted to do with their lives, Nevaeh witnessed many times how some chose to stay while others chose to go. They had a desire to do something grand, to be a part of something bigger, to venture into the big city and make something of themselves. It was almost baffling to her, but she watched it nevertheless.

Maybe it was because Nevaeh could choose where she wanted to go, maybe because she had seen so many different places in this world that she had figured out the best locations, or maybe it was because she had figured out what her own desires were, that Nevaeh decided to venture back to the town she had started from.

She asked her father about it one day, after bouncing from town to town and city to city over the course of many years. His response was fairly simplistic.

"Maybe you went back to that town because it's familiar, and because you have so many connections there already."

While she had accepted that as a good excuse, she kind of knew in the back of her mind that it wasn't entirely true. Over the course of the many years she spent traveling the world, visiting all of the various countries on each continent, getting to know the cultures and people, she knew one thing to be true – the people she had first met in that little town, were either quite old or had long ago passed away. The town had changed, and it had grown. It wasn't as big as a city, but it was busier than it ever was before. So many new buildings and houses and schools and roads had been constructed. The landscape she remembered had changed drastically. Suburbs touched the city and sprawled down the road towards other small towns; communities were annexed in.

From outer space their once speckled lights at night that dotted the terrain, became just as bright and overflowing as some of the other big cities. Her park bench where she had spent so many afternoons just sitting and watching the people had been removed, along with the park, for a shopping mall.

Nevaeh may have returned to the town she had first met, but the town had not returned to her. She journeyed to the edges of the metropolis, to smaller, outer communities and found moderate, isolated subdivisions that were scattered around landscapes of forests and glens. Floating above the communities, she could see how they kept spreading outwards. She watched them cutting down trees to pave new roads and foundations.

She did what she could for the people, but the growth was engulfing. It consumed everything in its place to make room for future generations. She was witnessing how the small cities became the big cities and how so many people would pack themselves into this crowded area. She watched them lose sight of what was important in life because there was so much to do to keep them busy. But then she caught sight of those who decided to move farther out, so they could be back in the simpler lives they so longed for. She followed them into smaller communities that seemed so familiar, but each day the city encroached on the outskirts. Growth was happening so quickly, it felt as if Nevaeh couldn't keep up. Every time Neveah returned to the Painting, so much time had passed, she felt as if she was a stranger looking in. When she finally went to her father about how she was feeling it reminded him of a story he had once heard.

"When I was living in the Painting I remember spending a good amount of time in one town that needed the extra help. They had built a dam to create a lake. It was a beautiful lake and brought a lot of happiness, but one overly wet spring that town got a lot of rain. They didn't think to let the water out of the lake until it was too late. When the water went over the top of the spillway, an area designed to keep the water from going over the top of the dam, it flowed across the land, sweeping trees and plants downstream. It cut into the land and carved out a deep gorge. It caused a lot of damage downstream."

"That's horrible Daddy, but what's the point?"

"In so many ways, life in the Painting is like water. It keeps rushing forward with such power that it can be destructive. There are times in life when the people can feel like they're drowning. Times when they have so much to do, so many tasks that are being asked of them, that it makes their course seem already cut out and out of control.

But there is also something else to take into account with water. Water, that can be so overpowering, so destructive, brings life. We need water to survive. We don't have the power to control it, but we can calm it. We can direct its path with planning and foresight. We can guide it and change the course it takes, and they could have done that, too.

With one simple act of caring, you can create an endless ripple."

Chapter 14

That evening Nevaeh returned to the Painting and soared over the lands looking for something specific, a gorge. When she found one, not knowing if it was the right one or not, she stopped to investigate. She scoured the land dotted by rivers and hills, large and small patches of trees, clusters of boats on the water and trails leading up from the lake into the forested areas.

That's when she spotted the lookout. A beautiful area at the top of a hill overlooking the gorge and the lake. It was a panorama of what should have been a postcard, a breath-taking sight to marvel at, and at the moment, the sun was setting and glistening upon the exposed stone of the gorge.

She was gazing out at the beauty when she heard the shuffle of someone's feet approaching. She turned and looked at the elderly man and watched him advance towards the guardrail at the edge of the cliff. He beheld the sight and breathed in the artistry of the landscape. He then pulled a picture out of his wallet and looked at it.

"Martha, do you remember that day? The day we watched the water just starting to trickle onto the spillway? I remember thinking how slow it was rising, that everyone on the news was over-reacting. But then the stories began to flow like the river that water was becoming. Before long the flood waters were ten foot tall and pouring over the landscape like a jack-hammer. They swept away trees, ground, rocks and boulders. The waters scrubbed the land clear of everything and then kept flowing. It connected to the nearby river and rushed downstream so fast. It overflowed the river beds, saturated everything downstream, picked up homes, and we watched those homes float down the rushing waters like an out of control canoe... that's how I feel right now... without you." He looked up from the picture clasped within his palm at the sight.

Nevaeh witnessed a tear slip from his eye. She wondered if Martha was his wife... she wondered if Martha was gone.

At that moment, the elderly man clutched his chest, and groaned in pain. His left hand grasped the railing as his knees began to buckle. Nevaeh realized he was in pain, and something dire was happening to his body. She looked around and saw no one. This man needed help and she couldn't do anything for him – she looked around, desperate to find help when she saw a deer.

He was staring at Nevaeh, his head and neck straight up, his eyes wide. Maybe he was concerned about the old man, who had just fallen to his knees, the strain apparent on his wrinkled face. Nevaeh looked back at the deer, who seemed to look right at her, and then he turned and ran into the woods.

"Wait!" She called as she flew after him. She flew into the woods and followed the path he was on. He leaped over the makeshift steps built from logs and tree roots. He ascended up a hill and then he disappeared over the top. When Nevaeh sailed over the top of the hill she flew right through a couple taking a walk on the nature trail. As she flew through them, her thoughts and worry for the elderly man went through them. She skid to a stop and turned to face the two.

"Did you hear that?" One said to the other.

"What?"

"That rustling, it sounded like a deer or something large running down the trail."

"Nope." He answered back. He turned to continue along the trail when he was stopped again.

"Are you sure that's the way? There's a fork in the trail here."

"Yeah, we go left." He pointed to the trail he was intending to walk down.

"But I thought we were going to see the gorge. Wouldn't that be up and to the right?" She inquired as she pointed the same direction she had heard the rustling.

"You just want to see if you can spot the deer." He chuckled.

"Well neither of us have been out here before, how can you be so sure that is the correct way?"

"I can't." They both looked at the trails ahead of them attempting to make a decision.

Nevaeh was screaming at them, "Go right! Go right!" She was desperate for them to go that way so they could check on the elderly man. So when she saw the man take a step towards the trail to the left, she panicked. She flew down the trail, turned and was about to fly through him again when her presence spooked a mother bird. She flew from her nest and towards the man stepping towards her and dive-bombed him. He ducked, covering his head and called to his wife, "Go right – run!"

The bird squawked and chased them up the path until they were far enough away from her nest to feel safe again. They continued to sprint up the path until they felt it was 'safe again' and then slowed to a stop.

Laughing at each other and the adrenaline escaping their system, they bent over to catch their breath. That's when the sound attracted their attention.

"Ohhh..."

They exchanged curious glances and proceeded up the path at a brisk pace. When they saw the elderly man huddled on the ground, they jumped into action.

Nevaeh was relieved when they found the man, helped him, called for help, and found assistance to help him off the mountain and to the hospital. She realized it had been a joint effort. The deer led her down the path, her determination to get them to choose the right path filled the bird with the desire to lead them away from the left, and his groan of pain pulled them closer.

They had never been here before, but their arrival saved the life of an old man whose loneliness was going to take him from the world way too soon.

CHAPTER 15

"What's wrong? Gerald asked of his son when Benjamin came to him.

"It's Nevaeh, something is wrong. She's stopped visiting the Painting. She hasn't talked about it for weeks."

Gerald walked over to Nevaeh, sitting in the yard, overlooking the tadpoles in the pond, and sat down beside her. "What are you doing?"

"Watching the frogs."

Gerald looked closely at the pond and then spoke. "I don't see any frogs."

"In the water." Nevaeh pointed.

"Those are actually tadpoles. They haven't become frogs yet."

"I know that Grampa, but why lie to ourselves? They will grow up to become a frog, so why wait to change their name?"

Gerald sat down next to her and was quiet for a long time. He watched the tadpoles swim, and eat, and sleep. He saw big tadpoles with legs starting to emerge and small tadpoles fresh out of their eggs. It took him back to a day he fondly remembered from his childhood.

He recalled watching the tadpoles, like he and Nevaeh were doing right now. He was fascinated with how they could breathe under water. He remembered how enchanting he considered their world, underwater, where all you could hear was the sounds of the currents. Where your vision was enhanced because your hearing was dulled, and how nice the quiet would have been to him when he was a child.

Then Gerald remembered the kids from school - how they all decided that day to go swimming. He heard them laughing and screaming. He watched them leap into the water, splash around, kick up the mud, disrupt the ecosystem and how their presence destroyed the tadpoles home. He tried to find them through the turbulent waters, to see them through the thick muddy mess but they had all been swept away.

He remembered how sad he was, and how angry he had become. He had yelled at the children for coming – but then he realized he was upset at them for playing, for enjoying their lives and for partaking in the world of which they were a part.

They didn't understand what his problem was, but he used that to understand what was going on in Nevaeh's mind.

"It's true. They do grow up. They come out of the water. They lead their own lives and they move on. That's just the way it is. It doesn't mean that we should skip this step though."

"Grampa, it's sad to see so much change. It's hard to watch them all move on so quickly."

Gerald contemplated his next words carefully, then spoke curiously. "You know, I haven't seen that pretty blue sweater of yours in a very long time."

Nevaeh looked over at him with intrigue. "My blue sweater?"

"Yeah, the one with the sparkles."

"Grampa," she smiled, "I got rid of that months ago."

"You did?" Gerald sounded disappointed. "It looked nice on you. Why'd you get rid of it?"

"I outgrew it."

"So you just threw it away?"

"No. I donated it."

"That's sad."

"Why is it sad? I'm sure someone else is wearing it right now."

"Well I guess that's a good thing. It can go on to be enjoyed by someone else."

"Maybe that someone else's Grampa could enjoy it, too?" Nevaeh offered.

"Maybe." Gerald smiled. "It's just hard to watch you grow up so quickly. It won't be long before you move on with your life, and I get to see you even less than I do now."

"I guess you're right." Nevaeh realized. "It's what's supposed to happen, even in your Painting." She took her Grampa's hand.

"So, do you want to tell me what's really on your mind?"

"I don't feel like I fit anywhere in there."

"How do you mean?"

"Everyone is so busy. It's like they are all strangers. To me, to each other... I feel so alone when I go there now."

"I can understand that. It is heartbreaking to know how easy it is for others to move on, to feel as though your presence is either over-looked, unnoticed or completely forgotten. I have felt that way many times throughout my life." Gerald admitted sadly.

"You have?"

Gerald nodded. "In the absence of a personal connection, lack of love or a feeling of belonging, there is always suffering. But it's those hardships that strengthen you. That discomfort you are feeling is because you need to find an attachment. Something or someone that connects you to what you need."

Nevaeh looked lost. She stared at Gerald for a long moment before speaking again. "How do I do that?"

"That's an excellent question." Gerald frowned, "But only you can figure that out."

Nevaeh turned to look back at the tadpoles. This wasn't helping, she was thinking.

"Loneliness leads to heartache."

"How did you get past it?" She inquired.

"Well...." Gerald thought about it. "I returned back to the places that made me happiest... and then I made new memories, found new happiness and grew with the changes that were coming at me."

"How can I do that?"

"I know you found a lot of happiness at one time within my Painting. I think it's time to go back and make a new happiness."

"The small town I once liked is now a large metropolis. It's so loud and busy – it makes me sad to see it now."

"So find a new happiness. Find a different small town to fall in love with."

"Grampa, I traveled the world, it's all the same. So many people, so many blurry faces racing by in their busy lives, not listening, not caring, not noticing one another or the beauty of your world. Why bother?"

"Because someone there still needs you."

"How do they need me?"

"Benjamin was raised in a small town that has long been forgotten. It grew a bit, over time, but the work dried up. Many people moved and the town was almost forgotten about. But a new company has started to build there. It's brought back jobs, and people, it's about to prosper."

"That's good, I guess." Nevaeh smiled. "But doesn't that mean it'll grow into a big city and lose sight of what's important, just like all of the others?"

"Maybe. Maybe not. You see, something just happened, something that could take it all away. The town needs you to help it survive."

"But what can I do?"

"Everything. Or nothing. You don't have to do anything, but I'd like for you to at least witness what's going to happen. I think it will be quite beneficial for you."

CHAPTER 16

Nevaeh was told to follow the bells and as she did, she flew into a familiar looking town as the sun was setting behind the nearby hills. The town was laid out like many towns she had visited. There was a square, where buildings of stores and restaurants were lined up along all four sides of the streets. Across the street, in the center of town, was a beautiful tree. A massively large tree, whose branches stretched out far and wide, curving towards the ground where they almost touched and then reaching towards the sky as if getting a second wind. There were floodlights shining onto the tree from the ground and picnic benches placed methodically in even increments along the outer sidewalk. It was a beautiful place, but no one was there. It seemed a shame.

Nevaeh looked around and saw that there were a few people heading towards the school gymnasium at the end of the street. She followed the people, and as she neared, she realized the entire town may have been here.

The building was packed full of people, and they were all talking among themselves.

"I can't believe we're even here talking about this. It's ludicrous to think we can save it."

"Ludicrous? It's the most important piece of history in this entire town! It must be saved."

"It's dangerous. It nearly killed that boy."

Nevaeh was intrigued. What were they talking about? She walked over to another conversation and listened in.

"I hear he's going to die."

"Stop spreading gossip, Mrs. Peabody, he's a strong young boy who's going to be fine."

"How do you know? Are you a doctor?"

"I'm a friend of the family. He's got a broken arm and two broken ribs and a slight concussion. But he's going to wake up soon."

"You can't know that. Nobody knows what's going to happen."

Nevaeh walked towards another group talking and listened to them.

"We need to tear it down."

"It should never have been let stand for as long as it has. It's a danger to us all."

"It's beautiful and historical."

"It's where some boy, maybe spent an afternoon talking about it, and the mayor decided to make a plaque commemorating its existence. It's truly nothing special."

"Nothing special? SOME boy? How can you say that? That tree is the tree the Painter's son talked about. He gave his first lesson about our creator using that tree as his diagram. The insight that young man had was marvelous. How can you possibly disregard that? How could you even contemplate saying that tree is nothing special?"

"Because the story was from generations ago, Dylan. We don't know if it was true."

"Of course it was true." Dylan countered.

"It doesn't matter. It took place so long ago that it isn't at all relevant today. There's no such thing as the Painter – and oh yeah, there's a boy lying in a hospital bed grasping to his life because of it. Anyone who's against tearing down that tree is as insane as the parents who begged everyone to ask Geody to help him."

Nevaeh was completely taken aback. Her father had told her the story about the tree. She saw the painting of it hanging on the wall in his den. She had always wanted to see the tree, to see with her own two eyes, the details he talked so vividly about. When she first arrived in the Painting there was so much to see, so many amazing sights and sounds. She had been overcome with the multitudes of different options, places, people. Her senses were flooded with so much opportunity that she had all but forgotten about really focusing on each and every minute detail. The universe, the world, the town was massive, to her, how could she focus so intently on the details of one little tree when she had seen a billion trees covering miles and miles of landscape across an entire globe.

Of course she had studied the trees. She looked at so many of them over her travels they blended into the environment. Short trees, tall trees, trees wider in circumference than a house. There were trees of various shapes, colors; so many types of leaves, or needles, some bearing fruit, others grew flowers... she never thought she'd ever find the one tree in all of the world that her father spoke so highly of so long ago, and yet, here she was, within walking distance.

"It's got to be torn down."

"It'll destroy the town."

"How could the loss of one tree destroy an entire town? That's preposterous!"

"Because, that tree is the only thing that's kept our town on the map all of these years."

"In case you haven't heard, we've got a great manufacturing company in town. THAT is what has put our small, dying town back on the map, not that overly large, dangerous tree."

"People," a booming voice came from the center of the room. Nevaeh made her way over to see a couple of people standing on stage by a podium. "We can't solve this problem tonight."

"Sure we will – tear down that tree!"

"No!" shouted a huge group of people from every section of the room. "You can't!"

"Watch me!"

"Both sides have valid points. There is a lot to take into consideration for a decision like this and we must go about making that decision in the best, most fair way possible."

The crowd all began to talk at once and Nevaeh's ears hurt from the noise.

"People!" The man spoke again, regaining the crowd's attention. "If anyone, goes near that tree or tries to destroy it, they **will** be arrested."

"Sounds like you've already made your decision. How is that fair?"

"No one has made any decisions. There are too many emotions surrounding this issue and until both sides are heard, in an organized, legal proceeding, we will not make any decisions regarding the fate of that tree. Once both sides have reasonably presented their case and rebuttals, our mayor will make his final decision based on the best possible outcome."

The murmurs and outrage began again, but the town sheriff stepped up to the podium.

"And please let me remind you all, that until the case has been made and the outcome decided, the tree will be under constant protection. If anyone comes near it, intending to cause it damage, defame it, or destroy it, they and anyone helping them, will be put in jail until the resolution of this case. Are we clear?"

Nevaeh was thankful for that. She would hate to see anything happen to that tree, especially before she could really see it in the daylight. She knew this tree was special. It was a historical symbol of her grandfather's love for the Painting, of her father's unsurmountable appreciation of his own father's creation.

While many were just looking at this tree as an obstacle that needed to be taken care of, a danger, it symbolically meant so much more. It was about the people's opinions of Geody. Whether some believed he painted the tree and the world they live in, and the thoughts of other's who couldn't bring themselves to believe. If they got their way, they'd destroy a valuable piece of history, a visual reminder that Geody painted them. But then again, they had the entire world to see that... To Nevaeh, it was about her father, the fact that he was born here, lived here, died here, to teach everyone about Geody's grand plan, about his love for this world. It was the fact that he pointed out that evidence in such vivid detail, one single tree that symbolized such painstaking detail and thought and caring that went into every brush-stroke... THAT was what needed to be remembered.

So instead of heading back home that night, she chose to stay in the Painting. She didn't want to leave until she had seen the resolution. One day in her world was, a year in the Painting. If she went home now, she wouldn't get to see how the peple resolve such a heated conflict. By the time she got back the tree would either still be here or it would be gone and there would be no trace of it having ever existed. She couldn't fathom that.

So she found Dylan, the person who so strongly believed in saving the tree, Geody's love, the man to whom she felt drawn. She followed him home and slept on his couch. Sure, she could have slept outside, nothing could see her, touch her, bother her, but it just didn't seem comfortable. Nevaeh had never slept in anything but her own bed, and she had a feeling she'd be here for quite a while. The next morning she awoke to the smell of bacon frying, the news blaring on the TV, and her unaware temporary roommate deep in conversation with someone on the phone.

"Yes, I'm going to be the one who speaks for all of Geody. I'm going to need everyone's help to gather as much historical and factual information as I can about the Painter. The other side is going to present this as a simple open and shut case. They're going to say it's an old tree and it must go, simple as that. But our job is going to be much more difficult. It's our task to prove beyond a reasonable doubt that this should be marked as a historical landmark. That it should be saved, cared for and upheld, because of it's historical significance."

As Nevaeh listened, she realized, maybe she'll be able to help.

CHAPTER 17

The hustle and bustle of the campaign office was confusing to her. There were dozens of people who filled the room, each at their own desk, either on the phone or computer or both. Some doing research, others calling around for information. She spent weeks watching, listening, admiring these people.

Their goal seemed impossible. While the tree already had significance to it and the mayor had already taken the first step to place the plaque next to it, commemorating its history, it wasn't enough in the eyes of the law. One person was writing a report about the exceptional value the tree's existence had and what that value does for the town. Another person was in charge of detailing the event that made this tree important, her father's story. A third person was showcasing how the tree represented a great ideal, the existence of Geody, the Painter of the entire universe. A fourth person was detailing the artistic merit with the beauty of this tree, writing down as much detail as they could, trying to recreate Benjamin's speech.

They shared information with each other as well as other researchers, working diligently to combine their data in the simplest most profound way. Their collaboration made Nevaeh's heart soar. However, on the other side of the room, there was another whole group that was in charge of bringing in conflicting points of view to destroy the first groups research.

At first it seemed counterintuitive, but then Nevaeh realized why they were doing it, so they could be prepared for the debate. They all brought in their own particular pieces of this puzzle, all representing their own sections. As each side presented their findings Nevaeh sat in awe. The conflict was real, and strong. Each side had such valid points. She could understand where everyone was coming from. Sure, she was partial to saving the tree, it meant more to her than most. After spending multiple afternoons just sitting underneath it, taking in all of its beauty and charm, truly taking the time to understand each detail her father had pointed out, she was filled with a passion for this tree unlike any she had ever experienced before.

She was so happy to be spending time with Dylan, being filled with his hopes and desires. Seeing this world in a way she hadn't taken the time to yet. Sure, she had seen the world, from the top of the mountains to the bottom of the oceans and everything in between, but all she saw was what was there; the final scene. She could marvel at the sunset as it dipped down behind the mountain range, but she hadn't simply looked down at the mountain, the ground she stood on, and taken in the unique topography of the soil.

She had seen fields of green that stretched along prairies so far that they seemed to fade into the sky, but she hadn't taken the time to marvel at a single wildflower, at the exquisite detail of each petal, how the leaves connected to the stems or how the stems were coated with a fuzzy layer of fur to protect it from animals that would want to eat it. And as she sat under the tree, looking at its limbs that seemed so tired, the thick, weathered trunk, and all of the dead growth just under the canopy of leaves, the balls of moss that had taken over, she realized, Dylan's job was going to be more difficult than anyone had expected.

This tree was tired. It had lived through and seen so much, so many generations, so many lives had come and gone, so many children had grown up around it, left their footprints on its ground and carved their memories on its trunk. Its roots had grown over and around rocks, had come up from under the ground, reached over obstacles and then submerged themselves back under the ground, only to come back up a few feet away and do it all over again. As the roots had been marred by lawn mowers and bicycles and deer horns and scuff marks, new life was starting to sprout from them, attempting to stretch up through the shade of its upper canopy in hopes of finding a ray of sunlight.

It was trying so hard to survive, to endure through the restrictions of its location and the interference from the humans. She saw where tree limbs had been struck down by lightning or broken by weight, where years of drought had slowed its growth, or where floods had rubbed its bark smooth. Taking the time to really see this tree gave an insight as to why things in this world must live and die. Why buildings come and go, why people have cycles, and that all things must eventually come to an end.

No, she did not want to see anything happen to this tree, for every reason Dylan had brought up and for every emotion she had tied to it, but she also didn't want to see it or any other child suffer under the weight of a broken limb or crumbling structure.

It had been many months. As the debate began, her fears, her worries, her doubt and aspirations filled the arena. She hoped her father and grandfather were rooting for them, watching from afar, filling the people with the ability to be open to see both sides, but only time would tell.

Nevaeh's mother was beside herself. As she stood by her daughter's bedside she held back the tears. "She's been asleep for so long." She spoke while holding Benjamin's hand. "How long will she be asleep?"

"I don't know." Benjamin voiced honestly after explaining that her presence was living inside of the Painting. He turned to see his father walking into the room. "Is this how you felt, when I was living in the Painting?"

Gerald nodded. He gave Nevaeh's mother a hug to calm her down. "She's going to be fine." He tried to confirm.

"She missed breakfast."

Gerald understood this mother's worry but he knew in his heart that everything would be fine. He just didn't know how to help her understand.

"Wake her up!"

"She will wake up when she is ready."

The pounding of the gavel on the outdoor podium brought the crowd to attention. The entire town, it seemed, had come out to watch. People had brought chairs and blankets, picnic lunches; it seemed they were here for a show. Some had chosen a side, others were here to judge, while others really didn't care about the outcome one way or another. It was difficult to absorb, but somewhat understandable. If they were unclear of the debate, ambivalent regarding the fate of the tree, or torn whether the child should have even been climbing on it in the first place, they'd all have indecisiveness about them.

Yet, as the moderator of the debate relayed the rules, detailing the necessity for a peaceful assembly and calm from the crowd, Nevaeh was consumed by something else. She could feel the tension building within Dylan. As he paced under his canopy, with his group of advisors encouraging him, his heart began to race. "I can't do this."

"Of course you can. You are the best chance we have to win."

"We have confidence in you."

"You can do this."

But Nevaeh could feel him doubting himself, fearing what was going to come of this, worrying about what others would say, or think or react to his passionate sureness of Geody's existence and the justification of keeping the tree no matter how the family or others feel.

Nevaeh stood by him. She placed her hand on his shoulder, even though he couldn't feel her. She willed her spirit to fill him with the courage he needed to see this through. "You can do this. I believe in you."

Dylan inhaled deeply, filing himself with the determination and tenacity to stand up for what he believed. Then he began with his opening remarks.

The debate was harsh and filled with emotion. The young child had awakened and was doing better, but his injuries were on-going and the testimony from his parents was moving.

The opposing side asked questions like, what would you have done if your son wouldn't have woken up? What if his injuries would have left him in a coma or paralyzed? The tears running down the mother's face as she contemplated the absolute worse was enough to sway any opinion, but Dylan was great.

"But your son woke up didn't he?"

"He did, thanks to Geody."

"Thank Geody." He smiled brilliantly. "In fact, your son's arm will heal soon, and he's expected to make a wonderful recovery, right?"

"That's right. I want to thank everyone for your well-wishes. It means a great deal to our family to know so many people were thinking about our son during this trying time."

"How do you feel about the tree?"

"I…" she paused, not knowing what to say.

"Do you blame the tree for hurting your son?" Dylan carefully inquired.

"I can't blame the tree, it's not like it was malicious in its attempts to hurt my son."

"Do you blame the city for not tearing the tree down, before anyone got hurt?"

"We love that tree. I've grown up with this tree. My husband and I courted under the tree. We picnicked under it. I looked forward to watching my son climb it."

"Even though it was so old and others worried about its longevity?"

"It has stood the test of time. I figured it would be around for my children and grandchildren, and even their grandchildren."

As they took their first break, Nevaeh was proud of Dylan. She looked at the opposing council and noticed them planning their next move. Curiosity got the better of her and she walked over to listen.

"Is our next witness ready?"

"She just arrived."

"Great." He said as he collected his notes.

An elderly lady slowly made her way up to the podium, she walked with a cane and was very shaky on the ground. After she introduced herself, he began with his questions.

"Can you tell everyone what happened to you in regards to this tree?"

"It was my own fault, really. It was dusk, the landscape lights hadn't come on yet and I was running late for my book club. I decided to cut across the square, and I tripped on one of the tree roots that stick up above the ground."

"That's horrible. What happened?"

"I fell. I fractured my hip bone, twisted my ankle, sprained my wrist and broke my nose."

"That's terrible." Council spoke as the crowd murmured. "But this wasn't your fault, you were walking in a protected park. The Mayor himself is responsible for the upkeep of the area, that tree."

"Well yes, he is, but I probably shouldn't have crossed under the tree. It was too dark to see the roots."

"So the lights hadn't come on yet. If they would have, you may have seen the roots?"

"I would have."

"So, tell me. What did the Mayor offer to do for you?"

"Oh, he was so kind! He felt so badly about the accident that he offered to pay for my hip replacement surgery."

"Oh, that is very generous."

"Yes it is. I certainly can't afford it. The medical bills are piling up." She added.

"So our town is out quite a bit of money because of this tree. Money that could have been saved if he would have just taken down the tree in the first place."

"Well, he did make the lights be on full-time so no matter when it starts to get dark, even during a storm, it will always be well-lit under the canopy of the tree."

"And what if the lights go out? What if someone else gets injured?"

"I-I don't know."

"Wouldn't it make more sense to remove the obstruction, the problem? Would you want this to happen to anyone else? Would you want any other person to get injured like you, go through the pain of a fractured hip bone, broken nose and hip replacement surgery?"

"It is quite painful. I wouldn't wish this pain on anyone."

"Yet, the Mayor won't tear down the tree."

As the day ended and everyone went home, Dylan knew he had his work cut out for him. The trial was only beginning, it seemed, and the town was already starting to turn in favor of tearing down the tree.

He had made many valid points today, but so did the other side. Dylan wasn't sure how he was going to sway everyone's opinions. And that's what would need to happen. He'd have to convince everyone not to tear down the tree. That suddenly seemed like an impossible task.

As he made himself ready for bed, Nevaeh heard him ask Geody for help and guidance. She added to his plea and then wondered if her parents were okay. She had been here for many months already. She knew in her world that wasn't very long but she did know that by now, her mother would be concerned. It was probably after lunch now.

CHAPTER 18

Sitting next to her daughter's bedside, she glanced over at the stone cold bowl of soup she brought in and wondered how much longer it would be before Nevaeh woke up. How many meals can she miss before she becomes too weak? When should she call in a doctor?

"I remember, as a teen, I went to bed on a Friday evening and woke up on a Sunday morning." Benjamin's words broke the silence. "Yes, I was hungry, but I was fine. Sometimes a little extra sleep is a good thing."

"Yes, but she's not JUST sleeping, is she?" She took her daughter's limp hand into her own. "What is she going through? What is she experiencing? I know you told me about how you lived in the Painting, but I never thought our daughter could get trapped there."

"She's not trapped, she is choosing to stay, to see this through." Gerald spoke up as he walked back into the room. "There is quite a debate going on in this little town. A moral dilemma, and my granddaughter is on the front lines, willing everyone to have heart, to listen and care and give everyone a chance to be heard. It's beautiful."

"But she's alone."

"She's not alone, we're with her in heart."

"She's alone in a huge world, surrounded by strangers who are in conflict." Nevaeh's mom added. "Conflict that can turn into a dangerous battle if the emotions get too high."

"She is perfectly safe," Benjamin added, "she can't be hurt by anyone. They can't see her, hear her, touch her..."

"So she has no one to talk to, to comfort her, to guide her or help her understand what is happening."

"She's a smart young girl." Gerald declared.

"She's a Young girl."

It had been over a week and the debate was getting more heated. They were no closer to a resolution that when they first started.

Since so many stories had been brought to light, the emotions were even more conflicted than before. The other team had made their cases, plural, for the destruction of the tree, and while Dylan had done his best to counter each one of their claims, his dilemma was the fact that saving the tree was more for historical and emotional purposes.

The town was divided. As each day progressed, it seemed to become worse. The division was pulling apart friends, families, co-workers. Anger was building and fears were growing. A team of people had begun round-the-clock vigils at the tree, in order to protect it from groups of people intent on destroying it.

Nevaeh kept trying to calm everyone down, it was her desire to help, to keep the peace, but it wasn't working. She believed harder, felt stronger, desired with everything she had in her and it seemed her spirit was failing. Maybe it was because she was hungry?

But she couldn't wake up now. If she was gone for just an hour to wake up, eat and come back, more than two weeks would have passed. This whole thing could have gotten so out of hand in that time, a war could have broken out. Nevaeh felt the only thing keeping the people's emotions at check, the only thing helping to maintain order, was her desire. When she felt someone's rage increase too much, she'd go to them, fill them with love, desire that they understood and not retaliate.

But she was growing tired. Weak. She was at it constantly, day and night. Even when most were asleep there were some who wanted to take things into their own hands. Trouble-makers who wanted to vandalize, to tear down the tree. Even with the threat of jail time looming overhead, they just wanted this to end. As did Nevaeh. As did Dylan. But if they gave up, who'd be left to fight for this tree?

As dinner time approached, the tears began to flow down her mother's cheeks. Both Nevaeh's mother as well as her grandmother, Tiffany, sat quietly by her bedside. "She looks so weak, so frail." Nevaeh's mother spoke softly.

"Come," Tiffany spoke, standing up from her chair. She offered her daughter-in-law a hand and led her from her granddaughter's room. She glanced back at her husband, Gerald, knowing very well how this felt. She too went through it with her own son, Benjamin. She watched her son sleep for almost a month, and while she tried not to worry, she did.

Sure Gerald had told her Benjamin would be fine, that he would return unharmed, and he did. There were no physical injuries to him and she was grateful for that. Miraculously, his body had survived without nourishment, but then again, Gerald did have this amazing ability, an enchantment to do things, that no one could truly comprehend.

However, a mother not only looks at the physical ailments of her child, she also sees the emotional conflictions. She knew what Benjamin had been through while he was in the Painting. She stayed with him after he returned, she assisted him as he worked through his inner conflicts, his emotions and strife.

Benjamin suffered for years with a feeling of betrayal and distrust. He had been so good and kind, so thoughtful and giving to Gerald's world, and he was hurt by them. He realized in the end why. He understood how his suffering helped others, how it began the healing, but it didn't necessarily help him.

Knowing all of the good he did, the reinforcement of the Painter's plan, he grasped hold of that tightly, but the brain and the heart are two separate things. His heart hurt. And it was his mom, Tiffany, that saw the change in her son after he came back.

As Tiffany and Nevaeh's mom sat down in the living room she attempted to take their minds off of the situation at hand.

"Benjamin used to tell me about the Painting and his friends and adventures. I think one of the hardest things for him to talk about, with me were his parents, the people who raised him and took care of him for so long inside."

Nevaeh's mom listened to Tiffany as she talked, watching her as she shifted in her seat and clasped her hands together.

"I don't think he wanted to hurt my feelings by admitting how much he loved them, but I was so grateful they were there to care for him, to look out after him."

"But my daughter doesn't have that. She can't talk to anyone."

"She is a part of their lives. She may not be able to interact, but they can feel her presence and she can feel their hopes. She is a part of something so much bigger than we can comprehend. She is lucky." Tiffany smiled.

"Lucky? Have you ever been ignored? Completely forgotten about? Have you ever talked and no one heard you? Have you ever needed something and no one knew to help?"

"I have." Gerald spoke as he walked into the room. "As a child I was isolated, lonely. I was misunderstood and ignored. When I wasn't being ignored, or feeling shame and disappointment, I was being bullied by those bigger than I. I wanted nothing more than to escape, to be anywhere else, and that's when I discovered something very important. In the absence of connection, love and belonging, there is always suffering. I didn't want that to be the case any longer. I wanted to create a world of possibilities, filled with my love.

I loved this world, even when it didn't love me. I wanted so much to provide a place that could overflow with my love, that could overlay hurt and fears, and fill everyone with hope and dreams. I wanted to create a place where I and everyone who felt like me, could be included, could learn and could be filled.

My loneliness and my heartache created a world full of possibilities. It gave me an incredible power and that is what I gave my son, and my granddaughter. They have the power to enact change, the potential to transform lives, to change futures and to see and feel and hear and experience this massive potential.

I understand your worry, your fear, but understand that a few missed meals was nothing in the grand scheme of things. Conversation is not the only form of communication. Love can be given in more ways than a hug, and your daughter, my granddaughter, has a power, the spirit, to bind a whole planet together for the good of it."

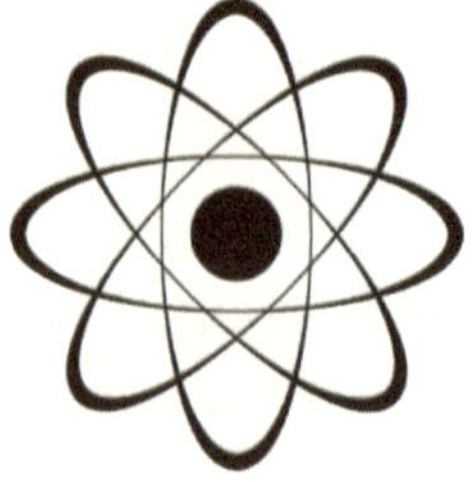

Chapter 19

As the storm clouds rolled in, no one noticed. The emotions were building, so strong, everything was about to burst. People were filled with anger and despair. Squirrels were more agitated, birds had flown away, wolves were howling in the distance, and the wind was picking up, whipping through the town like a rushing bull, charging at its captor.

Nevaeh was crying.

She was going from person to person, helping to smooth things over, willing them to understand, to not take things into their own hands, to not make a decision that would hurt others – but she knew – something had to give. She was standing in a minefield of emotion and the bombs were about to burst.

"People, you are friends, neighbors. You don't want to do this."

A thunder clap startled a child but his parents didn't notice. Lightning off in the distance was blocked by protestors' signs. The people were coming, gathering from every corner of town, culminating in the town square, surrounding the tree.

"Please, everyone. Please don't do this."

Officers and city officials were trying to hold back the angry protestors. Dylan's people were pleading with the people, yelling through a bull horn, beseeching those who would listen to be civil.

"Please hear him. Please calm down."

Nevaeh climbed the tree. She stood at the top of it. She saw the storm rolling in, heard the wind swishing around her, trying to knock her down, trying to defeat her. The thunder rattled her ribcage. The lightning lit up her eyes. The rain was starting and yet, the people kept coming. They were all so angry, ready to fight.

She only had mere moments before they all clashed. Her fears built within her. What was she going to do? How was she going to stop them? They couldn't even hear her! Her desire was peace, it flowed out of her with so much force it drained her of every bit of energy she had and still she persisted.

Someone pulled out an axe. She heard a chainsaw roar to life. She heard a scream.

The chanting and yelling and begging and pleading rose above her into the sky like a flood of hate that was drowning her. Her emotions were piercing her heart, her desire to end this kept growing and growing until it burst from her soul like an explosion in the night. Stomping her foot down with as much force as a child having a terrible temper tantrum she yelled at the top of her voice.

"STOP IT!!!"

At that exact moment a lightning bolt struck the center of the tree. The surge of electricity shot through the limbs and out through the sides. A large crashing sound built into a roaring disturbance that deafened the crowd. And as all turned to see, to acknowledge what was coming, they discovered a terrifying sight. It was too late – the tornado had touched down and it was heading right towards them.

Screams arose as the crowd panicked. Pandemonium filled the streets. The wind was pushing people over, into other people who were losing their footing, feeling as if they were being sucked up, being pulled away. The crowd clamored as confusion filled them.

Dylan barked into the bullhorn, "Get to the school! Help everyone get to the school."

Larger fellows grabbed the arms of smaller fellows, enemies they had been yelling at mere moments ago were now their top priority. They pulled each other close, protected strangers, and they all ran, together, towards the school.

Some people wanted to run the other way, towards their homes or their businesses, but they couldn't. Vehicles were being lifted into the sky and slammed down on the ground in front of them, forcing them to lurch, skid to a stop and turn away. Wind gusts veered around buildings, knocking people backwards, breaking apart fences and throwing the wood fence posts and planks at the crowd. Loose debris rocketed through the air like projectiles, herding the people like cattle, directing them away from the approaching tornado.

People helped people. They offered their hands, they pulled them to safety, they shielded the young with their own bodies. As the tornado closed in, Dylan and his team made sure everyone made it inside of the school. They pulled the doors closed. They held the doors, feeling like they were being pulled out towards the suction of the tornado, they hollered as their feet skid to the threshold, "I can't hold it!" Other larger men ran to the door. They grabbed part of the horizontal handles and pulled with all of their might. They worked together, opposite sides of the fight, coming together for a common good – survival.

Those who were yelling just a few moments ago, ready to start a war, reached for Dylan and pulled him backwards, helping to keep the doors closed. They came together to save each other, to save everyone. Enemies found comfort in each other, they held each other, protected each other.

The roar of the tornado barreled down around them. The air seemed to be sucked from within the gymnasium, women and children were crying, men began pleading for mercy. A child's voice cried out, "Help us, Geody." The words filled everyone's hearts, they all felt it. They all claimed it. "Geody, have mercy." Their hearts were pounding in their chests, the pressure was pounding in their eardrums, their will was strong and combined.

A barrage of hail began clashing against the building. Windows shattered as rain entered the room.

The people's fears merged into one. Their desires to survive, to live another day, blended into one massive request: "Geody, save us!"

Nevaeh had been watching the tornado barrel its way down the street towards the school. She had witnessed the people come together, to help each other. She watched as they all entered the school – the same place she had first met them when she arrived. She felt their faith growing as they helped each other, huddled together and pleaded for salvation.

Nevaeh felt that their desire to survive, all of them, together, was strong. She too desired that the tornado would cease, would relinquish its grip on the school and lift away, and at that exact moment – it did.

As quickly as it had begun, the tornado disappeared. The wind stopped. The debris that was spiraling around in the air, dropped to the ground. The clouds parted and a small ray of light shone down through the dark grey sky and in through the broken window of the school.

The huddled masses slowly looked up from their clusters. They saw the light, the clearing sky. They heard the silence and hesitantly, began to feel that it was safe. They checked on each other. They assisted those that had been injured. They helped the unsteady and weary to their feet, and they walked together, outside, hand-in-hand.

They were quiet.

They slowly made their way down the street, taking in the damage, benches thrown through windows, fence planks sticking out of walls like shot arrows, debris and tree limbs scattered all over the ground. That's when they saw it – the tree.

Or what was left of it.

CHAPTER 20

As the clouds cleared and the sun shined down on the destruction throughout town, the people surveyed the damage. They all walked up to the tree, the topic of such heated debates and confrontations for so many weeks, and as they gazed upon it, they cried.

The tree had been split down the middle. Its weak, heavy limbs, what was left of them, held up one side of the massive trunk.

Dozens of limbs had been snapped from it, yanked away and discarded throughout town like crumpled up trash. Leaves had been plucked from it, leaving so much of it bare, naked, weak looking. What had they done?

This once proud tree, that towered over their town, that symbolized life and love and the determination of Geody to provide for them, had been mangled and destroyed.

The people were heartbroken, ashamed. They held each other and cried. They were happy to have survived, grateful to still be a part of each other's lives, and yet saddened beyond anything they could have ever dreamed.

What had once seemed so important became anything but. Their family, their friends, neighbors – that's what was important. They had spent so much time and hate attacking each other over this tree, hurting each other's feelings, destroying friendships, for what?

They had forgotten how important the people were. Each of them had been out for themselves, their beliefs, their wants and desires. They didn't care what anyone else wanted or said, they refused to listen, to compromise, to try to get along. This tree that was supposed to be symbolic of love and beauty had torn apart a town, and a tornado, of such wild, uncontrollable destruction, had opened their eyes in under a few minutes time.

Had this been Geody's plan? An opportunity to disconnect in order to reconnect?

Nevaeh thought about this for some time as she watched the people of the town. They held each other, shook neighbors' hands, people that had been at odds – so angry – so full of venom, now shyly looking small, apologetic. Without saying the words, many people expressed their apologies through their actions. And then, when no other adult knew what to say, a child spoke for them.

"Mommy, I'm hungry."

Those three words lit up the town.

"The electricity is down."

"It'll be back up soon."

"I don't think so, the power lines are down, scattered across a hundred acres."

"I just got off the phone with the electric company – they've been slammed. Everyone has been redirected to the neighboring town to assist in *their* clean-up efforts. They don't think they'll be able to get to us until late tomorrow or even the next day."

The grocery store manager grimaced. "But our perishables, the milk, the meat?"

"The ice cream!" A child from within the crowd called out.

A few people chuckled, but a point had been made. Thousands of dollars of food was going to go bad. It was going to be a big waste.

A check-out clerk offered a creative suggestion, "Maybe it's time to throw a party. We survived a tornado. We should celebrate – say, with a bar-be-que?"

"Food and fellowship!" An older lady's voice lifted from within the gathering and a few others joined in cheerfully.

"How will we cook it?"

"I've got a grill." One of the men spoke up.

"I've got a camping stove."

"Me too." Other deep voices bellowed back.

"Okay, so we'll gather the perishables and bring them out here. If anyone needs ice to stock their freezers, come and get it while it's still frozen."

"Everyone who can assist, grab your coolers and head down to the grocery store to help. The rest of you go gather anything you have that you can donate to a town festival. We'll need tables, plates and utensils..."

"The church has a bunch of folding tables and chairs, we can set up a picnic area out here with them... by the tree."

The town all stopped their planning upon being reminded of the tree. They turned to look at what was left. They took in the destruction. Limbs had been ripped from the trunk. Leaves sprayed across the entire field. It looked bare. But worse yet was the lightning damage. The grand trunk, as thick as three people trying to hug it, had been chopped down the middle. It looked as if it had been pried apart by a clamp, and the insides were charred black. It was actually still smoking just a tad.

As they stared at what remained of the tree, a dead tree with broken limbs and a fractured body, they also remembered Benjamin and how his body had been fractured. They remembered the stories he told about the tree, his father's plan for the world. They were reminded of its promise, the hope they all felt when they had grown up around it.

The sadness began to take over, to consume them. A morbid silence took over the crowd – they shared a moment of silence.

Wow! Nevaeh thought to herself as she observed the people. She felt a tear fill her eye and escape down her cheek. It fell onto the trunk of the tree and splattered on the dark, charred debris.

Then just as suddenly as the quiet hushed them, they were back to planning and scattered to take care of their tasks. Within less than an hour there were over two dozen grills sizzling and smoking. There were hotdogs and hamburgers, grilled chicken, fish and even steak sizzling from all corners of the town square.

There were men, women and children fast at work collecting debris, chain-sawing broken limbs, raking leaves and cleaning up.

Over fifty tables were brought in. Hundreds of chairs and even more coolers were scattered across the grounds. Some of the mothers brought yard games to keep the younger children occupied. Musicians brought their instruments. They set up a makeshift stage across the street to provide a fun musical ambiance. Couples danced. Children laughed.

The people of the town had all come together, in the most miraculous way.

As the sun began to set, ingenuity continued, many people parked their vehicles around the square and flipped on their headlights. The local scouts built a campfire and used the trees downed branches as kindling to keep it going.

Some of the children started talking about making this into a campout. Next thing you knew tents were brought out and setup. Sleeping bags appeared. As many of the children fell asleep, the majority of the adults stayed up talking and socializing throughout the night. The people of the town hadn't done anything like this in decades.

As the morning sun began to rise over the hilltops, the grocery employees brought out the eggs, sausage and bacon. Breakfast aromas wafted into the children's noses, and they awoke from their slumber with giggles and joy.

Milk and orange juice flowed into glasses and cups of coffee were poured. When it seemed most everyone had a cup in their hand, the pastor of the church clanked his glass. As the crowd hushed, glasses were raised to neighbors, to friends and to loved ones. The Pastor cleared his throat and then took a deep breath. When he spoke, everybody heard him.

"Friends, neighbors, townsfolk, join me as we lift our cups to the sky. A sky that was painted for us by the great

Painter Geody. A sky that brings sunshine to warm us, light to guide our way, and a cool breeze on a hot summer's day. The same sky that brings rain that promotes growth and quenches our thirst, also brought the tornado – that brought us together.

We were down. We had knocked each other over with our words and actions. We had nowhere else to go but up – but we couldn't see it. So what happens when life knocks you over? When you're lying on your back, down and out – lost without a way? You look up! Look up to the sky and then find a way to touch it - get up and keep moving forward.

The Painter has given you everything you could ever need to succeed. He's given each of us the tools we require to help those around us. He's given us the knowledge and the common sense to see somebody's hardships, the compassion to acknowledge what they seek, and the love in our heart to assist those who lack. It is us, individually, who choose not to let that happen.

Just remember, you count. You have worth. You have been given the ability to enact change because each of you are significant in Geody's eyes. In each of your hearts, is a desire; a desire to do good. It is one of the most powerful tools you will ever have. It's the engine that ignites our will; the will to make good choices, to do good. We each have to make the decision to open our hearts to the needs of others, to use our judgement to find alternatives, compromises, and work with our fellow man.

We may not understand *why* things happen the way they do. We may not understand *how* things work out. But we all can find ways to understand *who* is in charge. We are no more in control of our lives than a tree is in control of the weather. We are solely dependent upon a higher power, upon each other, upon any number of variables that dictate what is going to happen in our lives.

We have to believe in ourselves. We have to work together to benefit each other as well as mankind. We have to work on it, to focus on our dreams, on our goals. Look at what we accomplished in one short night!

We got it done. We pulled together as a community. We looked out for one another, we shared time and music and food with our fellow man. We broke bread together. We proved to each other that silly arguments, conflicts, and disagreements, can't truly separate us from ourselves unless we let them. We can do anything we put our minds to, if we all work together.

Resolve, right now to keep moving forward, to keep working with one another. Let us establish a covenant of friendship and togetherness by doing FOR others. This is your moment - right here, right now, to appreciate what we have, to welcome our neighbors into our hearts and to thank Geody for the gifts he has bestowed upon us.

Thank you, Geody, for sparing our lives. Thank you for showing us the error in our ways. Thank you for bringing us back together again. Thank you for our friends and family and neighbors and community. Thank you for always showing us the way of good. We appreciate you!"

Chapter 21

The townsfolk cheered, they applauded the pastors speech and they hugged one another. They were happy, satisfied, wanting nothing because they felt complete. And as those feelings washed over a very satisfied Nevaeh, the rumble of trucks rolled into town.

"It's the electric company!"

With the knowledge that the town would be fine, that the people had come together - the hopes for a better future exploding within her heart. Nevaeh decided it was finally time to go home.

When she awoke, she saw that she was surrounded by all of her loved ones. Her Mom and Dad, her Grandparents, they were all sitting by her bedside.

"She's awake!" Gerald proclaimed joyously as Nevaeh slowly started to sit up.

Her mother pulled her into a great big hug as Benjamin hugged his own mother, Tiffany.

"We were so worried about you! You've been asleep for days!" Her mother cried.

"I'm okay Mom. Promise."

"I wasn't sure you'd ever wake up again."

Benjamin glanced over at Gerald who glanced over at Tiffany. They had all been through this, in one way or another.

"Mom, it was wonderful. Horrible and then wonderful." Nevaeh began as she turned to her grandfather to continue explaining.

"They were all so angry, arguing, fighting one another. I wasn't sure how to fix it, if I *could* fix it. It kept getting worse and worse until a storm began to build. The wind picked up and the clouds rushed in and they grew thick and dark. There was such vivid lightning and the thunder was so loud. And all it did was make the already angry townspeople angrier. They grew louder and more vicious, it was breaking my heart. I could see what it was doing to the children. I could feel the hate seething through their veins. I couldn't stand it any longer and I screamed for it all to stop."

"And did it?" Benjamin inquired.

"No!" Nevaeh sat up straight and looked at her father. "A wind storm, a violent funnel-shaped whirlwind poked down through the clouds, touched the ground and began tearing apart the town! It seemed to herd the people together, directing them into one direction. They all ran to safety, huddled up together in a nearby building and they were so afraid. I could feel their fear. It was over-powering, but it was also unifying. It was the first time in weeks that everyone was thinking and feeling the same thing. And do you know what happened when I felt that? When I felt their combined pleas for survival and safety?"

"What?" Her mother asked as she sat on the edge of her seat.

"The tornado dissipated. It dropped all of the debris it had collected and had been throwing around the town, and it just dropped it. It disappeared as fast as it had arrived. And in its wake, it left destruction. It destroyed the thing that had been the cause of all of their conflict, and when they saw what happened they all grieved for it.

"What was it that was causing so much conflict?" Nevaeh's mother inquired.

"Dad's tree."

Benjamin glanced at his daughter. "My tree? What tree?"

"The tree you taught your first lesson on. Your friends, spoke of that first lesson so much, to so many people. They shared the knowledge you gave them about Grampa's grand plan and the town saved that tree. For so long that tree stood and grew. Its limbs were so heavy, it tired of holding them up and when a small child tried climbing those limbs, they collapsed and the child got badly hurt."

"That's horrible." Nevaeh's mother voiced. "Did they cut the tree down?"

"That was the debate. Whether they should or not. The town was divided, half wanted it cut down, half wanted it saved. No one could agree so the tornado made the decision for them."

Nevaeh's head lowered. "What's wrong sweetheart?" Benjamin asked.

"The tree seemed so important. It was a visual representation that my father had been there. So many people shared fond memories of it, looked forward to seeing it, and now they won't be able to. It's so sad."

"What do you mean they won't be able to see it?" Gerald inquired coyly.

"The tornado destroyed it."

"There's nothing left of it at all?"

"Well," she thought, "Most of the limbs had broken off. It had been split down the middle of the trunk by a lightning bolt. Surely they wouldn't keep it in that condition... right? Wouldn't it be dangerous to keep it like that?"

"The people of my Painting can be quite the visionaries when inspiration hits them. Their artistic creativity is enough to marvel the most imaginative mind." Gerald spoke as he stood from his chair. He reached his hand to Nevaeh's hand. As she took his hand, he led her out the door downstairs. "Let me tell you about some of the stories while you have yourself a nice meal."

"I *am* hungry!" Nevaeh rubbed her belly with her free hand. "How long was I asleep?"

CHAPTER 22

That night Nevaeh couldn't sleep. Of course, she had had plenty of sleep recently to last a while. Still, she stayed up all night listening to stories from her father and grandfather. She truly understood how things worked in the Painting now, and she marveled at how much could change in such a short period of time.

As Benjamin would share stories of life one day at a time, Gerald would share stories of life one call at a time. Nevaeh, however, described the world one moment at a time. Each perspective was distinct and fascinating, but they were each separate. Each viewpoint was expressed in relation to how the other experienced it and Nevaeh realized how neat it would be if they could each share this experience together.

"Wouldn't it be cool if Grampa could see what you saw Daddy, from your perspective from the ground?"

"It would..." Benjamin acknowledged, "and wouldn't it be neat if we could soar through the universe like you had done and see all of your watercolor nebulas up close?"

"It would..." Gerald answered, then turned to Nevaeh "and wouldn't it be nice to feel the whiskers of a soft bunny tickle your nose?"

"Yeah!" Nevaeh agreed with delight. "Can we? Can we?"

"Nyos" Nevaeh heard both men speak alternate letters together.

With confusion, she asked, "Which is it? No or yes?"

"No." Benjamin spoke.

"Yes." Gerald clarified.

Benjamin and Nevaeh both looked at Gerald with wonder. "Yes?"

"Of course." He smiled. "I painted it. You, Benjamin, were born into it, and you gave Nevaeh the gift of visiting it. Of course we can all go there."

"I don't understand, Dad. How? You've never been able to visit it, not since you put the Painting inside of the Universe."

"Nevaeh can take us inside, and you can help us become a part of it."

"How?"

Gerald shook his head with a smile.

After a bit of explanation, which still didn't seem at all feasible, they accepted the possibility. Gerald was so certain as he explained, how could they possibly disagree? The three of them looked at each other with Cheshire smiles on their faces. Nevaeh was eager to show them everything she had seen. Benjamin was curious beyond compare and Gerald was just smiling from ear to ear.

"Will it be safe?" Benjamin inquired.

"I won't let anything happen to her," Gerald placed his palm on his son's shoulder, "or you."

Benjamin felt butterflies swarming in his stomach. He was nervous and excited. He trusted his father more than anything and he loved his daughter more than that. How could he not be worried? But also, how could he not want to go back and share this with his daughter?

This would be the experience of a lifetime.

"When?"

"What better time than the present?" Gerald stood and held out his hands.

So, the three of them stood side by side in front of the universe painting. Standing in the middle, Benjamin took his father's right hand and Nevaeh's left hand and closed his eyes. He thought fondly of the Painting, the world he had loved so much for so long, returning there, being a part of it again. When he heard Nevaeh's shriek of excitement he opened his eyes to see a sight he had never seen before.

"This is the universe Painting!" Nevaeh beamed brightly as she pointed with her free hand at the colorful clouds of watercolor paint she had added to it. "Aren't they beautiful?"

Benjamin marveled at the stars, at the size of the planets, at the nebulas and at the sun. They were shooting through the universe, speeding by so many marvelous sights that he had only seen from an extreme distance spiraling around his father's canvas.

Nevaeh was leading the way. She had seen all of this before, spent weeks observing it, exploring it. She was in a rush to get to her Grampa's world and while disappointed that he wouldn't get to truly spend the time he wanted exploring here, Benjamin was excitedly filled with the knowledge that he could come back any time he wanted.

"Over here!" Nevaeh squealed as she led her father and grandfather towards the most marvelous Painting in all of creation.

As they flew closer to the planet Benjamin heard the sounds of the world. An eruption of noise pierced his ears and he tried to slow them down. The pain was evident on his crinkled face and Nevaeh saw this.

"It's okay, Daddy. The closer we get to town the quieter the rest of the world becomes."

Nevaeh pulled her family through the stratosphere and rushed them through fluffy white clouds. Clouds that Benjamin had only ever seen from the ground – so far away, he was never able to touch them, only dream about.

Watching them pass by, Benjamin looked down at the world, at mountains he had spent days climbing, feeling exhausted at the end of the day. They were flying over them like they were minute drops of paint. They looked so different from this viewpoint. From this angle, looking down at the world was a phenomenon that he had never even dreamed of doing. He knew his father had painted the world, *He* had seen it, but Benjamin never got to see the Painting from his father's perspective. It had long been secured within the universe when Benjamin came along, and growing up within the Painting, was so much different than this experience.

"Do you know where you are going?" Gerald asked Nevaeh, who was leading the charge past cities, prairies, rivers and deserts.

"Of course! It's just past the ocean." Nevaeh giggled as she turned to her dad and caught his eyes. "Remind me to take you there, Daddy. It's so much more than you could ever imagine!" She recalled his stories about fishing and swimming but not being able to hold his breath too long.

As they landed in the town square Nevaeh's eyes beamed with delight as she stared at the scene in front of her. Her father, however, was looking all around at the town. He kind of recognized some things, the buildings surrounding the square were similar, but the businesses had changed. Facades and designs of the architecture had updated the look, but some of the framework was similar.

Gerald watched his son and grand-daughter stare at his world in amazement. He heard the birds singing. He felt the wind sweep across his cheeks. He smelled the aroma of the flowers… he felt Nevaeh pull from his hands and race across the street.

Benjamin felt her pull from his hand and he spun his attention to her quickly. She was racing across the street, in the direct path of an oncoming car. "Nevaeh!" he raced to her, sweeping her up into his arms and landing on the opposite side of the street.

"What did you do that for Daddy?"

"You aren't here in spirit today. You are here for real. You can really get hurt if you aren't careful."

"I'm so sorry!" The driver spoke, as he stood out of his vehicle. "She came out of nowhere."

"She's okay. Thanks!" Benjamin voiced back as Gerald made his way across the street to join them.

Benjamin helped Nevaeh back to her feet, and she immediately went to what had attracted her attention initially. "They made benches out of some of the downed tree limbs."

"Those are gorgeous." Gerald smiled.

"Look over here, they've carved animals into these." Nevaeh pointed at them.

"And scenes." Gerald added seeing two baby bear heads poking out of a cave with a momma bear standing watch over them outside. He loved how much time was obviously spent carving these scenes.

Benjamin noticed one that looked like a basket full of food, and a scene of a fishing boat on the water. "Such craftsmanship."

"This one has words carved into it and a design that looks like a paintbrush and palette."

Benjamin and Gerald followed Nevaeh as she scoured the grounds admiring all of the carved artwork.

"Tourists?" Someone spoke, as they walked up to the three. Benjamin looked over at the man surprisingly. "We get a lot of tourists these days – come to see the new tree and the saved artwork."

"What saved artwork?" Gerald asked.

"The carvings of initials and hearts and memories that had been collected on the trunk of the tree over the generations. One of our local artisans carefully carved each off the trunk and made them into decorative pieces of historical artwork that can be seen hanging on the walls of our businesses along the square."

"What a wonderful idea." Gerald smiled.

"New tree?" Nevaeh inquired, wanting to continue exploring but being held there by her father who was holding her hand.

"Not long after the great storm that struck down the tree and brought the townsfolk back together again, one of the local groundskeepers noticed new growth sprouting from the center of the destruction." The nice man led the three to the center of the square and pointed at it.

"A bolt of lightning split that massive trunk right down the middle and burned the center leaving only the outer shell of the tree. Little did we know, that shell provided protection and safety for the new sprout to grow and prosper. So, as you can see, we have a new sapling, the starts of the old tree bringing life to a new tree from within itself."

"It looks like two hands holding it." Nevaeh admired as she noticed how the artisan, after saving the carvings, had carved the remainder of the old trunk into what looked like two large old hands carefully cupped around the new tree sapling.

Benjamin noticed a plaque and leaned in to read it aloud. "The hands of the Painter protecting his children."

Gerald beamed, "What a beautiful representation of old life giving new life."

"It is," the friendly man agreed. They all looked at the tree for a moment and then the man spoke. "I'm Dylan."

Nevaeh's head turned quickly to see the man closer as Benjamin spoke. "I'm Benjamin, this is my father, Gerald."

"Hi," Gerald spoke as he shook Dylan's hand. "This is my son, Benjamin and that spirited young girl is my granddaughter, Nevaeh." Dylan kneeled down to introduce himself to Nevaeh at her level when she ran to him and give him a big hug. Startled, he looked at Gerald and Benjamin in wonder.

Benjamin kneeled down before Nevaeh and spoke, "Do you know Dylan?"

"Dylan is the one who stood up for...." Nevaeh slowed seeing an odd concerning look in her father's eyes. "The big debate... to save the tree? He was the one who led the side to save it."

"Wow! You know your history." He spoke proudly to the young girl. "But there are plenty of people in this world named Dylan..."

"But only one I know who felt so strongly about preserving the past."

Realizing this was the man Nevaeh had followed for months, Benjamin felt even more fascinated. He reached for and shook Dylan's hand again. "Sir, it is an honor to meet the man who stood so strongly to save the tree."

"I had a huge team to help - it wasn't just me." Dylan's cheeks flushed. He knew the story had stretched across the land, but it had been a couple years since someone recognized him as *the* Dylan from the stories.

Over the course of the day Nevaeh showed her father her favorite places in town. Some of them had already changed and her disappointment was apparent but Gerald didn't allow her to stay sad for long.

"Change is important. Growth is key. This world was designed to keep spinning. Motion, advancement, it's the dynamic I painted. I don't want the world to get complacent, to forget. I want them to appreciate this Painting, to explore it, to love it. To see everything..."

"Trust me Dad, that is not easy!" Benjamin spoke. I lived here for over 30 years and hardly scratched the surface."

"Exactly," Gerald added as the three of them walked down the beach. "It's impossible for a single human to experience everything the Painting has to offer – that's why there are so many humans. I gave every single one of them a gift, the gift of creativity. They each have their own unique imagination, a resourcefulness and a drive.

There are musicians who share the sounds and rhythms of the world, and artists who paint or photograph the landscapes we can't go see in person. There are the writers who detail the stories and describe scenarios that other-wise would never have been considered. There are people with disabilities who show us how to appreciate ourselves in all of our strengths or limitations. There are those with little who demonstrate appreciation, and those with more who offer giving. There are people with large families and those with none and so much more.

When I painted this world I focused all of my energy on its beauty, on the nature and plants, the environment and weather. I made sure everything worked in collaboration – even if from the human perspective it seemed like chaos. Storms brought rain for growth, fires provided a clearing for space, and earthquakes designed to shake things up to curb complacency. Everything had a reason, and so do the people.

Every person has a reason to be here - whether it be big or small. Each individual has their own part to play, their own story to live out, their own impact to make. Like ripples in the water, every human's story matters, they are all integral to the grand design. Even when they are no longer visible in this Painting their memories live on, their adventures continue, and they become a legend."

"Wow." Nevaeh expressed as she looked up at her dad to see him nodding his head in understanding, "Grampa, you're amazing!"

Gerald blushed. The three of them were silent as they continued their stroll out onto the pier. As the morning sun began to rise over the shimmering waters of the ocean it reflected the extreme colors in the sky. The pink, red and orange hues faded up into the dark blue as if the night had been a shadow and the universe was being washed away to create a new canvas of possibility.

Nevaeh watched a dolphin leap up out of the water and dive back in, then another. "Can we go see them?"

Benjamin's thoughts went back to his human limitations, that he couldn't hold his breath long underwater, that his arms tired of swimming after a while.

"When we are here on the Painting we can do anything we can imagine," Gerald conveyed, knowing what Benjamin was thinking. "Let's go swim with the dolphins."

"Yeah!" Nevaeh jumped up and down clapping. "And then, Daddy, I can show you the depths you never got to see before."

"That would be wonderful." Benjamin smiled in delight at his spirited young daughter.

"I can't wait to show you how I got to see the world. I'm going to teach you so much!"

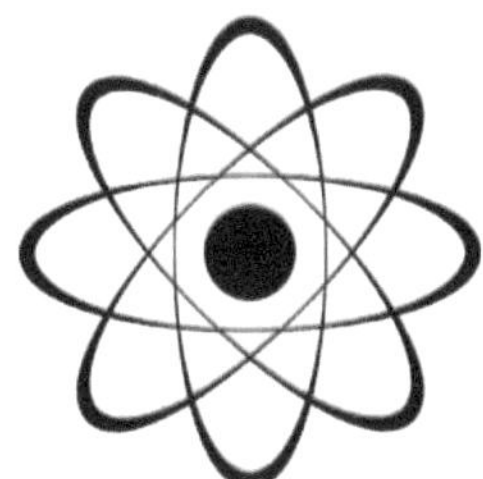

John 14:26 *But the advocate, The Holy Spirit, whom the Father will send in my name,*
will teach you all things and will remind you of everything I have said to you.

Who am I to write this story?

At the end of each book, this question was posed to me during prayer and I took the time to write down my answers. The first book, before there was even a dream of the next two books, it felt like a fitting tribute.

When the second book was complete, that question came back to me and my first thought was, nah, I don't need to answer that again, it's probably the same answer. But as I thought about it, I realized – I needed to write an answer. It shocked me how different the response was to the same question.

So when the third and final book was complete, I looked forward to answering the same question again – just so I could see what the answer would be. I even started my response with a "let's see how this goes" feeling. I was again pleasantly surprised with my response.

Writing is a form therapy. When you write you get to work things out. Scenes, reactions, situations from your life, they make their way into the book. There's a joke that is something to the effect of: *Don't upset a writer, you'll become a character in our next book.* It gets a laugh out of the writing community. But the fact of the matter is, it works a lot like prayer. As your life changes, your prayers change. Your perspective on each circumstance changes. Things from a couple years ago don't seem nearly as important or dire as things you are dealing with now.

You grow as a person, your understanding about life is altered. It's your reactions that make you the person He wants you to become. It was quite a neat endeavor to see how far I had come over the course of the past six years. A lot had happened. I changed as a person because of what had happened. Sometimes I remember how I didn't like who I had become, or how I missed the old me. Now I look back and realize – it wasn't the old me I was missing, it was the new me I didn't recognize.

Who was I to write these stories?

Just someone who listened and was willing to hear.

The Painting

Who am I to write this story?

That's the question I kept asking God for about a month after the idea came to me. During my discovery of the story's plot, formulation of the characters and outline creation, I felt I couldn't possibly be the best fit for this project.

This story idea came to me during a fairly low time in my life. I was lonely. I was annoyed and frustrated with the people of this world. The question of "What if God never painted the humans?" felt rather fitting. I was perfectly okay with letting the question hang there. However, there was a small nagging part of me that insisted it not be left unanswered and unexplored. My guess is that God was prodding me on. For the life of me, I couldn't figure out how I was supposed to direct this story out of this emotional situation.

So I asked friends, many friends, with many life outlooks and experiences, what they thought. An older grandmother of a rather large family, who seems to never be alone, was certain the character in the story needed to find love and have a family to share his life; to even become a father to understand God's love for us.

A wonderful yet sometimes truthfully harsh woman felt there was a need for devastating circumstances to change the perspective of the story. A direct loneliness would push him towards the search for companionship. It seemed feasible. It took a drastic, life-altering situation in my own life that helped me find God, so why not?

A rather, *in my opinion*, lonely young man loved the idea of leaving the question hanging as he too probably at times feels exactly like the main character… and while I, at the time, was right there with him, I knew in the back of my mind that the story needed to find a way to show God's love.

I was led to believe this child didn't need to become an adult before he understood. I truly felt that a plot of dire circumstances was an excellent way of bringing about the change, but I didn't want it to feel like it always has to be that way. So often, a devastating situation can place a fork in the road that can either lead a person closer to or further away from God. I didn't want this story to even hint of a possible fork.

If I were to write what I felt needed to be written, it would be a dark enough story as it was. So, since my pastor was busy with pastoral responsibilities and opportunities - digging a well in Africa, assisting flood victims, dealing with her own husband's heart attack - I sought answers on my own, through research of the Bible.

However, that research led me down dark alley ways. It brought about confusion and conflict. There were what seemed to be contradictions in the Bible, and that realization opened my thoughts to what the devil wanted – for me to lose focus on what the story truly needed to do.

So finally, I sat down with a pastor-in-training, someone who was just starting her education. I brought her everything I had on my mind; my ideas, my confusion, my questions and my quest. What if God never painted the humans? He loved us so much to create us, but why? And how could I prove it? This was a difficult thing for me to understand. I already had in me the answer 'He made us in his image' and 'He gave His only son,' but I had nothing else. I was searching for scripture that would prove his love. I was searching for examples, illustrations of his love and specifically – for why He started this whole "thing" in the first place.

One friend suggested the song 'Jesus loves me this I know, for the Bible tells me so,' and I smiled, knowing the song well. But then I realized the song was 'Jesus loves me' - I wanted proof of God's love. He gave us Jesus, yes, but that was much, much later. I wanted to know why he created us from the very beginning.

Then, my friends explained it in a way I understood: "because He wanted us to understand love." I've always felt alone. I grew up alone, with few friends. I'm a workaholic who works from home, alone, and then does a show selling books every weekend, surrounded by people, and yet feeling utterly alone. I'm not one to ask for help – so seeking out others' opinions for this story was out of the norm for me.

I realized I was missing the very Christian love that God wanted me to write about. That's what I hadn't understood. He wanted me to learn that humans are His way of showing His love. By making me question my story, I was forced to ask for help. It gave me the opportunity to see what others had experienced of God's love. It showed me that I don't know everything. I learned that He was trying to teach me so I could in turn help teach others.

But then I asked, why me?

I'm not a Bible scholar. I'm new to Christianity. I don't know what He wants me to teach and I'm learning as I go. Who am I to write this? And then my pastor preached that Sunday and said "God uses unlikely people to do his work," and it all made sense. He chose me to write this story, to learn from Him, to teach others about Him and simply to be His witness. What an honor. What a privilege. What a terrifyingly huge task for little ol' me… but what an opportunity!

So that is why I wrote this story. I hope that it helps to open your heart to God as it has mine.

The Painting 2

Who am I to write this story?

I ended the first book with this question and my answer was basically a dissertation of how I listened to God who led me. So now again, I find the need to ask this question. *Why me?* Because I wrote the first book and someone needed to write the second? That doesn't seem like a good enough answer.

I'm not a bible scholar, and recently I've felt out of place at church. I'm close to God, I feel as if ***He*** is my best friend - if you know me, you can understand how important that phrase "best friend" truly is... so the conflicting feeling I was experiencing; that church wasn't where I needed to be, caught me completely off guard.

I feel God everywhere. I look back and know which times in my life he walked with me. I see his signs and hear his messages, because we ALL can, if we try. However, church is the primary place you are supposed to go for God – right? Church is where I met God for the first time in my adult life. Church was the place I felt most at home; it was warm and inviting and filled with the love of a God I was hungry to get to know.

So why was it, these past years, that I was feeling pushed to go somewhere else? And pushed is definitely the correct word. I'd love to say I was being pulled, that God was taking me by the hand and pulling me towards something better - but I can't. He wasn't there in the church for me... and I could feel that emptiness deep down within my soul.

Now, I'm not saying leave your church. If you are happy and you feel His love there, or you are getting the insight and education you need there, then that is exactly where you need to be. It is where I needed to be for so long absorbing his word like a sponge.

What I'm saying is God was my teacher. He educated me, showed me how to love and then sat quietly and watched me as I took the test. My test being, writing this book.

But it wasn't simply sitting at a desk and referring to the Bible. No, my test took me across the country. It introduced me to new people, it reminded me of old. It brought me closer than I could ever dream with someone whom I lost shortly after genuinely getting to know them. And then, I turned the page and realized the test was only going to get harder.

It tested my faith, and made me grow stronger. It showed me that I had that strength within me. That life is not easy, we are meant to work hard, but the rewards are worth it. This test gave me the inspiration to finish this story.

Sometimes God tests us.

Will we take the test he's giving us, or will we walk out of the classroom?

The Painting 3

Who am I to write this story?

I ended the first book with this question and my answer was basically a dissertation of how I listened to God who led me. I ended the second book with this question and discovered that God likes to test you and your faith.

So I will now, end this book with that question for a third time, and what I've come up with is this: to believe is not enough.

I had my own small confrontation with a tornado one week after writing about it in this book. Watching the destruction first hand, how our heavy, sturdy building was pulled apart by the wind. Staring in awe as fragments lifted into the air and danced around like butterflies, weightless and beautiful. It was terrifying to know that even those small sections were too heavy for me to move by myself during clean-up. It's amazing to realize the power and strength of God.

Why did it happen? Oh I know – I was being taught by a higher power, or those lost loved ones above were looking out for me. It could have been worse – they simply brought to my attention things that needed to be addressed, and I think that's what this book is intended to do.

Your relationship with the Lord may be strong, you may wholeheartedly believe that, but is it really? I consider Him my best friend. I thought I talked with Him all of the time, but I realized I didn't. I neglected our relationship just as much as I neglected my own friends. The term 'being busy' is not an excuse, it is a way of living, and that is not a good thing.

When you are too busy to talk to friends, or even with God, you are making yourself unavailable. It's a good thing God doesn't get too busy for us. *Believe me when I tell you, there is definitely a plan and we will never know what it is, in life.*

The other thing I have noticed, while doing all of this writing and introspection, is that every new scenario in my life brought about new insight. Two weeks after writing about Nevaeh naming the tadpoles frogs (because that's what they will eventually become) I wrote a blog post with an entirely different insight – God doesn't tell us what we're going to grow up to become because He doesn't want us to think we failed Him.

I honestly don't know where this story came from – I mean – I KNOW – but I didn't plan it. How was it, that my life, my trials, my own uneducated insight brought to life a Painting that inspired so much with so little? How did everything tie together so perfectly, without an outline, strategy or agenda?

How was it that a name came to me out of nowhere, that when abbreviated, spoke volumes. That when sounded out became the entire theme for the next story, whose soul existence opened the door to a spirited story of goodness? How did I write the biography of the Father, Son and Holy Spirit without even writing a rough draft?

To believe is not enough. I believe we are all here for a reason. I believe that bad things are only bad in our eyes, and I believe that if we never give up on God's plan, He'll never give up on us. I also believe that thinking I believe all of that, even saying it out loud, doesn't truly mean I believe it. I don't think our minds are capable of understanding the depth of love God has for us.

I think the best thing we can do, the only thing, is to accept it. To be open to the changes that will come into our lives and look back to find that ah-ha moment.

I cannot even begin to tell you how many times in my life I've looked back after a trial and said, wow, was *that* the plan? How did He know I needed that? It's truly amazing to see how things turn out, but you almost can't ever look back right away and see the reason, that comes later – when you least expect it.

You just have to be open enough to see it when He presents it to you.

You just have to trust and believe.

Acknowledgements:

Thank you to my friends.

The wonderful perky grandmother who is never alone and yet is always showing me God's love through her family.

The bittersweet woman who always tells it like it is. She is not afraid to tell me the truth no matter what because I realize the truth is always the way.

The young man who I hope is able to draw something helpful from this story, who can so closely relate to this character. I pray you find some true friends with whom to share your life with.

The Pastor-in-Training who first read about my confusion and *I'm sure* prayed for my salvation before even beginning our conversation about the story. Yes, the devil always tries to block us from God, but you helped shine the light on the truth of His plan and you stuck it out.

My Pastor, whose absence forced me to do exactly what I was supposed to do – research the Bible and myself. Whenever it is easy, it isn't right. Also a heartfelt thanks for the suggestion of book 2 of this series (which was never intended to be a series but opened my heart to the possibility).

To my editor and friend, your insights give me clarity. You make me think. You make me work. You make me better. Without you, my readers would be just as confused as I am half the time. My world is better with you in it.

Conversations about faith, sharing God's love and reminiscing of our cherished loved ones whom are no longer with us. You fed me at that dining room table, body and soul. You listened, and gave me the opportunity to express myself when I thought no one was listening. You know who you are, because we are positively connected.

To my Grandfather who I was so blessed to have gotten to know in his end times. Whose scientific skepticism led me on a trek to understand and see God's love at work. Who reached for Jesus with his dying breath confirming that God loves us all and He always answers prayers.

The Pastor who suggested a book two which helped open my eyes to the possibility of this story becoming a trilogy.

To my readers, editors, narrator and fans who kept inquiring about this book and lighting a fire under me to finish it.

To "The Little White Light" who's story of a city come together after their own tornado sparked the inspiration and conclusion to this story. I had been struggling with what would bring people together because we so rarely see it in life. I should have known it was that easy.

To my Grandfather - who recognized the value of simple time spent with one another, not talking, just being. I will never forget those peaceful, musical evenings. It showed me how much could be conveyed without uttering a single word. It's a calm I will seek for the rest of my Earthly life.

God works in mysterious ways.
It's not a cliché if it is true.

About the Author

Kathleen J. Shields is an award-winning author having won First Place Best Educational Children's Series from the Texas Association of Authors for "The Hamilton Troll Adventures".

The Hamilton Troll series is educational and inspirational, teaching young children social skills, animal characteristics and how to handle real-life situations in a fun, entertaining way.

While awaiting illustrations, Shields' writes chapter books for her slightly older readers (tweens and general audiences). While still infusing education into each story, Kathleen endeavors to entertain young readers, igniting a desire to read (and maybe even write) that will span a lifetime.

Shields' also runs a website and graphic design company called Kathleen's Graphics. She designs colorful, eye-catching websites, custom logos and advertisements for businesses and authors. She enjoys being challenged to learn new things.

Additionally, Kathleen writes an inspirational and educational blog regarding her endeavors as an author as well as a business woman and Christian. Her views are always light-hearted and thought-provoking and are intended to get the reader thinking.

For more information about the author, and her books,
please visit: ***www.KathleensBooks.com***
or follow her blog at: ***www.KathleenJShields.com***

The BEST GIFT you can give an author
is a REVIEW of their BOOK!

Other Books by This Author

Ghost Dogs

As a toddler Jamie develops an amazing gift, the ability to see Ghost Dogs. They look just like our past pets, just transparent.

Dream World Defenders

Ryan and his friends enter the dream world where they can do anything they imagine. The only thing they can't do? Wake up.

Constellation Crimes

A Giant Scorpion, a Crab Attack and a Killer Wolf – What do these have in common? The zits on Jared's face! A boys will be boys with active imaginations, story.

Ally Cat, A Tale of Survival

Allison Catsworth gets knocked off of a cliff and instead of falling to her death, she transforms into a cat and lands on all four paws!

A Rainbow of Thanks

Kate walks into a rainbow and is transported to various places as she tries to get back home.

The Painting

Gerald is given a blank canvas to paint whatever he wants. So he paints a world, one that he loves so much – it comes to life!

The Painting 2

Benjamin, Gerald's son, discovers a way to be born into the Painting so he can tell the inhabitants about his father, their Painter.

The Painting 3
Nevaeh, Gerald's granddaughter imagines herself into the Painting while she's there in "spirit" her desire to help is contagious.

The Painting Trilogy

This Limited Edition Hardback book combines all three of the Painting stories to make one complete *"Trinity".*

Dandy Lion, A Legend of Love & Loss Dandy loses a strand of hair each time he helps someone. He sews the seeds of love by doing good deeds.

A Rhyme For Everything
A collection of rhythmic poetry for every mood, being an author, love, fun, music, story time, grief, inspiration and craziness.

Turtle Diaries

When a tortoise roams a turtle sanctuary, then writes a daily journal about his adventures and the other turtles he meets, fun, education and challenges ensue.

The Dog Who Cried Woof

Riley takes it upon himself to announce Daddy's return home, but turns it into a game that goes horribly wrong. ***Short Story***

Ethan's Reception

FiFi was not happy the day Ethan was brought home from the animal shelter... but Ethan was enthralled! ***Short Story***

The Day Hell Froze Over

When the inhabitants of hell begin praying for some cold weather, the devil finds himself in a horrible bind. ***Short Story***

Also be sure to check out

The Hamilton Troll Adventures

Twelve fully illustrated, rhyming educational stories for bedtime up to 2nd grade. They teach social skills, animal characteristics and even science. They also increase vocabulary by providing definitions to words. There is a Children's Cookbook, a Coloring book and a Curriculum workbook to continue the education. Perfect for home school and stay-at-home activities.

And for Young Adults:

The Kaitlyn Jones Trilogy

Kaitlyn discovers the gift of precognition, she's able to see things before they happen. She also discovers a telepathic bond with the guy who changed her life and the desire to help others with these gifts. Follow Kaitlyn through High School, her first job as a police officer. When she became a bodyguard, secret service and then secret agent!

Her Guarded Desire

Kristen must decide between her boyfriend and her bodyguard, when danger reemerges and they are forced on the run.

Erin Go Bragh Publishing publishes various genres of books for numerous authors. Their portfolio consists of a 1200 page Vietnamese to English Dictionary, Historical fiction, an award-winning children's educational series, multiple adult novels and memoires, tween adventure stories, as well as Christian Fiction. Their objective is to promote literacy and education through reading and writing.

www.ErinGoBraghPublishing.com
Canyon Lake, Texas

www.ingramcontent.com/pod-product-compliance
Lightning Source LLC
Chambersburg PA
CBHW020529310726
48979CB00014B/2262/J

* 9 7 8 1 9 4 1 3 4 5 4 5 0 *